Praise for Pat...

'A sensational romp with an e...
plot, and a thoroughl... ...
Leigh Russell on *Hattie Brings the House Down*

'This warm-hearted theatrical thriller [is] a real joy to read.
It's Simon Brett on steroids'
**Alex Coombs, author of *Murder on the Menu* on
*Hattie Brings the House Down***

HATTIE STEALS THE SHOW

PATRICK GLEESON

NO EXIT PRESS

First published in the UK in 2025 by No Exit Press,
an imprint of Bedford Square Publishers Ltd,
London, UK

noexit.co.uk
@noexitpress

© Patrick Gleeson, 2025

The right of Patrick Gleeson to be identified as the author of this work has been asserted in accordance with the Copyright, Designs and Patents Act 1988. All rights reserved. No part of this book may be reproduced, stored in or introduced into a retrieval system, or transmitted, in any form or by any means (electronic, mechanical, photocopying, recording or otherwise) without the written permission of the publishers.

Any person who does any unauthorised act in relation to this publication may be liable to criminal prosecution and civil claims for damages.
A CIP catalogue record for this book is available from the British Library.
This is a work of fiction. Names, characters, places, and incidents either are the product of the author's imagination or are used fictitiously, and any resemblance to actual persons, living or dead, businesses, companies, events or locales is entirely coincidental.

ISBN
978-1-83501-005-1 (Paperback)
978-1-83501-006-8 (eBook)

2 4 6 8 10 9 7 5 3 1

Typeset 10.5 on 13.8pt Minion Pro
by Avocet Typeset, Bideford, Devon, EX39 2BP
Printed and bound in Great Britain by
CPI Group (UK) Ltd, Croydon CR0 4YY

The manufacturer's authorised representative in the EU for product safety is Easy Access System Europe, Mustamäe tee 50, 10621 Tallinn, Estonia
gpsr.requests@easproject.com

For Iggie and Ari

THE FOLLOWING MEMORANDUM IS CONFIDENTIAL AND INTENDED SOLELY FOR THE USE OF EMPLOYEES AND DIRECTORS OF GEOFFREY DOUGRAY PRODUCTIONS ('GDP') LTD. IF YOU HAVE RECEIVED THIS MEMORANDUM IN ERROR YOU MAY BE COMMITTING AN ACTIONABLE OFFENCE BY READING FURTHER.

Louise,

After everything that's happened I think we should take stock re the workshop. Here are my current notes about attendees:

Creative:
Writer: **Jala**
Composer: **Teri** (I think she's locked in now. She'll need some prep, so maybe she joins a few days later than the rest.)
Repetiteur: **Calvin**.
Director: ~~Hashi H~~ (turned it down, can you believe it?!) **Mel**

Set and costume design: **Maxine**
Projection design: **Gareth** and **Tom** (I know, I know, it's a bit premature, but I *really* want projection on this. And Tom is such fun.)

Cast:
Hera
Pip
~~James N~~ (has a clash) **Dylan**
Delphine (not ideal, but she's free, it'll smooth things over, and we can re-cast at the next iteration)

Crew:
Tinca's agreed to cater, so that's all sorted at least. Meaning the last little niggle is the stage manager. (Note, for your ongoing theatrical education: *Do not underestimate the importance of this seemingly inconsequential role!*) Here's what we're up to:

~~Donna~~ Stuck on *The Guilty*
~~Leah~~ Too good to stage manage, apparently. She thinks she's a producer now!
~~Louis~~ In America
Hattie (Cocker)??? Bumped into her on the off-chance. Getting on a bit, and she's not well known any more, but I wonder…

Let's catch up in the morning.

Geoffrey

Prologue

The door did very little to advertise its presence. From the mouth of the alley that led unobtrusively off Shaftesbury Avenue, all you could see above the cluster of bins was the box with the frosted glass sides that housed a dim bulb and from which the black lettering that spelled out STAGE DOOR had rubbed off many years before.

But it was a door that didn't need much signposting. If you knew what you were looking for it was precisely where you'd expect it to be, at the rear of the Revue Theatre. And if you didn't know what you were looking for, you probably had no business with a door like that anyway.

Hattie Cocker did indeed know exactly what she was looking for, having passed through this door many times over the course of her career. She didn't need to look for it at all; she could simply instruct her legs where to go once she got off the bus at Piccadilly Circus and allow them to make the journey on autopilot. Or at least, that was her expectation. It turned out that her legs had developed an unfortunate confusion concerning the relative placements of the Revue and the Apollo – she had a great deal of practice at walking to both – and so it was only when she was raising her hand to press the doorbell of the stage door of the latter that she realised her legs had brought her to the wrong place.

This minor situational mishap addressed, she still managed to ring the *correct* doorbell a full five minutes before the time she had agreed to arrive, thanks to her innate habit of building in contingency buffers to all travel plans, and after a short wait was duly admitted by a familiar face.

'Hallo, lovely,' Donna greeted her with a broad smile that somehow lacked warmth.

'All right?' replied Hattie, with as much positivity as she could muster. She liked Donna, she really did, it was just... well, never mind that now. 'It's nice to be back here.'

'Which show did you do?' enquired Donna.

'It was an Ayckbourn... *Man of the Moment*, I think?'

'That never ran here. You're thinking of the Gielgud,' Donna corrected her, a trifle sharply.

That was it, wasn't it? It was almost impossible to have an interaction with her without coming away feeling like you'd been slightly told off by teacher. A manner like that was no bad thing, professionally, but it always made social chit-chat slightly strained.

'You're right, I'm sure. It must have been something else. It'll come to me.'

Donna nodded. 'Thanks for helping out,' she offered, perhaps by way of reconciliation.

'You know me. I never turn down paid work if I can help it,' said Hattie as she signed in on the clipboard hanging by the door. There were only a handful of names on the sheet that weren't marked as signed out: Donna of course, a Lel Nowak, which was a name that rang a bell, and then someone called Colin McDermot, which was a name that definitely didn't. Lots of other people had been around at some point then left again (there had been a matinee performance earlier in the day), so the building was quiet, although Hattie could hear muffled voices from somewhere in the auditorium.

'Well I'm very grateful. Everyone else is so busy at the moment.'

It wasn't meant as a barbed comment. Probably. Of *course* Hattie was more likely to be free for a gig at short notice than other stage managers. She was in the very unusual position, thanks to her current gig tutoring at a drama school, of being a jobbing stage manager whose evenings were normally free. And of course, she only had that gig because Donna, the previous SM tutor, had missed the industry so much she'd gone back to it, leaving a vacancy. So it was only fair that Donna might call on Hattie for a favour, as Hattie was in a rare position of being able to oblige.

It was just that Hattie had only had to *take* the SM tutoring gig because she'd found it increasingly difficult to find regular work. In this industry it was all about who you knew, and once injury forced Hattie off the touring circuit she realised that her social-professional circle in London had mostly retired or moved away. It didn't *matter* of course, as the tutoring put food on the table, but still, she didn't like being reminded of how she'd slightly lost her footing.

'Shall we get on with it, then?' asked Donna.

She led Hattie along a low-ceilinged corridor that jinked left and right a few times, opening out suddenly to a much larger space, the bulk of which was walled off by some extremely makeshift-looking timber-and-canvas 'flats' – the tall, narrow panels that are the building blocks of theatre scenery. Hattie knew that on the other side those flats were carefully finished and painted with enough delicacy that, from a dozen yards away, under stage lighting, they looked like the solid walls of an imposing cityscape. Like everything in theatre, scenery could be as flimsy and ramshackle as you liked so long as the bit the punters saw looked the part.

There were still voices coming from somewhere. The sounds came from above, raised but distant, although Hattie could make out none of what was actually being said. Perhaps some actors were running lines in a dressing room. They worked their way along the back of the set, then ducked through a gap between two overlapping flats to emerge abruptly onto the stage, where an angled floor and some clever forced perspective tricks made a six-metre rectangle feel like an expansive swathe of London's South

Bank. Even under the harsh fluorescent working lights it was still quite something.

'Who designed the—' she began, but was interrupted by Donna who called out, sharply: 'Excuse me!'

Hattie followed her gaze up to the balcony that ran round the backstage area, from which the various pulleys that 'flew' scenery in and out were operated. Much of it was obscured by long black drapes that hung all the way from the ceiling to the sides of the stage, and from behind one of those drapes were coming occasional metallic clonking sounds.

'There shouldn't be anyone on the fly floor at the moment. Come down please!' commanded Donna sternly. The clonking stopped. They waited in silence for a few moments, listening for any further sounds, before Donna relaxed. She turned back to Hattie, rolled her eyes and muttered, 'A couple of stage hands dragged a massage chair up there to sit in while waiting for their cues, and now the crew spend half their time fighting over getting turns in it. Honestly, you wouldn't think they've all been doing this for six months with the way they go on. There's no discipline with some of this lot.'

Hattie made a sympathetic face. Donna was a famous stickler for discipline, and while this was entirely right and reasonable, Hattie felt she could be slightly more free with the dressing-downs than she needed to be. Was being up on the fly floor between the matinee and the evening show really such a terrible sign of decadence?

'Now, we've got cue lights on all the entrances except upstage left. That's because…'

Donna launched into an extremely thorough overview of everything that Hattie would need to know the following week while Donna was away. The show, a musical called *The Guilty*, had opened earlier in the year. It was produced by feted impresario Sir Geoffrey Dougray, and while the reviews were positive, the general consensus was that it wasn't *quite* the smash hit return to form that Geoffrey had been chasing ever since the last of his run of hits in the early 2000s. It was booked to run in the West End until November, and the rumour was that it was unlikely to be extended. Instead, it would be packaged off on a regional tour, and then either taken abroad or retired. A perfectly respectable production, in other words, and therefore a huge disappointment to Sir Geoffrey.

Donna was taking a week off mid-run, to look after her daughter after some surgery of some sort that had been unexpectedly scheduled at short notice. Hence the need for someone to step in and stage manage the show during her absence. Hattie was now here to get the full rundown from Donna, and would in a couple of hours' time shadow her during the evening performance, so that she could be ready to take over the next day. It was quite a lot of bother for what was, from a stage manager's perspective, a very straightforward production. But over-preparedness was the watchword of her profession, and Hattie and Donna did these things by the book.

When Donna had finished her introduction, she took her round the rest of the set to help get her familiar with everything, pointing out which exits led to where, along with the various trip hazards, props tables and other minutiae with which an SM concerns themselves. As there was one moment where an actor needed to enter through the auditorium from behind the audience, Donna twitched aside the lush stage curtain so they could poke their noses out at the rows of seats. All was quiet out there, as the ushers had long since finished sweeping up spilled snacks from the stalls and had now gone on break. In fact the auditorium was entirely empty save for—

'Mind the plasterwork!'

A very large and jolly-looking man in a tweed suit was leaning casually against the side of the proscenium arch – the big wall dividing the auditorium from the backstage area, containing the large hole through which the audience could see the stage. It was to him that Donna had just addressed the rebuke. She was right to make a fuss, in that the 'prosc' was covered in ornate, gold-painted plaster twirls and swirls that were nearly a century old, and in Hattie's experience things like that crumbled as soon as you breathed on them. The weight of a large man's shoulders could do some very expensive damage.

But unlike Donna, Hattie would probably not have dared utter an admonition had she been first to see the leaner. Because this particular man, as it happened, was Sir Geoffrey Dougray, and he owned the whole damn theatre, plaster and all.

Well, technically his production company owned a controlling stake in the corporate group that leased and managed the venue, but the gist was the same. Hattie hadn't seen his name on the sheet by the door, but she considered that he was probably the one person in the world who mightn't get an additional dressing-down from Donna for not signing in.

Geoffrey, who appeared to be lost in thought, slowly rolled his head towards Donna, wearing a completely blank expression. After a second or so his eyes seemed to focus, and he heaved himself upright.

Donna, perhaps mindful that the person she had just upbraided was the person who ultimately signed off her, and everyone else's, payslips, offered with a half-shrug, 'You know how Colin will be if it gets damaged.'

'Quite so, quite so,' murmured Geoffrey pleasantly. He didn't move away, but he offered nothing more, so after a second or so Donna turned her attention back to the task in hand.

'Now, the auditorium doors are a bit noisy, so—' she began, but was then immediately interrupted by Geoffrey, who called out, 'Hattie! It's Hattie bloody Cocker! How marvellous!'

'Hullo, Geoffrey,' replied Hattie, genuinely astonished that he remembered her. She had worked on the Broadway transfer of one of his shows a full two decades earlier, and had had very little direct contact with him during the process. Or at least, very little contact while either of them was actually working. They'd got chatting during a couple of messy, boozy parties around the opening and closing of the run, but Hattie had assumed the parties were messy enough and boozy enough that Geoffrey wouldn't remember the particulars.

Evidently, though, she had made more of an impression than she gave herself credit for, because here came Geoffrey, beaming from ear to ear, looking like an overgrown puppy who'd just found a playmate. For all that he was a shrewd businessman with a legendary ruthless streak, Geoffrey was immediately likeable by virtue of being so perennially enthusiastic.

'This is the woman,' Geoffrey proclaimed excitedly, 'who persuaded me to revive *Roses*! Do you remember, Hattie?'

Hattie didn't, and would have admitted as much had Geoffrey given her a chance to speak. He trundled on. 'Do you know I think of you every time I drink Riesling? Where on earth have you been for the last twenty years?'

'Oh, you know. Lots of touring. I'm tutoring at ACDA these days.'

'A teacher! Wonderful! Moulding a whole new generation of mini Cockers and sending them out into the industry. What on earth brings you to my theatre tonight?'

'I'm shadowing Donna, so I can cover for her next week.'

Geoffrey raised his hands skywards dramatically.

'Fate!' he proclaimed. 'True serendipity. It's the sheerest happenstance that has me in tonight myself. I was just meeting...' here his smile faltered, just momentarily. 'Well anyway, I may have a job for you. You'll say yes, won't you? Do say yes.'

'It depends on the job,' said Hattie cautiously.

'My assistant is around here somewhere, I'll get her to... oh never mind the boring details for now, I'll have her get in touch with all of that tomorrow. It's a fun one,' he assured her conspiratorially. 'Oh, this will be wonderful.'

'Shall I give you my number, or my email, or—' began Hattie, but he interrupted her with a wave of his hand.

'No need, no need. I can always find people when I want them. À bientôt. Hattie Cocker? Marvellous.'

And with that he was off up the central aisle of the stalls, still muttering to himself as he went. Hattie and Donna exchanged an amused look.

'I didn't know you were pals with Geoffrey,' said Donna, and Hattie thought she detected a certain something in Donna's tone, but wasn't sure if it was jealousy, or disapproval, or something else entirely. Either way she just nodded, and said, 'You know how it is.'

They carried on with the tour. Donna showed her the prompt desk, the prop tables, and the dressings rooms. Then, as she was leading Hattie round the stage left scenery dock, a man in jeans and a hoodie came out of nowhere and barrelled past them in the direction of the exit, causing Donna to stumble.

'Hey!' she called out, but the man kept walking, his head bowed. Hattie had only caught the slightest glimpse of his face, and now she could see nothing more than his back, but there was something familiar about his gait...

'Eoin?' she said, noting how unfamiliar the name felt in her mouth after all these years. So was the sudden rush of guilt and shame that she had, for such a long time, so strongly associated with that name.

The man stopped and stood stock still for a moment. Then his shoulders sagged and he turned, giving Hattie a proper look at a face that, last time she had seen it, had belonged to a teenager. Now it was worn by a man of maybe fifty, who was using it to carry a pained expression, full of anxiety and stress.

'My goodness, Eoin, it's Hattie. Hattie Cocker.'

His expression slowly changed, and what seemed like a genuine, albeit small, smile appeared at his mouth.

'Hattie! Wow. I'm' – he blinked heavily, then took a deep breath – 'I'm so sorry, I didn't mean to barge into you. I've got a lot on my mind… I can't stop… It's really good to see you, Hattie. Maybe we can catch up another time?'

And before she could respond he was off again, striding towards the nearby stage door, through which he was already leaving before Donna could finish calling after him, 'I didn't see anyone called Eoin on the sign-in sheet, you know…'

'Well that's strange,' said Hattie, as much to herself as anyone else. 'I haven't seen that boy in over thirty years. I wonder what he's doing here?'

This time the disapproval in Donna's face was readily apparent. Hobnobbing with producers was one thing, but fraternising with people who charge round backstage without having completed the correct paperwork was quite another.

'We'll need to do an inventory of valuables,' she snapped. 'You might know him, but I don't, and if he's been walking round here unsupervised then who knows what he's been up to?'

'Of course,' said Hattie. 'He's called Eoin Norell. He's a playwright. Or at least, he was. I don't know if he still is. He was a techie before that. I'm sure he wasn't up to any mischief but… well, far better to be thorough, eh?'

That last suggestion was uttered without conviction and simply to appease Donna, who agreed wholeheartedly with the sentiment. The pair started retracing their steps, with Donna pointing out the various things in the theatre that were both potentially valuable enough to steal and not bolted down. Of these there were fairly few. With the exception of various bits of uniformly bulky and heavy technical kit, more or less everything you found backstage in a typical theatre was flimsy, knackered, and held together with string. But they diligently checked everything anyway.

Nothing was amiss, and Donna's agitation gradually lessened as each new area was discovered to be as it should (it takes some skill to detect agitation in a stage manager's face, but Hattie knew the signs). Once they had completed a full sweep of the ground level Donna said, 'All right. I think we're all set. Let's just check the fly floor, then we can get in a quick bite of food before the half.'

Hattie glanced up apprehensively at the vertical ladder leading up from stage right, unsure that her duff hip would forgive her for such exertion, and was quietly relieved when Donna led her through a door stage left, where a small stairwell offered them a more sedate ascent.

There wasn't much to the fly floor, comprising as it did a C-shaped, scaffold-railed steel walkway running along the sides and back of the stage at a height of around twenty feet. On one side was a counterweighted pulley system that allowed an operator to hoist scenery up and down between the fly tower above and the stage below. On the other were banks of connectors from which a spaghetti of cabling sprouted, leading to the lights and speakers mounted at all angles on every point that allowed a purchase. At both ends of the 'C' the walkway widened to form little booths nestling in the upstage shadow of the big proscenium arch. The near one of these was a storage space containing cables, spare lanterns, and several bolts of thick black cloth. Nothing here appeared to have been disturbed.

They ambled round to the far booth, which on first glance was empty save for a shelf on one side containing an assortment of cast iron blocks used as counterweights for the scenery pulleys, and an extremely large, heavily padded, black leather armchair with a set of buttons built into the armrest. It had seen better days, and was patched at various places with gaffer tape. This was evidently the massage chair Donna had mentioned. It was positioned oddly in the room, sitting a good foot forward from the wall, not leaving much room for anything else.

'Oh God, Lel!' said Donna abruptly, and rushed forward.

She knelt on the floor, and Hattie suddenly saw why the chair wasn't up against the wall. Poking out from behind it on one side were two legs, and from the other was a head. Hattie felt herself assailed by a twin surge of both horror and déjà vu as her eyes made sense of the scene, and she realised that the owner of these extremities, stuffed as he was behind the chair, was completely still, twisted at a horribly unnatural angle, and covered in blood.

Act One

1

We have thus established that, dialectically speaking at least, theatre IS trauma. How do we, as practitioners, respond to this? Must we turn every rehearsal into a traumatic experience? No. Rather, we bring with us into the rehearsal room the trauma that we ourselves embody, in order that, through performance, we may release it. Thankfully it is a commodity of which there is no short supply.

– From *Advanced Theatre Practice*
by Jala Senguel, MA

'I wish I could tell you that you'll all be successful. You all deserve to be. You've fought for this, and you'll keep fighting. I know you will.

'It's easy to read the statistics, as an actor, and be downhearted. And look, I can't promise that you'll all make it. Of course I can't. But what I can tell you is this: hard work does pay off. You have to throw yourself into it every single day, but it pays off.'

'What a pile of absolute badger todgers,' muttered Rod, and Hattie, sitting next to him, had to suppress an involuntary snort.

They were in the back row of a bank of seats temporarily installed on the stage of the main auditorium at ACDA, west London's most prestigious drama school. (The new principal was known not to be hugely fond of this epithet and had drily noted that, west London not being famed for the quantity of its drama schools, such a geographical restriction somewhat lessened the impact of any superlative. However, RADA, squatting over central London, cast a long shadow, being older, more famous, larger, better funded, and with a richer history of turning out successful actors. So ACDA made do with whatever claims it could make that managed to avoid direct comparisons with its higher-profile neighbour, and the students and faculty consoled themselves with the thought that at least they weren't as snobby and self-satisfied as they imagined the dreadful RADA lot to be.)

Today was a big day in the ACDA annual diary: today the final-year students were graduating. To mark the occasion the whole school, along with many tearful mums and dads, had squeezed itself into the main auditorium for a ceremony that tried to mimic the pomp of graduations at more academic institutions but couldn't quite bring itself to submit to anything so dry as caps and gowns, certificates and scrolls, handshakes and bows. Instead, the graduating actors performed scenes from their showcase productions from earlier in the term: those with the best singing voices boomed out a couple of full-throated Sondheim renditions; the stage combat specialists got over-excited and narrowly avoided taking chunks out of the building with assorted mediaeval weaponry; and the most talented dancers among them did their best while implicitly reminding everyone that dance wasn't really ACDA's forte.

And the stage management and technical theatre students... sat there. No one wanted to defuse the energy of the day with a showcase of lighting techniques, or a demonstration of exotic sound effects.

But no matter. When the performances were done, at which point everyone felt in need of a breather, Principal Jolyon Jones was wheeled on to say a few encouraging words about how well the school had done in getting the students this far, and hint that they should remember ACDA should they ever be in a position to make philanthropic donations in future.

And, as was traditional, they also got a successful ACDA alum to make a speech. This year's was a barrel-chested man with hair trimmed short, a loud shirt, and unexpectedly tight jeans. He had recently had a recurring role in a BBC police drama that had been cruelly overlooked in the latest crop of BAFTA nominations. This was the man whose confident assertion that 'hard work pays off' was earning him inspired smiles from the acting students and murmured derision from Rod, the senior sound tutor.

'I dunno,' Hattie murmured back. 'At least badger todgers have a purpose.'

'*Two* purposes,' pointed out Rod with a chuckle that was loud enough to turn heads in front.

'Hush, you,' Hattie hissed. She was well aware that Rod already had a reputation for being a troublemaker, and Hattie was on her way to being tarred with the same brush. Rod deserved his reputation, Hattie thought, being a cantankerous old git who didn't pay nearly enough mind to what other people thought of him. Hattie wasn't a cantankerous old git, she'd simply made *friends* with one. Sitting at the back and leaning into their perceived roles as the two old codgers of the technical department was fun and all, but if Mark, their head of department, caught them at it, he'd give them a Look and possibly a Talking To, and Hattie had been hoping to make it to the end of term without any more of those.

Either way, Rod was right: it was a brutally unfair industry, whatever Mr Barrel-chest said. It was estimated by the number-crunchers that a full three quarters of all those actors who graduated from a drama school in the UK would never once in their lives receive a professional pay cheque for their craft. And by this point, on graduation day, several fates had already been sealed: some, by dint of their performances in the showcase productions, had managed to attract the attention of a decent agent, and had a shot at being put up for serious roles on stage and screen. The rest would have to spend the next couple of years desperately trying to find some other way of getting onto the industry's radar, be it through fringe shows, the lottery of open casting calls, or relentless networking. And even the ones who had agents already were no shoo-in. If their looks were too distinctive there'd be very limited roles they'd be put up for. Too generic and they'd be drowned in a sea of hungry competitors for every audition.

It was cruel, Hattie thought, for one of the lucky ones who'd happened to make it to tell this lot that all it came down to was hard work. Because the majority of them, who didn't make it, who would one day have to make the painful decision to walk away from the dream, would forever hear this pillock's voice in their head asking them if their failure was their own fault, if really it was because they hadn't tried hard enough.

'Look,' whispered Rod, gesturing with a meaty finger at one of their students. 'I think Tina's pissed already. Couldn't even wait until after the ceremony. She's almost falling off her chair!'

Hattie shushed him and pushed his hand down. 'Stop distracting me,' she whispered back, although she'd barely heard a word of the speech in the last five minutes, so deeply had she been distracted by her own thoughts. She looked over at the newly minted batch of acting graduates. They had no idea what they were getting themselves into. And that was just the actors. Things were even worse if you wanted to be a director, or a writer, or, God help you, a composer...

Ah. That was it. That was why she was in such a black mood, and so dismissive of the speech and so down on the industry as a whole. It was because at the back of her mind she was thinking about a composer. A composer, indeed, by the name of Lel, whose career penning musicals had been beginning to take off, only to be cut short in the most tragic circumstances.

Hattie gave an involuntary shudder, masked by a very deliberate shake of the head. Now was not the time to dwell on such thoughts. She turned her gaze towards her lot: the techies. They, at least, would have an easier time of it. Not because the work was easy: far from it. But because the work was there to be had. And more importantly, because once you were in work there was no concept of 'making it' as a techie. A tiny paid gig in a fringe theatre counted for no less than calling the show on opening night at the National, or the O2. You weren't constantly competing to get more prestigious roles in more prestigious shows, hoping to hit the 'big time', because there was no big time: the money was terrible no matter where you worked. No, professional development was about, every day, trying to do a better job than you'd done the day before. That was all. Which wasn't to say that this latest batch would all stay the course. Some of them had already realised that they weren't up to scratch as a techie, and were even now planning their exits from the industry. Some of them *hadn't* realised it yet, but Hattie was grimly confident that they would have that realisation thrust upon them soon enough. They might get hired once, but they were unlikely to get hired *twice*.

Some of them would be fine, though. And anyway, no matter what the future held, today was as much about celebrating their collective survival through two intensive, arduous years of training. Hattie wouldn't begrudge them a day of joy, even the numpties.

The speech wound to an end, gaining a standing ovation for the speaker (it was a drama school after all – you barely had to sneeze to have people leaping to their feet and shouting 'Bravo!'). The ceremony morphed into a drinks reception, and soon enough Hattie found herself gravitating towards a cluster of her departmental colleagues: Rod, construction tutor Shane, Angharad from the lighting department, and Mark, the head of technical training. Hattie, who had spent much of the last week in a daze, found her attention kept wandering. With a frown she tried to drag it back to the conversation around her.

'… really *feel* the collective energy,' Shane was saying. 'You know?'

'If we could harness the collective energy of a gaggle of acting students somehow, we could power the whole building and sell the excess to the national grid. Maybe we could make a profit for once,' observed Mark.

'When you've been here as long as I have, you'll stop worrying about money,' put in Rod. 'It has a way of cropping up whenever it's truly needed.'

'At this rate I won't get the chance to be here as long as you have: I'm not sure ACDA will survive that long,' was Mark's rejoinder.

Rod raised an eyebrow and exchanged a brief glance with Hattie. Everyone let their guard down a little bit on graduation day, but even so, Mark was never normally this forthcoming, or this gloomy, about ACDA's finances. Was this a sign that things were genuinely bad?

Hattie was still trying to find the words to probe Mark more on this topic when a trio of newly graduated stage managers bustled up to them, all three of them giddy with triumph and the help of several glasses of the fizz that had been laid on to mark the occasion.

'So,' one of them began with a waggled eyebrow. 'What's the goss?'

'I beg your pardon?' asked Mark.

'The goss. The latest. The inside line. Come on, we're not students any more, you don't have to be all professional around us. What's the stuff you've not been telling us?'

The tutors exchanged blank looks.

'Sorry,' said Hattie. 'I'm afraid we're all very boring people, really.'

'Well that's not actually true, is it? Hattie, you've got some massive gossip haven't you?' announced Angharad.

'Do I? Oh... I don't know that—' Hattie began, but Angharad, perhaps in subtle retribution for being labelled as 'boring' by Hattie just now, was already away: 'You heard about the Revue last week? The dead body? Hattie was there.'

'What, when they found it?' asked a student, breathlessly.

'Not just when they found it. She was on stage *while he was being murdered*. And the guy who did it ran past Hattie as he was escaping!' Angharad exclaimed. She was the member of the technical tuition team whom Hattie knew least, but what Hattie did know of her, she didn't really like: Angharad was a shameless scandalmonger, for one thing, and while Hattie liked scandal as much as anyone, she felt there was a time and a place for such things, and a time and a place for discretion.

'*Seriously?*'

All three students looked awestruck at Hattie, making her feel deeply uncomfortable.

'Well, no... it wasn't like that...'

It was like that, though. It hadn't taken long for the police to join the dots: the sounds Hattie and Donna heard up on the fly floor while they were on stage; Eoin's appearance out of nowhere and his rush to get away. When it was confirmed that the dead man was the composer Lel Nowak, the police asked no further questions. They were quite sure they knew exactly what had happened.

Which irked Hattie. It had been a long time since she had last placed her trust in a police officer, and on the whole she considered that if you were looking for the truth, a good place to start was considering the complete opposite of whatever the plods said. For example, by the time they'd arrived and rounded up everyone in the building (including large numbers of company members who had started to trickle in in advance of the evening performance), a quick audit of the sign-in sheet showed that Colin McDermot, who had signed in *before* Lel had died and not signed out again, was missing from the building. But once they'd heard Donna's story about Eoin, had they even followed up with that? Not as far as Hattie could tell. In fact, they'd seemed to treat the whole thing as a tick-box exercise. Which wasn't just lazy, it was also pretty disrespectful to the victim, in Hattie's book.

'That poor man,' Hattie found herself murmuring. Although she wasn't entirely sure, she realised guiltily, that she was thinking about Lel when she said it.

When it became clear that Hattie wasn't going to divulge any sordid details, the over-excited graduates soon lost interest and the talk turned to other topics. Hattie allowed herself to peel away from the group and gently drift to the edge of the room, and then out into a corridor and back to the quiet of the stage management office. She wasn't in the mood for conversation.

What it came down to, she found herself thinking, was a disconnect. On one side of it was a straightforward, if rather grim, story: Eoin Norell and Lel Nowak had, for many years, had a creative partnership, creating shows together where Eoin wrote the script and lyrics, and Lel wrote the music. Their work had received some critical acclaim but no commercial success. Then, in recent years, Lel had started to make friends in higher places in the industry and found work with other collaborators, work that led to bigger shows, more recognition, and finally a bit of genuine income. Meanwhile Eoin, left to his own devices, had languished in obscurity. They had met up backstage at the Revue, home to Lel's latest project, *The Guilty*. Eoin, driven perhaps by frustration, by resentment, by a misplaced sense of betrayal, had attacked and killed Lel, clumsily shoving his body behind an armchair to try to conceal his crime before making a break for it through the stage door and disappearing into the night. He would, doubtless, soon be apprehended, charged and convicted, and justice would be served.

That was the story on one side. But on the other side… on the other side was a rather different story. A story, pulled from deep in

Hattie's memory, about an unusual young man, troubled certainly, but hugely kind and compassionate, who had escaped a life of abuse, finding solace in the theatre. A story about a friendship that had been formed, but then allowed to dwindle, until a chance meeting years later had raised the heartening possibility of rekindling it, only for that possibility to be immediately snatched away.

These stories were both, apparently, true. And both revolved around the same central character. But try as she might, Hattie couldn't reconcile the two of them in her head. Like two magnets with matching poles pointing towards one another, they just wouldn't stick together.

It didn't help that the discovery of the body had also ended Hattie's hopes for a proper theatre gig. It was selfish, she knew, but when Donna had got in touch to ask her to cover for her for a week at the Revue Hattie had jumped at the chance. She hadn't had a proper gig since her slightly ill-fated work at the Tavistock the previous autumn, and while tutoring students was fine, it didn't quite scratch the itch Hattie had. She'd been aching to get back out there, even if it was only for a week. Now the Revue was a crime scene, for the very worst sort of crime, and the police and the producers had agreed to suspend the show for seven days, with performances resuming on the day that Donna had intended to return to work anyway.

And then Geoffrey had said he would ring Hattie the next day, but he never did, so she got her hopes up for nothing.

She was interrupted from her thoughts by a knock on the office door. After a second it opened, and in poked the head of Abua, one of the new graduates. A quiet and cerebral young man, he had worked hard over the course of his training, performing respectably in all technical departments, but excelling at stage management and earning himself a distinction as his overall grade (not that anyone in the industry cared remotely about what kind of qualification you had, Hattie always noted, but still, it offered driven ones like Abua some well-deserved validation of their efforts). He should be as jubilant as anyone today, and no one would think the less of him for spending the afternoon getting royally plastered. Yet here he was, skulking into the SM office, a look of anxious despondence on his face.

'Hullo, lovely,' Hattie greeted him warmly. 'What are you doing here?'

'I just wanted... Er hi, I mean. How are you?'

Hattie smiled. 'I'm very well, thanks. How about you?'

'I'm good, I'm... I just wanted to ask you something. If that's okay?'

'Of course! Come on in.'

Abua shuffled into the room and closed the door, then hovered nervously for a few moments, seemingly marshalling his thoughts.

'I just wanted to ask... You've been so helpful to me, and I've learned so much from you, so... thank you. I guess that's the main thing. I wanted to say thank you.'

'Well, you're welcome,' said Hattie, flushing slightly. 'You've been a pleasure to teach, and I think you have the makings of an excellent stage manager.'

'I know, but... I mean, uh, that's very kind of you to say so. Thank you.'

There was an awkward pause. The young man clearly had something else he wanted to say, but for now his nerve seemed to have failed him.

'Are you happy to have graduated?' asked Hattie, knowing it was a daft question, but unable to think of anything else to fill the silence.

'Oh yes,' replied Abua. 'I mean, it's been hard work, and it's nice to have a qualification to show for it.'

'Just remember, the qualification is just a piece of paper. What matters is what's up here,' said Hattie, tapping her temple. 'Once you're out in the industry, people will only care about whether you're a safe pair of hands. It's all about getting on. Getting on with the job and getting on with the people around you. But you're good at both, so you'll be fine.'

'Um… yeah. Thanks.'

Somehow everything Hattie said seemed to be making Abua more miserable. He was now practically in tears.

Hattie frowned. 'Abua, what's going on? What am I missing?'

'I just… I was just wondering… what if I *didn't* go into the industry? I just don't think I'm cut out for it. Maybe. I thought maybe I'd be better off doing something else entirely. Like recruitment, maybe.'

Hattie suppressed a snort. 'Abua, I don't know much about the world outside theatre, but I do know this: you'd be wasted as a recruiter.'

'I know, but… I mean, I just…'

He tailed off, and it finally started to click for Hattie: he was terrified. He wouldn't be the first. ACDA worked its students hard, but they were still in one sense coddled by the safety of a college environment. The 'real world' could seem a very scary place. Hattie felt a wash of protective feelings surge through her as she considered this poor student of hers, at the threshold of a new career and dreading it. He was so young, after all. Still just a boy really.

'Oh Abua, don't worry, it won't be as bad as you think.'

'No?'

'No. I promise you. I know it seems scary for now, but you'll get through it. And I'll tell you how and all: one day at a time. Right?'

Abua nodded, uncertain. Hattie continued. 'You've got something lined up over the summer, haven't you? Was it the Donmar?'

'The Young Vic,' he murmured.

'Well then. Your first day will be fine. They're a bunch of sweethearts at the Young Vic, they'll be sure to ease you in slow.

Your second day will be fine too, but we're not worrying about that yet. Just think about the first day first, and I promise you, the first day is nothing to worry about. Now, I'm going to give you my number. At the end of your first day, you're going to call me and tell me how it went. And then we'll talk about the second day. Okay?'

'Thank you,' he sniffed, and Hattie realised his eyes were wet with tears.

'That's no problem. And if at any point you need a chat, you just let me know. I'm not your tutor any more, but we look out for each other in this industry. If you need anything, you tell me about it, and I'll see what I can do.'

It took a few more encouraging words to get him smiling again, but eventually, newly armed with her phone number, Abua left her office with the stated intention of rejoining the celebrations with his fellow graduates, and Hattie allowed herself to relax. She didn't find that the pastoral side of stage management, and in particular of stage management tutoring, came naturally to her. But she'd never considered that a reasonable excuse not to do her best when she was called upon. Abua was perhaps a little quiet, perhaps a little shy, but all of that could be overcome. What he needed now was just a little bit of help taking the first steps, and if Hattie was in the right place at the right time to provide that help, then her duty was clear.

The noise from the drinks reception on the other side of the building, which had been steadily getting louder as the alcohol continued to flow freely, had now reached a pitch that confirmed to Hattie that she had no desire to rejoin the proceedings. So she gave the office a little tidy, picked up her bag and keys and let herself out from the ACDA back entrance.

2

There was a young woman loitering outside ACDA as Hattie stepped onto the pavement. She was short, stocky and stylishly dressed, with a broad, ruddy face and her copper hair in a high ponytail. She started slightly when she caught sight of Hattie and looked as though she was about to offer a greeting, but then, seemingly changing her mind at the last moment, shrank back.

Hattie, who didn't recognise the girl in the slightest, considered this behaviour somewhat odd but not noteworthy and would have thought no more about it except that, at the tube station a few minutes later, waiting for her train, she looked along the platform and saw the same girl hovering awkwardly a few yards further down. Hattie smiled at her, and the girl smiled shyly back. They enjoyed no further interactions on the platform, and when the next train arrived they got on in silence and sat down at opposite ends of the same carriage.

It's easy, in moments such as this, to let your imagination run away with you. Hattie, though she took a quiet pride in being sensible and down-to-earth, nevertheless sometimes found the anxious part of her mind indulging in bizarre paranoid fantasies. In this case, fully aware of how absurd the notion was, she found herself imagining that this girl was following her, and in her mind's eye pictured the girl getting off at the same stop when Hattie needed to change lines, then following her onto the new train, then tailing her out of the station and all the way back home, leading to a confrontation, maybe even an altercation, outside her front door.

Even the most paranoid part of Hattie's psyche struggled to come up with a credible motive for the girl: she didn't look remotely like either a mugger, a terrorist or a lunatic. She mostly looked embarrassed, and a little worried. She kept looking up and briefly making eye contact with Hattie, then looking away again. Hattie thought this was a tad suspicious until she realised that the only reason the girl kept making eye contact was that she, Hattie, was now continually staring at girl. No wonder the poor thing looked worried and embarrassed.

Hattie chastened herself for her rudeness and resolved not to look in the girl's direction for the remainder of the journey. She told herself to stop being so silly and forced herself to think of other things.

It was with a great deal of surprise, therefore, that Hattie, having changed to the District Line at Earl's Court, discovered that the girl really had followed her off the first train and onto the second. The surprise turned to alarm when the girl alighted at Chiswick Park, just like Hattie. And when, two streets' walk from the tube station, the girl was still shuffling along behind Hattie at a few yards' distance, the alarm gave way, very suddenly, to anger. Hattie found herself, abruptly, stopping dead, turning on her heel and marching up to the girl.

'Oi!' she snapped. 'I don't know what you think you're doing, but stop it. Do you understand? Just sod off. Go on!'

'Sorry!' cried the girl, cringing.

The sudden spike of adrenaline was already wearing off and faced with such a submissive response, Hattie found it hard to stay cross.

'Look… what are you doing?' she asked.

'I'm really sorry it's just that Geoffrey didn't know your address and he told me to find out and I've just started and I didn't want to let him down and ACDA wouldn't tell me and I couldn't think of another way so I followed you and I'm really sorry please don't tell him!' blurted out the girl, all in a rush, in a high-pitched Mancunian accent. Then her face crumpled up and she started to cry.

'Oh… bother,' said Hattie. 'Look, I'm… well I won't say I'm sorry, because I'm not sure I am, but I'm… my flat's just round the corner. Come and have a cuppa.'

It took a strong cup of tea, three Hobnobs and several careful words of comfort before the girl, who turned out to be called Lorna, was ready to be coaxed into a fuller explanation of her actions. But when she was, Hattie managed to gather the basics of her story: she had secured a three-week work experience placement with Geoffrey Dougray's production company. She considered this role, despite being entirely unpaid, to be a much vauntable position, as she was apparently chosen out of a pool of over two hundred applicants (all of them, Hattie imagined, bright young things looking to make their way in the world of theatre and hoping that some of the Dougray magic would rub off on them if they could spend enough time in his presence).

Her first day had been all about making cups of tea, stapling, tidying and so on, and as is so often the case with work experience, from her second day onwards no one could think of anything actually useful for her to do, so she mostly sat in the corner trying to look keen. But on the third day Geoffrey's assistant, Louise, said that the big man wanted to track down Hattie's postal address, and this assistant had decided that this was a task that could be delegated to Lorna.

Lorna had trawled through the contacts database and the old address books in the stationery cupboard but drawn a blank. Terrified of having to admit failure to Geoffrey's assistant, certain that any chance at turning the work experience into a paid internship or even a proper job one day would evaporate the moment such an admission were made, she had decided to show her initiative and Googled Hattie. That had led her, logically and then geographically, to ACDA, outside which she had loitered for an hour before recognising Hattie as she came out from the back entrance of the main building.

'Did you consider that you could have just *asked* me?' asked Hattie, trying not to sound too reproachful.

'I lost my nerve,' said Lorna. 'I thought you might say no and get angry with me.'

'I… well, next time maybe consider it. I'd much rather be asked where my home is by a stranger than followed back to it by one.'

The girl nodded, earnestly.

'I don't suppose you know *why* Geoffrey wanted to get hold of me?' Hattie added, a note of hopefulness entering her voice unbidden.

'I think it has to do with the workshop for… Oh! No, sorry, I can't say,' yelped Lorna, her hands flying up to her face.

'I beg your pardon?'

'It's… it's confidential. Everything in the office is. They gave me a whole talk about it. I hadn't realised just how secretive they have to be. Someone actually broke into the office at the beginning of the week, but didn't take anything. They think it was a journalist or something, trying to sniff out what Geoffrey's next project will be. Anyway, I'm not allowed to say anything, basically. To anyone.'

Hattie stifled the urge to grimace. 'I see,' she said neutrally. 'But either way, why on earth would he want my address? Why couldn't he just call me?'

'Oh, I know that one,' said Lorna, enthusiastically. 'At least… I don't think this is confidential. Any time Geoffrey wants to work with someone he sends them champagne first, that way when he gets in touch it already feels like a done deal and it's harder for them to turn him down.'

Hattie snorted. That did indeed sound like the Geoffrey she knew of old. He was a showman through and through, flamboyant, manipulative and very accustomed to getting his way. She couldn't remember him doing precisely this back in the day, but pre-negotiation champagne as standard sounded very much his style. Perhaps he hadn't yet been successful enough to afford such flourishes back then.

'Well look. You know my address now. Go ahead and tell Geoffrey, and I promise not to tell him *how* you found out if you promise never to stalk strangers across London again. Deal?'

'Deal,' said Lorna.

Hattie showed the girl out and, closing the door behind her, found herself indulging in a quiet chuckle. The girl was... well, not exactly gormless, but daft as a brush and clearly riddled with anxiety. All young people seemed to be nowadays, she thought, remembering her earlier exchange with Abua.

She was also a little bit flattered that the great Geoffrey Dougray was following through on his indication the previous week that he wanted to get hold of her for something. And with term at ACDA ending and a long, empty, boring summer stretching out ahead of her, she was more than a little bit excited at the idea that maybe he would have some work for her. It was the end of a long and tiring day though, so for now she would do well to put all such thoughts to one side and concentrate on dinner, a relaxing shower and an early night.

Dinner turned into more of an ordeal than she had intended. She had already put the pasta on to boil by the time she spotted that the pesto in the tub in the fridge was well past its sell-by date, and that it wasn't just basil that was contributing to its green colour any more. There were no other tubs of sauce available, but there was an onion in the fridge, a tin of tomatoes in the cupboard and a jar of Italian seasoning in the spice rack. Hattie would be the first to admit she was no great shakes in the kitchen (actually, she might be the second: Nick would probably say it for her before she could get a word in edgeways), but committed as she already was to conchiglie, she thought this might be within her culinary capabilities.

So she was trying, with the aid of a frustratingly blunt knife, to hack up the onion when she heard the door open and Nick let himself in.

'Hullo!' she called, but she received no reply. Instead she just heard his soft wheezing as he pulled his boots off, and a few moments later he stomped past the kitchen doorway into the sitting room.

'It wouldn't kill you to at least say hi, you know,' she said, sharply, then immediately regretted her tone. When it came to basic human niceties such as covering his mouth when he sneezed, picking up his toenail clippings, and acknowledging the existence of his life partner, Nick was hopeless, and Hattie didn't feel at all bad about pointing out that he was hopeless and insisting that he try to do better. But the thing was, he wasn't hopeless on purpose. In his own way he did try. It was just that absentmindedness wasn't something that could be solved by willpower. The only thing that worked was patient, habit-forming encouragement and reinforcement, and over the years Hattie had had some successes in training him out of his worst tendencies that way.

Whereas snapping at him just made him act like a stroppy teenager for twenty minutes until he got distracted again and forgot about it.

Hattie sighed. Maybe it was the mental image of the corpse at the theatre from last week still looming large in her consciousness. Maybe it was the memory of that fatuous speech from that fatuous actor earlier today. Maybe it was this sodding onion that preferred to slide apart into its constituent layers as soon as she grasped it, rather than submit to the ministrations of the knife blade. But either way, she was in a grouch.

'Sorry,' said Nick, reappearing at the doorway. 'I was miles away.'

'It's all right,' she replied, adding as a peace offering, 'at least you remembered to take your boots off. How was the warehouse?'

'Fine. Well, except that I nearly ended the day two inches shorter than when I started it, no thanks to Min-Su…'

With that, Nick launched into a detailed retelling of the events of his day. In a rare gap between touring shows he was filling time helping out at a lighting kit hire warehouse, preparing endless flightcases of lanterns, dimmers and cables for distribution across the country, taking receipt of yet more flightcases, and unpacking, storing and taking inventory of their contents. It ought to have been mind-numbingly humdrum work, but being Nick he had previously crossed paths and made friends with ninety per cent of the people who were now working there, and within days had befriended the remaining ten, and they spent each day joking and gently teasing one another, while devising ever more bizarre and overcomplex ways of shunting kit around in the name of 'efficiency', all fuelled by quantities of tea that would kill a normal person. (Mind you, Hattie reflected, with the amount of sugar Nick put in his tea, she was pretty sure it'd kill him too in the end.)

Nick rambled on and Hattie half-listened. His narrative was a welcome distraction from her own thoughts, and even when the content was a bit dull, the light-hearted drone of his delivery made for a pleasing background noise. Together they tackled the pasta sauce, producing something that, when covered in enough grated cheese, was at least inoffensive. Nick started to lay the table, but readily acquiesced when Hattie suggested that perhaps today could be a telly supper day. So they set themselves up on the sofa, and Nick was scrolling through a list of sitcoms when, very unexpectedly given the time of night, the doorbell rang.

They exchanged glances.

'Jehovah's Witnesses?' suggested Nick.

'They haven't been round in years,' replied Hattie with a shake of her head.

'Oh, I'll tell you who it is: it's Anoor. He wants to talk about… you know… the pipework thing in the basement.'

'Can you get it then? I've never understood what it is he's on about.'

Nick scowled, but he picked himself up from the sofa and wearily stalked out into the hall. She heard him walk out of their door and down the communal stairs, and then open the front door. There was a long pause before he called up to her in a slightly strange voice: 'Cockatoo? He wants to talk to you.'

Surprised, Hattie got up and poked her head out of the flat, peering down the short staircase at the front doorway of the building. But the man hovering awkwardly on the doorstep, visible behind Nick's oddly defensively positioned form, wasn't their neighbour Anoor at all. It was Eoin.

'Can I come up?' he called to her, a definite note of urgency in his voice.

'Am I committing a crime if I let you?' she replied.

He laughed, but she hadn't meant it as a joke. Nick turned round and looked at her, questioningly. He'd never met Eoin before, and at best could have only very tentatively connected the grim story Hattie had told him about the previous week with this stranger on the doorstep. But he knew something was up.

'Come on, Harriet. I just want to talk to you,' pleaded Eoin.

Hattie sighed. 'All right. But when I tell you it's time to leave, you leave. And if you try anything funny I'll… well, I'll be very disappointed in you.'

Nick stood awkwardly aside and Eoin, smiling gratefully, hurried up the stairs. Hattie led him to the kitchen table, got him to sit down, and reflexively put the kettle on, before sitting herself. Nick stood in the kitchen doorway, miming confused gestures at Hattie.

'Eoin, this is my husband Nick. Nick, this is Eoin Norell, who I used to work with back in the day. He's…'

She found herself faltering, and Eoin cut in with: 'He's the one who everyone thinks murdered his writing partner last week.'

Hattie winced. That was indeed what she had been trying to say, but it sounded very ugly out loud.

'Right,' said Nick, frowning 'I'll um… I'll…'

'Could you give us a few minutes to talk?' suggested Hattie.

'I'll be in the living room, then,' said Nick. With a last anxious look at Eoin he trudged uncertainly away, and after a moment Hattie heard him slump down on the settee.

'So, what have you been up to these last few decades?' asked Eoin, breaking the silence that had started to crystallise around them.

Hattie shrugged. 'Touring, mostly. Mostly UK, bit of Europe, some America. A few West End stints, but I preferred the road. I've had to give that up, though, recently. My hip.'

Eoin made a sympathetic face. 'Whoever would have thought Harriet Fowler would get so old? Wait, it's Hattie Cocker now, isn't it?'

Not that old, she thought. *And besides, look who's talking!*

Eoin had changed a lot. He'd been such a skinny boy. Now, while his frame was still stick-thin, he'd filled out, around the face at least. His cheeks were puffier, his jaw was jowlier and his forehead wrinklier. But, buried in the middle of all that extra flesh, the same features poked out. His hair was grey and thinning, and he'd swapped baggy jeans and angrily sloganned hoodies for chinos and a nondescript woolly jumper. Hattie didn't think middle age suited him, but maybe she just needed time to get used to this new incarnation.

But that was beside the point…

'Eoin,' she said, 'What's going on?'

'Well, my life is ruined, I'm a wanted man, and the last of my friends have abandoned me. Other than that, it's business as usual.'

'And... I don't know how to ask this,' said Hattie uncomfortably, 'but—'

'I didn't kill him,' Eoin said, forcefully. 'I could never. I loved him. I mean, he was awful in many ways, and at times I absolutely hated his guts too, but I loved him.'

'But then what happened? We heard a struggle, then you were running away, then we... found... him,' Hattie finished, shuddering involuntarily at the memory. Behind her, the kettle started to rattle as it heated up.

'I honestly don't know what happened. I went to meet Lel, we talked, it got pretty heated, I got very upset – *very* upset, I will admit – but talked him round before I left. He was alive and well. He even got the last word in. He said, "I just hope we survive this" if you can believe it. I would have left straight away, but then I saw that bastard Geoffrey in the way. I knew if he saw me it would get ugly – he's someone I really *could* have murdered that day – so I hid in a prop store for a few minutes until I was sure he'd gone, then I tried to sneak out the back without him spotting me. That's why I couldn't stop when I saw you. Then the next thing I know the police are calling me and I'm all over the bloody news.'

He sat back and looked at Hattie defiantly, as if daring her not to believe him. It was a moment of tension, broken by the sudden ping of the kettle switching off, at which both Eoin and Hattie twitched.

Eoin chuckled. 'Jesus, we're both on edge, aren't we?'

Hattie nodded, stood up and started to make the tea. Eoin's story was... well, it sounded sort of plausible. It was certainly easier to imagine him *not* murdering Lel than murdering him. But, given that *someone* had killed the poor man...

'I don't suppose you could get this cleared up if you talked to the police?' she asked, half-heartedly.

Eoin laughed again, noisily and bitterly. 'Oh come on Harriet, you of all people... No, I mean, I was in the right place at the right time, I've got a motive, I must have fingerprints all over the crime scene, and the body too, and no one's going to vouch for my character. The fact that I simply couldn't possibly have done it… the good fellows of the Metropolitan Police aren't going to let a little detail like that stand in the way, are they?'

'You say you couldn't have done it,' prompted Hattie, hearing as she said it the note of hopefulness that appeared in her own voice.

'I read the news stories. Someone physically overpowered him, bashed his head in with a stage weight, then picked him up bodily and stuffed him behind a chair. Does that sound like something I could do? You know me, Hattie. I mean, it's been a while, but you know what I'm like.'

Hattie thought about it as she put the milk away. 'You were the worst stage hand we ever had,' she said, slowly teasing out the memories. 'Any time a flat needed shifting, if you were holding one end of it no one wanted to be on the other, cos they knew it'd probably get dropped on their foot, or fall over, taking half the set with them. You weren't exactly weak, but you were never the physical sort, were you? And you were… scared of heights? You were, weren't you? We couldn't get you up a ladder, let alone the fly floor.'

'That's right! Oli said I was the worst stage hand in the history of the Tree.'

'To be fair, he said I was the worst assistant stage manager too, so we had that in common. Do you remember the time we spilled five litres of stage paint from the fly floor? We managed to splatter the entire stage and half the auditorium.'

'God almighty, yes. Oli made us stay and clear it up, and said we couldn't leave until everything was immaculate. But then we lost the bloody keys so couldn't get out—'

'All the white spirit fumes went to our heads, didn't they?' Hattie interjected.

'That's right, we spent half the night giggling uncontrollably, covered in paint. And eventually we gave up and passed out in the green room, and the next morning you found the keys in your back pocket.'

'Yes! I'd slept on them, and woke up with a ruddy great bruise on my bum! I can still picture Oli's face. I was sure he was going to fire us.'

'I'm amazed he didn't.'

Hattie smiled at the shared recollection, but as that image gave way to others, the smile faded. Because it hadn't all been silly adventures with Eoin. There had also been the other thing. The serious thing. And that was the thing that had shown Hattie who Eoin really was. She remembered what they had been through, or at least what Eoin had been through, in the time that they had known each other. The bond they shared was old, but it was forged in fire.

'You never lifted a finger, did you? Not even to defend yourself, when… well, I reckon if you were ever going to hurt anyone, it would have been *him*.'

Eoin nodded solemnly, and she could see his eyes moisten.

'You *remember* me,' he whispered. 'The real me. I don't think anyone else does. I barely do myself. Oh Hattie, I've been so lonely.'

He dissolved into tears, and thirty years melted away and once again he was that scared boy who'd turned up out of the blue at her door, crying and alone and with no one looking out for him but her. It was the same boy whom she had seen at his most vulnerable, whom she had come to think of as a younger brother, who was a victim, not a villain, and who had responded to violence with dignity, to anger with grace. In that moment Hattie knew, with absolute certainty, that Eoin was no killer. She put an awkward hand on his shoulder, and he put his hand on top of hers. They stayed still in that sad tableau for a few moments, then she handed him his tea and sat down.

'So what do you need?'

3

The first day that Eoin walked into the backstage area of the Beerbohm Tree Theatre in Knapesfield, Oli Tressel and Jude Zytinski were deep into a feud about chisels. It wasn't his first day of hanging round the theatre or even of watching the goings-on in the backstage area: the weather was almost unbearably hot, so the team had the big hangar doors at the back of the building rolled open, and sandwiched between the far side of the car park and the near bank of the river was a little hummock of grass where Eoin had spent much of the last two days, sitting and watching as the get-out for one show ended and the get-in for the next show began.

But it wasn't until the chisel thing kicked off that he got closer. It all came about because Oli was the theatre deck chief, and as such was responsible for the big case of tools owned by the theatre, maintaining them and making them available to people like Jude, a freelance production carpenter. Jude, in turn, was responsible for using those tools appropriately and responsibly and returning them to the case when she was done with them. And this was all normal and proper and a system that had worked since time immemorial.

But, in the workshop, alongside the case of theatre tools, was a smaller box. In this box lived Oli's personal tools, including a set of tempered Japanese carbon steel wood chisels. And these wood chisels had gone missing.

Jude categorically denied having taken them. And this would have been assurance enough for Oli, had she not followed up her denial with a throwaway line about how it really shouldn't have been a big deal, as there was a full set of chisels in the shared case. This put Oli into a state of great agitation, and he accused Jude of not understanding the significance of personal tools, citing one of the great unwritten rules of carpentry, namely that you never mess with another man's chisels. Jude took exception to the implicit sexism of that 'rule' and counter-accused Oli of being 'a precious little bitch', and things went downhill from there.

So when Eoin first made his entrance, carefully picking his way around half-constructed pieces of scenery, no one at first noticed him: the entire crew had downed tools to watch the barney between the two chippies. And when he drew attention to himself, by way of a light 'excuse me', he was perhaps unfortunate in that the person who responded to him first was Oli, who, already having lost his temper, immediately yelled at this unexpected and uninvited scrawny teenager to get out and get lost, without giving the poor boy a chance to get a word in edgeways.

But then, despite this unfortunate introduction, Eoin managed to turn things around. Instead of walking back out of the door as directed, he took a short detour towards a small pile of sound equipment in the corner. He lifted up a loop of cables and from underneath produced a small wooden case, inside which five highly valued and personally owned chisels were to be found.

'That lady put them on the floor there yesterday when she was making room for the mermaid tails on the workbench,' he said, pointing apologetically to a young assistant stage manager who was supposed to have been working on photocopying pages from a 1920s newspaper (so that the main character could rip their paper in half in Act 3 without costing a fortune in replacement props), but had of course given that up when the Oli-Jude bust-up became too noisy and exciting to ignore.

There was a moment's pause.

'Oh for God's sake, Harriet,' said Oli, but, with the reappearance of his chisels, the venom had gone out of his voice.

'Sorry,' said the young Hattie. 'I'd completely forgotten I'd put it there. Next time I'll check with you before moving anything. Sorry Oli, sorry Jude.'

'That's all right,' said Oli awkwardly, while behind him Jude offered a smile and a shrug. Then he turned to the newcomer: 'So who are you, anyway?'

'I'm Eoin. I was just watching what you've been doing, and I was wondering if I could help out? In some way?'

And that was how Eoin Norell got his first taste of the world of professional theatre. Well, professional in every sense apart from him being paid. Even in the carefree nineties, for an under-aged kid with no ID to be allowed to work in a hazard-filled environment when everyone suspected he should really have been in school took some bending of the rules; to *pay* him as well would have been, it was generally felt, pushing it.

Not having any recognisable relevant skills, he was at first passed around the crew to whoever needed a dogsbody. More often than not this meant he ended up footing ladders (always at the foot, never at the top – he suffered from extreme vertigo) or taking orders from Hattie, as an ASM's duties needed less specialist knowledge than, say, a stage electrician's. However, Eoin was curious and intelligent and quickly picked up enough knowledge to allow him to cut a gel for a lantern, tape down a cable run, or screw two battens together. He came across as very confident, but there was something rather defensive about him, and he seldom offered up much information about himself. His caustic sense of humour got him in trouble a few times, but in general he was well liked, and by the time a few shows had opened and closed he was officially designated a stage hand, with responsibilities assigned to him for each performance, and the understanding was that they'd be able to find uses for him for the rest of the season.

And then came the awful day when he turned up on Hattie's doorstep, his face puffy from crying, announcing he'd run away from home and begging her to let him stay, and Hattie... well, Hattie failed him.

But now he was back, and once again throwing himself upon her mercy.

'I'm so sorry, Hattie. I owe you so much already. It's completely unfair of me to ask you for more favours.'

'Don't worry about it,' Hattie reassured him. 'After everything that happened, I still... I owe you.'

She was trying to sound calm; in reality though she was anything but. The memories dragged up from years ago, the creeping fear that the police might somehow show up any minute, the noise from next door as Nick stood up and paced heavily back and forth, puttering and sighing, it all meant that the situation felt thoroughly volatile.

'So what should I do?' she asked. 'Do you want me to help you get somewhere? Or say something to... someone?'

Eoin shook his head. 'They'll catch up with me eventually. It's only a matter of time. And once they do I'm going to prison. I'm sure of it. That's okay. I never thought I'd make it past my thirties anyway, so all this is just... well, it's bonus time. If I spend it in a cell that's no great loss. It's the show, Hattie. I need my show back.'

'What do you mean?'

Eoin sighed, closed his eyes for a moment and scratched his head. 'Lel and I were... partners. Creatively. You know about that, right? We did *Total Hell*, *Martin Chuzzlewit*, *I'll Never Tell*, loads of things. I did the book and lyrics, he did the music. We had some misses, and a lot of our stuff was a bit rough round the edges, but when it worked it *worked*. We did best with adaptations. I suppose we benefited from the structure of an existing story.'

HATTIE STEALS THE SHOW

As Eoin was speaking, Nick turned up at the doorway. He was still looking worried, and made some agitated head nods in the direction of Eoin alongside some questioning gestures. Hattie held up a pacifying hand, hoping he would interpret it as a request for patience, and calm. Nick gave her a sour look in return, but retreated again.

'But it was a slog,' Eoin was saying, apparently unaware of the exchange that had happened behind him. 'A lot of what we did wasn't particularly commercial, we never found a producer who truly got us, we got buggered around by some agents, and it meant that every show we did, we had to carry it all the way ourselves. And Lel… began to lose heart. He began to lose faith. In us. So he took on some other work. He was so *nice* that people liked him and always wanted to work with him again, even if his actual output was a bit… Anyway. He got onto Geoffrey's radar, and long story short, a few years later they're opening *The Guilty*, and Lel's finally got his name up in lights.

'And I was happy for him. I genuinely love to see him succeed, even if it's without me. There's so little space these days for composers in theatre. Producers are only interested in jukebox musicals, rehashing old pop music from a big name artist, you almost never get to write original songs. Lel found a way, with Geoffrey, and that's great.

'But we had unfinished business. Did you ever read a book called *The Fall of a Thousand Hopeless Stars*?'

Hattie shook her head. The name rang a bell, but when she got a chance to read, her taste in fiction was, she was sure, a little less highbrow than Eoin's.

'It's an amazing work. Incredible. I mean, flawed as a novel, but its potential, dramaturgically, was… well. We weren't the only ones to see it, but we went after Tahmima, the author, and we pitched her, and we persuaded her, and with a bit of luck and perseverance we got the stage rights. And it took ages, I mean *ages*, to crack it, but eventually we got there, and we were sitting on an absolute firecracker of a show. But that's when Lel went to work on *The Guilty*, and he left me to try to put together the production by myself. And I... I've run out of friends. It's my own fault. I can never resist giving people my honest opinions, and as a result I've pissed off everyone I ever met in the industry, I've got myself a reputation. No producer would touch me, no backer would meet me.

'As a last-ditch thing, I asked Lel to pitch the show to Geoffrey. It was stupid of me, I should have known what would happen, but I was desperate. So Lel goes off and pitches the show to Geoffrey, shows him my script, plays him his music. Geoffrey sounded pretty excited, said he wanted to get some more opinions, but he'd get back to us.

'And then nothing happened. I was constantly pushing Lel to talk to Geoffrey, get him to give us a yea or a nay, and Geoffrey kept stalling. And it was only after this had been going on for a frankly comical amount of time that I realised what was going on. You see, we didn't get the rights in perpetuity. We got a five year window. If by the end of five years – by the end of *this year* – we hadn't opened a production, the stage rights would revert to the author. I don't know how Geoffrey came to find out about it, maybe he'd been talking to Tahmima directly, but he was winding down the clock, *because he wanted the rights for himself.*'

'Why though?' asked Hattie with a frown. 'You were asking him to produce the show anyway while you had the rights to it, wouldn't that amount to the same thing?'

Eoin shook his head. 'No, because so long as it was us holding on to the rights, he couldn't fire me as a writer. He liked the book, he liked Lel's music, I'm pretty sure he liked what I'd done with it, but he hates me. I said the wrong thing too many times, gave him opinions that were too honest, and couldn't bring myself to fawn over him the way that Lel did. He wanted the rights himself so he could cut me out of the show.'

Eoin sat back. 'That's why I was at the Revue last week. To persuade Lel to tell Geoffrey to go screw himself so we could mount the show ourselves. We'd have to do it small scale, but all we need to retain the rights is to open it *somewhere*, even if it's a ten-seater above a pub in Staines. And he agreed to it. It took a lot of persuading, because Geoffrey's someone you don't burn your bridges with lightly, but he came around. We were finally going to do it! And then he was murdered.'

Nick was hovering in the corridor, just out of sight. Hattie could hear the floorboards creak as he shifted his weight impatiently.

'So… what now?' she asked.

'I'm going to put the show on. I have to. It's what Lel would have wanted. And it's all I have left. At the very least, it's all I have left of him. I know a director who's… well, she's good enough. If I can just put it into her hands I know she'll get it staged even if I'm… you know. Not around. I mean, maybe they'll let me go see it on day release or something. But frankly, if I know our show – his music, my words – has been performed, just once, I'll be happy.

'The problem is I don't have the music. Lel was old-school, he hand-wrote everything on manuscript paper. He kept everything in these big binders in his studio, in this mad Georgian woman's house, and like everyone else she loathes me and I know she wouldn't even talk to me, let alone let me in. I hate to ask, but I need someone to go there and get Lel's score.'

Nick was on the move again. Hattie saw him walk past the doorway, then heard the click of the bedroom door closing. She tried to concentrate on what Eoin was saying.

'How though? I'm assuming you're not asking me to do any breaking and entering?'

'No, no, nothing like that. Say… say anything. Say you were sent by his agent. Or his lawyer, or by Geoffrey. But you'll need to do it soon, because any one of those will be turning up for real any day now. You just need to get her to let you in. She's drunk most of the time, she'll leave you alone after that. Upstairs in her house is a room, Lel's room. It's got a piano, and all his music is on shelves. You just need to find his score for *The Fall of a Thousand Hopeless Stars* and bring it back to me.'

'I don't know...' said Hattie, uncertainly.

Eoin looked at her sadly. 'I'm not going to try to twist your arm. I know how big an ask it is, and I know I don't deserve your help. I'm not going to tell you to do it for Lel's sake either. You know me, Hattie, I'm not a panderer. I'm not asking you to do this because I think you *should* do it, I'm asking you because you're my only hope.'

Hattie was torn. She dearly, dearly wanted to help her old friend. But there was something about this that wasn't sitting right. She realised that she was afraid.

'Sorry. I'm hesitating because... Lel *was* murdered. And blagging my way into rifling through the personal effects of someone who died from natural causes, say, is very different from doing it for someone whose killer is still at large.'

'I know what you mean,' said Eoin, nodding fervently. 'I can't stop thinking about what might have happened, and who could have done it. And look, of all people I'm the least keen to go around making accusations based on how things look, but... Geoffrey was there, wasn't he?'

'Geoffrey?' echoed Hattie, incredulous. 'I saw him a few minutes after it must have happened. He didn't exactly look like... well, like he'd just offed someone.'

'Maybe you're right. But then who?'

'There was a name on the sign-in sheet. Colin McDermot. He was in the building before it happened, and he disappeared at some point without signing out. I've no idea who he is but I can't help wondering, you know?'

Eoin shrugged. 'I don't know the name. But I didn't know a lot about Lel's life at the end. I'll look into it, if I get some breathing space when it comes to saving my own skin. In the meantime... well. I've never been in a situation like this before. I don't know what to assume, I don't know what are reasonable precautions to take. So I suppose, if you do go to his studio... do it soon, do it surreptitiously, but also do it in daylight so you can watch your back.'

'Okay,' said Hattie. 'Let me think about this, all right? Can I take just a little bit of time to think?'

But there wasn't time, because Nick reappeared again, looking anxious and apologetic, with his phone in his hand.

'I called the fuzz,' he said, his voice cracking slightly. He was never comfortable with conflict. 'They're sending someone over.'

4

It became apparent afterwards that they needn't have hurried: it was more than an hour after Hattie and Eoin said their flustered goodbyes and he disappeared into the Chiswick night that a knock on the door heralded the arrival of the self-important police officer who had clearly been only partially briefed on what exactly it was he had been called out about. Hattie was unsure how to play it: on the one hand, she wanted to give away as little as possible, keen as she was neither to incriminate herself nor do anything to help them catch up to Eoin. On the other hand, she could feel Nick's worried gaze on her, and she feared that if she wasn't forthcoming enough he would fill in the gaps for her, and if these things were to be told she would rather control the telling of it.

In the end, it was the dimness of the officer that did it: he was almost comically slow to grasp even the basics of the matter – that Eoin Norell, who did not live here, had nevertheless just *visited* here, and that while they had let him in of their own volition, since they knew him, Nick had *also* called the police on him – and so in large part in frustration at his idiocy, Hattie found herself spelling out the events of the evening in far more detail than she had intended. The only thing she held back was the detail about the missing score for *Fall*, and the nature of the help for which Eoin had enlisted her.

Eventually, satisfied at last that neither Hattie nor Nick could tell him where Eoin was now and where he was planning on being next, the officer departed, leaving behind him an ominous silence that claustrophobically filled every inch of the flat. Nick made himself scarce in the sitting room while Hattie worked out a series of emotions on the washing up in the kitchen before taking a quick shower and turning in.

As she was getting into bed Nick appeared in the bedroom doorway.

'I'll sleep on the sofa, then, shall I?' he offered.

Hattie sighed. 'No, you silly bugger, you can sleep here. I'm not angry with you. Well, I am, but… I mean you did the right… at least, you didn't do the *wrong* thing. Okay?'

Nick's face broke out into a big, relieved, crinkly smile. 'Okay,' he said, and half an hour later he was lying beside Hattie, snoring heartily.

Hattie, though, couldn't sleep. Her mind was too mixed up, and she replayed the conversation with Eoin over and over in her head, trying to make more sense of it. Eoin was innocent, of that much she was certain. Why was she so certain? Two reasons. First, the police were so lazily confident it was him, and that alone made it pretty likely that it wasn't in Hattie's book. Preconceptions about the effectiveness of the constabulary aside, however, Hattie knew Eoin. Not in the superficial sense, not any more. They hadn't seen each other in decades, after all. But in a more profound way, Hattie *knew* Eoin. She understood what motivated him and how he thought. She knew the fears he nursed in his soul, the emotions he kept locked up in his heart. Eoin could no more bring himself to murder than a puppy could.

So: Eoin hadn't killed Lel. That in itself raised the worrying question of who *had*, but leave that aside for the moment. The urgent question was what would happen to Eoin. He seemed resigned to being convicted eventually, and that sat uncomfortably with Hattie: she conceded that it seemed likely, but bridled at the idea it was an inevitability. There wasn't much she could do to help with that, though. She *could*, however, help with what Eoin was asking her to help with: getting his and Lel's final show mounted. Hattie was a theatre person through and through. She could see why the show was significant, why getting it produced mattered. In which case, the way forward was clear. Why, then, did she feel so uncomfortable about it?

The next morning, once Nick had headed off to the warehouse, Hattie found herself sitting at the kitchen table considering two possible shapes to her day. The first was an appealing one: with the term at ACDA officially over, there was nothing Hattie needed to do today. So she could have a quiet morning, maybe clean the flat, nip down to Chiswick High Road to buy some bits and bobs, and perhaps treat herself to one of the over-the-top chocolate and meringue creations they served at the coffee shop at the end of the road. In the afternoon she might scratch an itch that she'd been building up since April, by buckling down and sorting out her and Nick's self-assessment tax returns, and by the time Nick came back she could have supper on the table, a glass of wine in her hand, and a warm sense of self-satisfaction at a day productively spent.

That was the first option. In hindsight it was no wonder Hattie chose the second. She brushed her hair, re-packed her handbag, checked the weather and walked to the tube.

The address Eoin had scrawled for her (on a piece of paper she had chosen to show neither to Nick nor to the police officer) led to a three-storey terraced house just north of Clapham Common, around the corner from Battersea Arts Centre. It was a little bit run-down from the outside, in contrast with the other properties on the street with their fresh white paint and carefully coiffed topiaries. Hattie's first instinct was to find a secluded spot from which to survey the house, but she realised that there was nothing in particular she would be looking *for*, and the urge to linger was really just an expression of nerves. So instead, she steeled herself, walked straight up to the door and rang the bell.

After a prolonged wait it was opened by a woman of around Hattie's age, wearing a string of pearls, a floral chiffon blouse, joggers and Crocs. Wild black hair poked out from under a half-heartedly arranged headscarf, dark eyes peered out beneath heavy lids, and a large mouth sagged under the weight of its own lips.

'Yes?' she said, sleepily.

'Hello,' said Hattie brightly. 'Is this… I mean, was this… Did Lel Nowak use to work here?'

'Yes?' the woman replied, in exactly the same tone she'd used before.

'Ah, right,' said Hattie. 'I assume you know what happened? To him?'

'Yes?'

The woman's tone was unreadable. Was it confusion? Suspicion? Either way, the next bit was the hard part. Choosing her words carefully, Hattie continued. 'I'm here about Lel's work with Sir Geoffrey Dougray. I've been talking to Sir Geoffrey about the state of some of his projects – obviously he and Lel worked together a lot – and I'm trying to get my hands on the score Lel wrote. It's about protecting his legacy, now that he's gone. I was told I'd find it here?'

The woman frowned for a second, and Hattie's heart raced. Then she finally replied, in a thick accent that Hattie couldn't place: 'You… see… Lel… room?'

Hattie nodded.

The woman shrugged and, letting the door swing open, turned and wandered back inside the house. Hattie followed, closing the door behind her, as the woman led her down a tiled hallway that smelled faintly of mildew. She gestured up the stone stairs and muttered, 'Up… left,' then, without waiting even for an acknowledgement, pottered through a doorway from which filtered the sounds of a television broadcasting in what Hattie thought could be Georgian.

Hattie made her way up the staircase and, after a couple of false starts (the first door on the left turned out to be a bathroom), found herself in what must have been Lel's studio: it was a small room with cream walls, a scuffed dado rail all the way round, exposed floorboards, a high ceiling and a large sash window on the far wall. Most of the room was taken up by a large, black grand piano (Hattie found herself wondering how they'd even got it in in the first place) that had seen better days. There was a tatty blanket spread on top of it, over which were strewn various music books, notepads and a few packets of biscuits, mostly opened and spilling crumbs. To the left of the piano was a small writing desk, replete with more paper and snacks, with a bit of stationery thrown in for variation, and a small piano stool, worn and saggy enough that Hattie got a pretty clear sense of the shape and size of Lel's posterior.

The only other piece of furniture was an enormous free-standing set of shelves in the corner, about the size of a double wardrobe. While everything else in the room (as well as what other bits of the house décor Hattie had seen so far) looked a hundred years old and falling apart, the shelving looked like it could have been built from an Ikea flat-pack the previous week. It was divided into a grid of short but deep slots, most of which housed stacks of flipchart-size paper. It didn't take much investigation to make clear that these were all musical scores, mostly handwritten, sometimes accompanied by scripts, programmes and notebooks. This was it then: the catalogue of Lel's life's work. It was meticulously tidy and arranged such that every set of papers was easy to reach and peruse. The only other thing Hattie could have wished for was for the shelves to be in any way labelled. But there was no use sulking that they weren't. Instead, Hattie put down her bag, rolled up her sleeves and starting with the left compartment on the top row, began to browse.

It took her about ten minutes to suspect that the score to *Fall* wasn't there, and another ten to feel confident that her suspicions were correct. Each cubbyhole contained documents pertaining to a single show, with all papers marked in the top corner with the show's initials. Near the bottom on the right was the score and script for *The Guilty*, all marked with 'T.G.', up at the top on the left were a set of sketches for a show called *I'll Never Tell*, all marked 'I.N.T.' and so on. Right in the middle was an almost empty compartment, containing a single notebook that had inscribed in the corner 'T.F.O.A.T.H.S.', and a single paperback copy of *The Fall of a Thousand Hopeless Stars*. The notebook was almost empty, containing a few pages of indecipherable handwritten scrawls, and the paperback was well-thumbed, with certain passages heavily underlined throughout, and extensive pencilled marginalia. But there was not a single musical note written down in any of it, and eventually Hattie had scoured the rest of the shelves enough to be satisfied that the score hadn't simply been misfiled.

Crestfallen, she eventually admitted defeat and made her way back down the stairs. She poked her head into the room to which her peculiar host had retreated. There she still was, sprawled across a large cream leather armchair facing an enormous TV that was spewing out what appeared to be an eastern European news show. In one hand she held a large plastic cup, through whose lid poked a long straw, and her eyes were closed.

'Er... I'm finished upstairs,' Hattie said tentatively. The woman gave no indication of having heard her.

'I didn't actually find what I was looking for. I don't suppose there was somewhere else that Lel also kept his documents?'

Again, the woman didn't react.

'Well,' said Hattie. 'Never mind then. I'll let myself out, then, shall I?'

At this the woman's head shifted, and she murmured, '*Diakh,*

diakh, madloba...' before shakily lifting the straw to her lips, her eyes remaining closed throughout.

Feeling rather confused and more than a little bit frustrated, Hattie made her way to the door and went out to the street.

There was a familiar face waiting for her when she got home. Lorna the intern was sitting on the steps of her building, wearing a sheepish expression and clutching a very small wicker hamper.

'Let me guess,' said Hattie, 'Another slow day at the office, so when they asked you to arrange a courier, you volunteered to do the delivery yourself, right?'

'Pretty much,' said Lorna. 'I wanted to—'

'To show initiative,' Hattie finished for her, and Lorna nodded. 'Well, what do you have for me?'

The box turned out to contain a bottle of champagne and nestling next to it on a bed of curly wood shavings, a small debossed card that said 'Geoffrey Dougray Productions Ltd' in neat sans serif on one side, and an almost convincingly handwritten-looking 'I look forward to working together! Call me – Geoffrey' on the other, above a phone number.

Hattie, once she'd thanked and dismissed Lorna, put the champagne in the fridge, made herself a cup of tea and rang Geoffrey. The call was answered almost immediately by a woman, who said curtly, 'Geoffrey Dougray Productions, Louise speaking.'

'Oh hello,' said Hattie, 'Geoffrey asked me to call him. I got sent a hamp—'

'Your name please?'

'Hattie Cocker.'

'All right, I'll see if I can put you through.'

The line went quiet for a few seconds, and then Geoffrey picked up.

'Hattie! Wonderful! Did you get the champagne? Listen, I can't talk, but it's a workshop. Two weeks. Utterly thrown into chaos by the tragedy, of course, but we press on, don't we? It's going to be very close, very intimate. We're doing it up at Trevelyan House. You've been, haven't you? It's as much a house party as a rehearsal, so obviously I'm only inviting the right sort of people, but I need a stage manager who'll keep the twirlies in line, and naturally I thought of you. You'll do it, won't you? Starts Thursday next week. But like I say, I can't talk, so I'll get Louise to call you back and talk you through the details. Wonderful, 'bye now.'

And with that he hung up. He'd delivered everything at such a gallop that Hattie had barely had a chance to take it all in, let alone get a word in edgeways. With his words still ringing in her ears she pulled out a notebook from her handbag and jotted down everything she could remember about what he'd said. A two-week workshop, starting in a little under a week, taking place somewhere called Trevelyan House. No mention of what the show was, or what the workshop was *for*. No mention of pay either, so unlikely to be more than Equity minimum, but that was as good as you could expect anywhere, these days. All in all, without knowing the details it sounded as good a gig as Hattie could hope for, and given the summer break the timings were ideal. So why wasn't she more excited about it?

She spent the rest of the day quietly fretting. She did tidy the flat, she did nip to the shops and buy groceries, she even made a start on her tax return, but the day felt like a failure nonetheless. Even a ganache-filled rose meringue whirl wasn't enough to make her feel better. She found herself compulsively checking her phone, just in case she'd missed a call, although of the two calls she was half expecting today, she wasn't sure which one she was anxious about. When the phone actually did ring at about 5 o'clock she nearly jumped out of her skin, and was both frustrated and relieved to see that it was Angharad from ACDA calling.

'Have you heard?' asked the lighting tutor as soon as Hattie picked up.

'I don't think so. What?'

'Jolyon's formally proposed to cancel the technical course. As part of a complete overhaul of the school. They're going for more corporate training and things like that instead.'

Jolyon, the principal at ACDA, was a one-time director who had early in his career gravitated towards the administrative side of the arts, and who had made a name for himself primarily as an effective fundraiser for various ballet and opera companies in the Midlands before joining ACDA a few years previously. He had apparently been unimpressed by the technical department since his arrival, on the grounds that it didn't add to ACDA's prestige, didn't generate any wealthy or famous alumni, and required a lot of expensive kit that could otherwise be sold off.

'What, just like that?'

'Just like that. The intake for next year will be cancelled, and the current first years will be given a one-year diploma and turfed out – technically the first and second years are separate qualifications, it's one of the hoops we had to jump through when the accreditation system changed. So there's no binding requirement to let them finish the course. Anyway, it means from September we're all out of a job.'

'Oh,' said Hattie. It didn't feel enough of a response, given the circumstances. She had a thousand half-formed questions to ask, and more than that, she very much wanted to wail and rail, but none of that would have been very helpful at the moment, so she made do with 'Oh' until she could think of something more useful to say. Then, once her brain had had a chance to get into gear, she added, 'You say he's proposed to cancel it. Who needs to sign off on that?'

'Well… the board, presumably. I only know about it from Zain in the finance office, I haven't seen the details. But I think that's just a formality, then we're all out of a job.'

There was something annoyingly gleeful in Angharad's tone.

The pleasure of being able to gossip seemed to outweigh any concern she had about being made redundant. *She'll be all right, though*, thought Hattie. *She can find work back in the industry.*

The same went for most of them, in Hattie's opinion. Shane in construction, Francine in costume, Chris in production management, they were all eminently employable, and all the temporary assistant tutors who worked at ACDA had barely dipped out of the normal theatre circles anyway. Old Rod was stuffed – he had been out of it too long, and was too old to learn new tricks – but he'd been increasingly open to the idea of retirement anyway.

And Mark, their boss? What does a head of technical training do when there's no more technical training to head up? Hattie wasn't sure he'd be willing to go back to his old life as a stage manager. Would another drama school take him? Hattie couldn't imagine him anywhere else. If you cut him he'd bleed... well, red as you'd expect, but specifically the shade of red used in the ACDA logo.

'I don't think he'll stand for it,' said Hattie, thoughtfully. 'Mark, I mean.'

'It's not up to him, is it? He's not on the board.'

'No, but... well, we'll see. Thanks for letting me know. And do keep me posted if you hear anything more.'

'Will do. I'd better get on, I haven't told Shane yet,' said Angharad, and they said their goodbyes.

Hattie put her phone down and gave a little snort of frustration. The call hadn't done anything to improve her mood.

When Nick came back she told him her about her day – or at least, those bits of the day that didn't involve searching a dead man's papers on false pretences. He was appropriately alarmed about the ACDA news, but considered that the offer from Geoffrey did a great deal to ameliorate the situation.

'It could be just what you need,' he said, encouragingly. 'Get in with Sir Geoff again and that'll open up doors. And who knows, if this workshop turns into his next West End show then you're sorted. Perfect timing, really.'

Hattie didn't share his enthusiasm, but found herself unable to articulate why, resorting instead to getting increasingly grouchy and snappish until Nick gave up and changed the subject. They were both uneasy. There was a lot to be uneasy about. Hattie ended up on the sofa, pretending to watch the TV, willing her phone to ring.

5

The first of the anticipated calls came at a little after 7 o'clock. The number that flashed up on Hattie's phone was not one she recognised. They'd arranged it so that he would call her, and not vice versa, meaning that he didn't need to give Hattie a phone number that could be used to track him down somehow if it fell into the wrong hands. But in the rush of parting they hadn't agreed *when* he would call her, which was one of the reasons she'd spent much of the day feeling agitated.

'Are you somewhere safe?' was the first question Hattie asked.

'More or less,' replied Eoin. 'I don't think anyone will be able to work out where I am. Not fast, anyway. And I'll keep moving around.'

'Good.'

'Er… I hate to ask, but…'

'I went to the studio this morning,' Hattie confirmed. 'But I'm afraid I have bad news: the score wasn't there.'

'Are you sure? There's a lot of paperwork there, and maybe your eyesight—'

'I went through every bit of it. The score is gone. I tried to ask the lady, but she wasn't exactly talkative and… I didn't press her. Sorry, I should have been more persistent, but I was nervous, what with the whole… lying thing.'

Hattie felt the words pouring out of her like a guilty confession.

'Don't worry, Hattie,' Eoin said reassuringly. 'You wouldn't have got anything out of her. Madame Kuznetsova. She only knows a few words of English. I've no idea how Lel found her, he doesn't speak any Georgian. *Didn't* speak any Georgian. But they'd spend hours together: he'd sit and play the piano; she'd sit and drink. They were best friends, it was the strangest relationship.'

'Okay. Thank you. But then… where's the score?'

'I don't know. That's a lie. I do know, I just don't want to admit it: Geoffrey must have it still, from when Lel showed it to him. Which means I'm buggered, because I've got no way of getting to it. It'll be locked away in a safe somewhere, in his office or in that bloody country estate of his.'

'Hang on,' said Hattie, her brow furrowing. 'Would that country estate be Trevelyan House?'

'That's the one.'

'Funny thing, that. I might actually be going there soon.'

Hattie briefly explained Geoffrey's invitation to his workshop, and Eoin listened in silence. When she had finished she heard him take a deep breath.

'That is… well, that's an astonishing stroke of luck. Or at least it's an astonishing coincidence. It's only luck if… Hattie, I hate to ask – and I know I keep saying that – but… if the score is in Trevelyan House, and you're going to be in Trevelyan House…'

It was Hattie's turn for a deep breath.

'I'm getting less and less comfortable with this,' she said awkwardly. 'But here's what I can do: I can keep an eye out. Okay?'

'Oh Hattie, that's massive. That's truly wonderful of you. Yes, please, and I wouldn't ask you to do anything more than that. But you've given me hope.'

'And to think, I was really half-considering turning down the gig.'

'Really? Why?'

'I don't know. Just a gut feeling, maybe. I'm not looking forward to being in close quarters with Geoffrey. I know what I said last time, and I still don't think he could have killed Lel, so maybe I'm being silly, but—'

'I don't think it's silly at all,' cut in Eoin. 'In fact, I've been thinking about it more and more. What if Lel met Geoffrey after I spoke to him? And what if he told him that he was taking *Fall* back, to work on it with me? Would that be enough for Geoffrey to flip out? He's a big man, after all.'

'But I mean, I know Geoffrey,' said Hattie, doubtfully. 'Or at least I knew him, back in the day.'

'Look, I don't think it's right for me to point fingers, not with so many fingers pointed at *me*. I'm sure you're right. I'm sure Geoffrey didn't kill Lel. But equally, if you don't feel entirely safe, for *any* reason, then I don't think you should go to Trevelyan House.'

Hattie found herself setting her jaw in determination. 'I'm being silly, that's all. I just got spooked by the whole thing. I'll go do the workshop. I'll do it, and I'll see if I can find you that score. It's too good a stroke of luck to turn down.'

That decision made, Hattie felt a weight lifted from her shoulders, and she found herself looking forward with more enthusiasm to the second big anticipated phone call of the day: the follow-up with details of the workshop from Geoffrey's assistant Louise. It was therefore perhaps inevitable that that call did not come. Hattie waited for it all evening, and then she waited again all the next morning, and then, just as she began to wonder whether the whole thing had in fact been called off, she received an automated email from Geoffrey's company, Geoffrey Dougray Productions Ltd, requesting her electronic signature on a contract.

Hattie suppressed a sigh of disappointment. The champagne had been a lovely personalised touch, but perhaps it had unreasonably raised her expectations about how much individual attention she might receive.

Still, the contract answered the concrete questions she'd had about the job: it would run from lunchtime the following

Thursday to the Tuesday twelve days later. They'd be working on the Saturdays and have the Sundays off. The pay was middling, but board and lodging were included. Any discussion of the contents of the workshop with any outsiders, for any reason, would result in the most severe penalties.

She clicked the button that counted as a signature, and turned her mind to the practicalities. Trevelyan House was seemingly in the middle of nowhere up in Norfolk, so she'd need to borrow the Astra. And the accommodation provided was apparently a 'shared private room' which, as well as being a prima facie contradiction in terms, suggested she might do well to pack some earplugs.

And speaking of things to pack, her stationery supplies were running a bit low. In particular she didn't have, and would probably need, at least one lever arch binder.

Now, ordinarily Hattie would simply have nipped to the Ryman on Chiswick High Road to solve that particular problem, but before she got very far into getting ready to go out, there popped into her head a memory of a binder, a nice grey one, sitting in the corner of her desk in the stage management office at ACDA. She'd bought it ages ago and meant to use it to keep copies of the handouts she prepared for her students for use in future years, before discovering a stash of school-owned folders in a cupboard, and using one of those instead. So now a folder that exactly met her current needs was sitting in the office waiting for her.

By itself, the small-but-not-trivial cost of buying a new one wouldn't have been enough to motivate her to go all the way to ACDA. But alongside that consideration was the thought that, if Angharad was right, there was a possibility that she wouldn't get the chance to see that binder again in the normal run of things. And that didn't seem right.

So Hattie found herself, slightly to her surprise, heading eastwards on the tube, and walking to and then inside the ACDA building. Lacking the regular student bustle it was quiet but, oddly, not completely silent. She could hear a thumping noise coming from the stairwell that led down into the basement. Her curiosity piqued, she followed the sound to its source, which turned out to be Rod, on his hands and knees at the entrance to the sound studio, a hammer in his hands.

'What on earth are you up to?' she asked him.

Rod, who'd evidently not heard her approach, startled and nearly dropped his hammer. He looked momentarily alarmed until, recognising her, he contracted his expression into a conspiratorial grin.

'Welcome, comrade Cocker,' he said. 'Come to join the resistance?'

'Hey? What are you *doing*?'

'Being proactive. More specifically, I have no intention of letting that sneaky so-and-so Jolyon shut up shop and change the locks on me over the summer. So I'm changing the locks myself before he gets a chance. Or I would be, but the bloody thing is jammed.'

Looking closer, Hattie could see now that next to where Rod was kneeling, the door was lying ajar with the face plate of its handle removed.

'That is the daftest thing I've ever heard. You think that if you stage a sit-in they'll let you keep your job? They'll just change their minds and things will go back to how they were?'

'Of course not. Although it did occur to me that maybe if we all refused NOT to teach the poor buggers who are half way through their course, we could get through at least a term of guerrilla training before we were finally evicted. Anyway. I know I can't win. But that doesn't mean I won't put up a fight.'

'I thought you'd come round to the idea of retiring, anyway.'

'Maybe, but if I'm going to go I'm going to go on my own terms.'

'Rod, this is daft even for you.'

Rod sat back on his haunches. 'Not as daft as you might think.

Jolyon's trying to make a clean sweep of this. He's waited until the end of term to make his move, and he wants it all wrapped up by September. If he gets his way, everything in my sound basement will be sold off or skipped in short order. But what he doesn't care to consider is that half the stuff in here is mine. Now, if it comes to it I'm more than happy to take a careful inventory and work out what belongs to who, and I'll even give him the benefit of the doubt whenever it's not obvious where ownership lies. But I'm damned if I'm going to give him a chance to chuck my eight-tracks in a skip just because he fails to see the value of them.'

'Well, good to see you reacting in your usual calm and measured manner.'

'And you? Are you simply going to sail serenely through the storm, propelled by the wind of equanimity?'

Hattie shrugged. 'I'm not taking a hammer to the building, if that's what you mean. It's awful news, but there's not anything I can do about it, is there? There's nothing any of us can do. Door vandalism aside.'

'Tell that to Mark.'

'What do you mean?'

'I'm just saying he's not taking this lying down. He's upstairs right now.'

'Doing what?'

'Doing his thing. Politics. Influence.'

Despite herself, Hattie was intrigued to see what this might look like, so after one more half-hearted plea for Rod to recant and put the hammer down, she bade him adieu and took herself up to Mark's office, where she was disappointed to see that Mark politicking looked very much like Mark at most other times: hunched over his laptop, typing clinically.

'Ah! Hattie,' he greeted her, looking up with a brittle smile. 'We've almost got enough people in for a departmental meeting this morning. I take it you've heard the news.'

'Well, I heard a rumour. I actually just popped in to collect something.'

'Well look, let's not get carried away. We're not at the stage of clearing our desks yet, no need to try to rescue your personal belongings.'

'No, that's not what I mean,' said Hattie, but she had to admit to herself that it was sort of what she was doing, even if it was a stretch to call a lever arch binder a personal belonging. Still, she'd not been at ACDA for long, so she had had less time to settle in than the others. And she wasn't the sort to put a soft-focus shot of Nick in a frame on her desk. So there were precious few other belongings of hers in here that were *more* personal than a piece of unused stationery.

'Rod said you were going to try to do something about it,' she offered.

Mark shrugged. 'No promises, but we're not sunk yet. I've been building up some good will with the powers that be for the last seven years, and I'd like to think I've got a line of credit, as it were. I'd hoped to spend it getting a tension grid in the auditorium, maybe a motorised fly system. I'll settle for us all still having a job come September. But...'

He paused, which was unusual for Mark: words, and the right words, came naturally to him, so Hattie had learned to watch out for the moments when he had to marshal his thoughts.

At last he continued. 'I know your financial situation has been a little precarious in the past, and your health has closed off some avenues of work. I would hate for you to jump ship prematurely, but I can't in good conscience promise that the job will be here in September. You might be wise to at least start thinking of a plan B.'

'Well, it's funny you should say that. I've had a little bit of work come through. With Geoffrey Dougray. It's just a workshop for now, but it might turn into something bigger.'

'Ah,' said Mark, and Hattie immediately realised this wasn't the answer he'd been hoping for. Maybe what he'd wanted her to say was 'Don't you worry about me, boss, you just focus on saving all our jobs and I know we'll all be all right.' Instead she'd made it sound like she was indeed preparing to jump ship, and now he looked like he thought she'd committed a gross betrayal. Hattie cursed herself: it had taken months of careful effort to try to get Mark on side in the first place. Trust her to put her foot in it with him, just when she needed him most.

She left the binder in the ACDA SM office in the end. It was a daft gesture, and one that no one else would notice, but after her run-ins with Mark and Rod she felt as though scurrying away with the thing would be an admission of defeat, while leaving it there would in some small way symbolise her faith that everything would be all right in the end.

That symbol cost her twenty quid at Ryman though (a fiver for a replacement binder, the rest on some spare pens, post-its, propelling pencil leads and highlighters – all things she didn't technically *need*, but it would have been practically criminal *not* to pick up given she was in the shop anyway). And six more at the nearby Costa, because mornings like that call for big sticky drinks to calm the nerves.

Hattie had mentally dedicated every day until Thursday to getting ready for the workshop. Despite having last stage-managed a show the previous October, she felt oddly disconnected, and a little nervous about throwing herself back into it, so she wanted as much time to prepare as possible. But by the end of the afternoon, having meticulously inventoried her stationery supplies, made a start on packing a suitcase, and even re-read some of her own course notes on how to run a rehearsal room, she had to admit to herself that there wasn't very much preparation she could meaningfully do. No one had told her what form the workshop would take, who else would be participating, or even what show it was they were workshopping, and short of calling up Sir Geoffrey to interrupt him from his day to ask – which was obviously an absurd idea – she had no way of finding out. Presumably it was all hush-hush for a reason. Hattie could believe that Geoffrey was as serious about secrecy as Lorna had intimated.

But whatever the case, all Hattie could realistically do was show up at the appointed place at the appointed time and take things from there. For now, she could turn her attention to other things. And at the top of Hattie's list of other things to consider was the mystery of who killed Lel. Despite what everyone thought, it wasn't Eoin. But *because* that was what everyone thought, no one seemed to be putting any energy into investigating the alternatives. Not, Hattie had to concede, that there were many other likely candidates. The only people Hattie had seen in the building at the time Lel died had been Donna, who was by her side the whole time, Eoin, and Geoffrey. Whatever Eoin said, Geoffrey didn't seem a very likely candidate. Not least because he wasn't a fit man, and if he'd just committed a brutal murder on the fly floor before high-tailing it back down to front of house, Hattie would have expected him to be at the very least out of breath when she came across him leaning against the proscenium.

In fact, there was only one remotely viable lead that Hattie could think of pursue, but pursue it she was determined to do: it was time to learn about the one other name on the sign-in sheet, this mysterious Colin McDermot.

6

Having decided to investigate, Hattie wasted no time in starting her researches. By no means a regular netizen, she nevertheless managed a piece of digital reconnaissance of which she was quietly proud: by Googling the words 'Colin McDermot Revue', she established that he was a front of house manager at the theatre. That made sense: Donna had said something to Geoffrey about how Colin would be upset if he damaged the plasterwork.

Hattie's first move was to ring the venue. The theatre had gone dark for a week following Lel's death, but by now would have been back up and running for a few days, so its normal routine would have resumed. With that in mind she picked her time of day carefully: most of the time when an FOH manager was on-site they'd be busy with their duties relating to the day's performances. While it would in theory be possible to interrupt these with a high-priority phone call, doing so would disrupt the smooth running of the show, a notion that Hattie found abhorrent. No, far better to find one of those brief windows when there were no active front of house duties to be done but the manager would still reliably be on site. *Let's see now*, she thought. Curtain-up was at half past seven, the first act lasted just under an hour, and Donna had told her that latecomers were admitted at the end of scene two, around fifteen minutes in. Build in a buffer of ten minutes for miscellaneous admin, and to Hattie's mind that suggested that the ideal window of opportunity was between seven fifty-five and quarter past eight.

So at 8 o'clock precisely Hattie rang the Revue box office and asked for the manager. She was put on hold for a couple of minutes, and then a male voice answered with a cautious, 'Hello?'

'Hullo, is that Colin McDermot?'

'Er... no.'

No further details were offered, so Hattie prompted, 'May I ask who I'm speaking to?'

'Er... I'm Giles.'

Another pause. Giles's voice sounded nervous. Was he just crap at phone conversations, or was he being evasive? Either way, Hattie realised she needed to take the lead in this interaction.

'May I ask, are you the front of house manager, Giles?'

'No, I'm the front of house assistant.'

'I see. I did ask to speak to the front of house manager. Is he around?'

'Er... no.'

'Do you know when he'll be back?'

'Er... no.'

'Okay. And just so I'm one hundred per cent clear, is Colin McDermot the front of house manager?'

'Er... yes.'

The conversation was like pulling teeth, but the more she heard of Giles's voice the more she was sure: he sounded scared.

'All right, Giles,' she said, trying to sound firm but not aggressive. 'I do need to speak to Colin. Can you tell me how I can get hold of him? Do you have his mobile number?'

'Er... yes...'

With a little more coaxing, the hapless Giles read out a number and Hattie jotted it down. That done, she thanked him, coldly, for all his help, and rang off.

How curious. A quick look at the Revue website confirmed that there was indeed a Giles Caperton listed as front of house assistant and volunteer coordinator. On the balance of probability, that was who Hattie had been talking to, although it did cross her mind that perhaps it had been Colin himself, using an assumed name. That seemed unlikely, but it might have explained some of the caginess.

Still, she had made progress. She made herself a congratulatory cup of tea and then dialled the number she had been given. A new voice answered.

'Hello, Colin speaking.'

'Hi, Colin, my name's Hattie, and—'

'Are you the one who rang the theatre just now?' he asked abruptly.

'Yes,' Hattie replied, taken aback that in the time it had taken the kettle to boil, Giles had apparently spoken to Colin – despite having claimed Colin wasn't at the theatre – to warn him to expect her call.

'Then may I ask what this is regarding?'

Hattie took a breath. 'It's about the night Lel Nowak died.' Was that the right approach? Simply to come out and say it? Maybe not, but she couldn't think of a better way to go about it.

There was silence on the other end of the line, then Colin said, 'And who are you?'

'My name's Hattie,' she repeated. 'I was at the theatre that night, with Donna. You were signed in, but I didn't see you. I wanted—'

'All right, all right, look, I don't want to talk about this over the phone. You want to talk, you come talk to me in person, okay?'

'All right. But where are you? Your colleague said you're not at the theatre tonight.'

There was another pause, and then he gave her an address.

She went alone. It did occur to her that Colin McDermot was quite possibly a murderer, and therefore walking into his house late on a Saturday night was not necessarily the greatest plan ever concocted by a stage manager, but there was no one else she could realistically bring with her: Nick was spending the evening at the pub round the corner and would have come if asked, but he would inevitably have asked *why* she was visiting this man, and there was no way she could tell him enough to satisfy his curiosity without also sending him into a panic and make him refuse to let her go. So she went by herself, but brought a kitchen knife in her handbag.

It was a flat halfway up a dingy tower block in Shadwell, accessible via a rather terrifying lift whose walls were defaced by graffiti and half of whose buttons were mismatched, as though they'd been repaired on the cheap, in a way that did not inspire confidence in the integrity of the elevator system as a whole.

But it got her to the right floor, and she made her way to the right door, which she found ajar. Reaching into her handbag and finding comfort in the knife handle therein, she knocked on the door and called in, 'Hallo?'

'I'm through here,' came the reply.

'Oh. Are you not going to come to me?'

'No.'

Red flags were waving directly in Hattie's face, but driven by curiosity over self-preservation, she chose to ignore them. Thankfully, not every bad decision leads to a bad outcome, and Hattie, having made the foolish choice to walk into the apartment of a possible murderer, found herself proceeding down a dark and ominous corridor, only to emerge in a small living room upon whose sofa lay a very pathetic-looking individual. His face was puffy and swollen, some of his hair had been shaved off where several lines of stitches adorned the revealed scalp; his left arm was in a sling, and a crutch leaned by his side. He was slumped sideways in an angled recline, surrounded by a mess of food wrappers, wearing a tatty T-shirt and food-stained tracksuit trousers.

'Oh,' said Hattie. It wasn't what she'd meant to say, but perhaps in part due to the relief of being reassured that she wasn't in imminent personal danger, it was what came out.

Colin nodded. 'I got banged up.'

'What happened?'

'Motorbike accident. I'm lucky to still be here.'

'It looks… painful.'

He nodded again. 'You should have seen me three weeks ago.'

The cogs started to turn in Hattie's head. 'You've not been at the theatre since it happened, have you?'

Colin shook his head.

'So how come your name was on the sign-in sheet?'

Colin gave her a long look, then sighed, and said, 'Giles. He's been signing me in and out. They check the sheet when they're signing off timesheets.'

Hattie frowned. 'You're still submitting timesheets?'

'Can't afford not to. GDP contracts. I don't get sick pay. I'm a carer for my mum, but like this I'm having to pay someone else to do it. I can't afford not to be getting paid.'

'Surely someone's noticed that you're not there?'

He shook his head. 'It's a good team, for the most part. Giles is covering for me, and he had a word with the others to explain what's going on. Well, most of the others,' he said, his brow lowering. 'The ones we can trust.'

Hattie thought for a moment. 'I can't imagine Donna would stand for something like this.'

'No indeed,' Colin replied darkly. 'I've been praying she wouldn't get wind of it. In the normal run of things we don't see each other except in passing. So long as nothing out of the ordinary happened I thought I could get away with it. But then there's an honest-to-God murder in the building, and I knew it was just a matter of time until the gig was up. So. This is me. The question I have is, who are you?'

'Well, I'm Hattie. Er… I'm not with the police. Or GDP. I'm just trying to understand.'

'Okay. But you said you know Donna?'

Hattie nodded.

'Then I suppose I need to throw myself on your mercy, don't I? Not to tell her, or anyone, what's been going on. Like I say, my mum—'

'It's all right,' said Hattie, hastily. 'I'm not going to tell anyone. I just wanted to be sure that you… well. I won't tell. How long before you can get back to work, do you think?'

'I've probably pushed my luck for too long. I'll give the office a ring in the morning, say I fell off my bike tonight, take the rest of the week unpaid, go back next Monday. So long as I can physically make it to the Revue I'm golden. I won't be able to do much actual work, but like I say, Giles can cover for me, and I'll just add it to the pile of favours I owe him.'

'Well… good luck. I won't keep you. I hope you feel better soon.'

'Thanks. And… thanks.'

Hattie nodded, and started to leave.

'Oh!' he called after her. 'Could you close the door firmly on your way out? I used up all my strength opening it for you earlier, I can't face getting up again.'

Once Hattie was back out on the street she found herself breathing a big, ragged sigh. She had gone to the apartment and she *hadn't* found Lel's killer, and she was as relieved for herself as she was disappointed for Eoin. Well, she thought, that was that. There was nothing more she could do to help him, not for now at least. Once she got to Norfolk perhaps she could carry on investigating the score. But in the meantime, she could relax.

Well, 'could' as in 'had the time and space to', not 'had the emotional capacity to'. There was too much going on. So over the next two days Hattie completed her tax returns, tidied the flat, *cleaned* the flat, completely rearranged the sitting room, repainted the kitchen, defrosted the freezer, steamed the carpets in the hall, and was on the verge of retiling the bathroom when Nick finally twigged that things were amiss and on his day off gently but firmly insisted they take a picnic to Epping forest.

'Well, this is nice,' he said, as they sat, swatting at mosquitoes while they munched on those fancy sausage rolls from the market, in the shade of an expansive oak tree.

'Mm,' agreed Hattie, distractedly. 'How do you spell "parallel"?'

'Rs first, then Ls,' he replied. 'Why?'

'Oh, no reason. It's one of those words I'm never sure if I've got it right. You shouldn't really make spelling mistakes as a stage manager. Written communication, that's half the job. It's unprofessional if you can't get the words right.'

'It's never bothered you before.'

'No, but that's no excuse. You've always got to be improving.'

'Bloody hell,' Nick marvelled. 'You've really got stuck in your own head this time.'

'I have, haven't I?' sighed Hattie. 'I've got spooked about this gig, what with… you know… everything.'

'Makes sense. But Geoffrey already *knows* you're good at the job, eh? If the show goes forward you're a shoo-in. So, however the ACDA drama plays out, you're sitting pretty.'

Hattie nodded, but that ACDA drama wasn't the 'everything' she'd meant. What *she'd* been thinking about was Eoin, the unlikely but not impossible notion that her employer had actually killed Lel, and the daunting prospect of snooping around looking for a contested musical score in her free time. But all those topics were off limits with Nick for the time being. As far as he was concerned, Eoin was very obviously a murderer, and Hattie had cut ties with him. Hattie didn't like keeping secrets from her husband, but she knew she didn't stand a chance of talking him round, at least not as things stood now.

'Tell you what,' continued Nick. 'How about a nice bit of devil's lettuce to take your mind off things?'

'Well you can't; you're working tomorrow. Rules are rules.'

'That's true. To be honest, I was thinking we might need to extend the window to forty-eight hours anyway. Maybe I'm getting old, but last time I had a smoke on a Saturday I felt bleary the whole of Monday. Well, you have a spliff, I'll have a beer.'

Hattie thought about it. 'No,' she replied sadly. 'It just wouldn't be the same.'

The final couple of days before the workshop trip passed largely without incident. Nick's efforts, clumsy though they were, were not entirely ineffective, and Hattie found that she was able to attain at least a modicum of calm. She still turned their little flat upside down, scouring places that had never hitherto seen the light of day. But she successfully stifled the urge to retile the bathroom.

On the evening before she needed to leave for Norfolk, she became aware that there was just one thing niggling at her. Okay, one *more* thing niggling at her: she hadn't heard from Abua. Wasn't he supposed to have started at the Young Vic by now? And hadn't he been going to call her?

Perhaps if she had been feeling more generally equanimous she'd have let it slide. He was under no obligation to get in touch, and in fact maybe it was a good sign: Hattie's offer had been one of support, and maybe it was support he didn't feel he needed once his surge of graduation jitters subsided. Interaction complete; no further action required.

But, spurred by her supply of excess nervous energy, in Hattie's present mood she wasn't quite content to leave it at that. She found herself rooting through her emails for the crew contacts list from the last ACDA production Abua had worked on, retrieving his number and composing a text message. She stopped herself before she pressed send. Was initiating contact with a former student, even with the best intentions, transgressing a boundary? It felt somehow less appropriate than simply making herself available if *he* chose to get in touch. She deleted the message and put away her phone.

Then ten minutes later she rang him anyway, but he didn't pick up, and he didn't call or message back.

She did, however, receive a message from a number not saved in her phone. It was Eoin, wishing her luck on the new gig. He didn't say anything more: there was no reference to the missing score, no attempt to encourage or persuade her to help him. But the fact that he'd messaged at all showed that she was at the forefront of his mind, that he was counting on Hattie to find a way of helping him. Maybe he knew the effect his message would have, maybe he didn't, but either way, Hattie felt the pressure.

It was perhaps unsurprising that she couldn't sleep that night. Nick's snores seemed louder than normal, the glow from the bedside clock brighter, the sheets scratchier. Hattie kept convincing herself that this time she really was getting tired, and rather than get up she should simply force herself to relax and she was sure to drop off and go to sleep, only to realise that ten minutes had passed and she was well down another mental rabbit-hole of worry. Eventually, though, she began to properly succumb to sleep, and her last thought before she finally drifted off was: *How did Eoin know the specific start date of the workshop, anyway? I'm sure I didn't tell him...*

Act Two

7

The room where we create theatre is a sacred place, and once inside it we are transformed, from laypeople to celebrants. It is our sacred duty to express our truth in that room and, harder, to accept the truth that those around us express. It is this, the bond of shared acceptance, that causes the transcendence of action into performance. Without it, we are merely empty vessels.

– From *Advanced Theatre Practice*
by Jala Senguel, MA

It didn't take Hattie long to form a mild but persistent dislike of the A12. As the major artery into East Anglia from London, it had no right to be so small, so roadwork-beset, and so resolutely devoid of a place to stop for a pee. Hattie, by no means a frequent driver, had learned to use a satnav but never got the hang of taking directions from an app on her phone. Not least of her problems was finding a way of perching the thing somewhere in her eyeline where it wouldn't slither down into the footwell on every sharp turn, and, the Astra not being equipped with Bluetooth, she had trouble hearing the audio instructions over the noise of the motorway. Consequently, she had missed the turning for Thurrock Services where she had planned to make a loo stop to break up the drive, and her discomfort had been steadily increasing ever since.

Nevertheless, chuntering steadily further north and east, she found the nervous agitation of the last few days subside slightly as the monotony of the drive imposed its own form of soothing balm upon her soul. Even a ropey moment at a roundabout outside Ipswich didn't throw her entirely. And the instructions Louise had emailed through that morning for how to reach Trevelyan House, once she passed the border into Norfolk, were pleasingly straightforward and unambiguous: they had clearly been written by and for the sorts of people who didn't expect to rely on technology to get from A to B.

When she finally turned into the drive, she felt a brief surge of apprehension, but this quickly gave way to awe: Geoffrey was filthy rich, it was widely known, so she'd expected his country pile to be pretty grand, but this…

It was a Tudor manor house. Or at least Tudor-style: Hattie wasn't convinced that any residential buildings actually built in the sixteenth century were ever quite so big. If it was a modern imitation, though, enormous care had evidently been taken to make it look appropriately rickety. Maybe it was an optical illusion brought on by all those diagonal zebra stripes of plaster and tar, but none of the walls seemed quite vertical, and none of the doors and windows looked quite square. It crouched heavily on the top of a very slight hill, in the middle of a huge gravel circle, away from which rolled a set of short-cropped lawns, broken up by a tennis court, a swimming pool, flower beds, follies, outbuildings, and what appeared to be a small maze. The drive veered lazily around the outer perimeter of the grounds before swinging inwards towards the garages at the back of the house, allowing any new arrival to get a pretty clear sense of the opulence on hand at Sir Geoffrey's country palace.

Just before reaching the house the drive forked. There was a sign at the cleft, with an arrow pointing towards the house and, in jaunty lettering, the words: 'Welcome to Geoffrey Towers: No unsolicited dramaturgists.' A piece of laminated A4 was affixed to the bottom of this sign. This had an arrow pointing the other way, and said 'GUEST PARKING'.

Hattie followed this second arrow and eventually found herself driving through a gateway into a small, unkempt field at the back of the grounds, around whose edges a few other cars were parked. The ground was bumpy and it took Hattie a few attempts to find a space where she was confident the Astra would be able to go both in and out. She was acutely conscious that Nick very much thought of it as his car, and he had packed her off under strict instruction to treat it with respect accordant with its advanced age.

By the time she had parked to her satisfaction and stretched out the worst of the soreness in her spine, another car had arrived in the field. This was a grey, shiny SUV, and even from a distance Hattie could see that the back seats were down and the whole thing was filled to the brim with kit: flight cases, tool boxes, baskets of cables, all were pressed up against the windows, looking as though they might explode from it any moment.

From the driver door alighted a young, slim man wearing a plain white T-shirt, black cargo trousers and chunky steel-toed boots. His hairline was receding, he wore a brace on his right wrist, and he eyed Hattie up with a mischievous expression.

'Hello hello,' he said. 'Are you here for the shindig?'

'I am,' she replied. 'Hattie Cocker, stage manager.'

He shook her by the hand. 'Tom Lovell, I'm running video.'

'Oh, you're an AV person? I didn't know we'd got projection for this.'

Tom stiffened visibly, and while the tone of his reply was light, the smile on his face was frozen: 'We *don't* tend to call it AV. AV technicians get tellies working in conference rooms. Video engineers use cutting edge visual technology to blow people's minds in arenas and stadiums. We specialise. If you want some excellent V I'm all yours, but if you're looking for the A you'll need to go see a soundie.'

'Sorry,' said Hattie, 'I've put my foot in it already, haven't I? Tell you what, how about you call me the director's secretary, make us even?'

He smiled, more genuinely this time. 'If you really want to make it up to me, you can find me some strapping young men, the burlier the better, and ideally Italian, to hump all this kit for me. I've got a wonky spine and RSI, and my doctor has said she'll never speak to me again if I lift more than ten kilos at a time.'

'I'll see what I can do. Do you know where we're setting up?'

He didn't, so they walked together in the direction of the main house for a recce. In the space of 200 sauntered yards Tom managed, by way of a rather long-winded anecdote about his orthopaedic difficulties, to fit in a fairly comprehensive precis of his professional CV: he had started off as an all-purpose techie, gravitating towards video because it was more complex and less understood than other disciplines, and he liked a challenge. He'd fallen in with a small company that specialised in ambitious projection design for high-end productions – mostly for musicians' arena tours – and through them managed to get involved with two of Geoffrey's shows, first a revival of *The White Hotel*, and then the last show before *The Guilty,* called *Airportland!.* Apparently, when securing this company's services for the workshop, Geoffrey had asked for Tom personally. ('Mostly it's because he wants to sit at the back with me and say snarky things about the actresses, I'm sure.') Hattie decided that she tentatively liked Tom, but that she'd keep her guard up around him until she had a better sense of how he ticked.

They reached the house and in the absence of any signage telling them what to do, made their way to the front door where Hattie gingerly tugged on the polished brass bell pull. They were greeted by Geoffrey himself, who beamed when he saw them.

'Tom! Hattie! Two of the absolute greats! Do you know each other? Of course you do, of course you do, come in, come in. Drink?'

Just inside the hallway was a small round table, covered with a white lace tablecloth and set with a tray of champagne glasses.

'I've got the whole thing catered,' Geoffrey explained. 'Don't get used to bubbly and nibbles, that's just to kick us off. After this it's hardtack and water all the way, so make hay now, eh?'

Hattie accepted a glass of fizz to show willing, but was careful not to drink much of it – she was about to make (and receive) a lot of first impressions, and she wanted to stay as sharp as possible.

Geoffrey directed them through the house to a large but low-ceilinged sitting room, whose walls were filled with bookcases. A grand piano sat in one corner, and an enormous taxidermied bear (complete with jaunty top hat) reared in another. Two women and a man were in the centre of the room, chatting animatedly. Hattie didn't recognise any of them.

The first woman was tall and broad, with dark eyes and sweeps of black hair. She was wearing a tight-fitting black jacket with shoulder pads, and wedges that added a good four inches to her already impressive height. Geoffrey introduced her as 'Mel, our director'. The other woman was much more informally dressed in jeans and a faded T-shirt. Her hair was up in a greying bun, and the brown skin over her high cheekbones was pleasingly weathered. Her name was Maxine, and she was apparently a designer.

The man was short, pale, and a little tubby, with shaggy, mousy hair and chunky spectacles. He was wearing a buttoned shirt with a floppy collar, and a small assortment of leather bracelets. He winked at Tom when he saw him, and was introduced to Hattie as Gareth, a video designer.

Hattie was a little disappointed with herself at first that, despite her leaving plenty of contingency time for the drive, so many people had arrived before her. She was used to being the first to arrive at any professional gathering and felt that that was as it should be. However, as the conversation continued, it became clear that these three had been at the house since at least the previous evening, and Hattie forgave herself.

Geoffrey and the two women mostly talked about fine art – a topic on which Hattie had very little to contribute – and theatre gossip – a topic where Hattie would have felt more comfortable had she recognised *any* of the names being dropped. She felt very much an outsider. Gareth was fairly quiet, interjecting with a wry remark here and there, and Tom spent a lot of energy trying to work his way into the conversation, but was hampered by the fact that despite Geoffrey chuckling at most of his jokes, Mel and Maxine largely ignored him.

'Circus!' Geoffrey exclaimed emphatically to the assembled group during a lull. 'That's what it's all about. For this show.'

Maxine wrinkled her nose thoughtfully. 'You could do a lot with silks. Aerial work. And fabric on stage opens up the possibility of projection, but I worry about precision. How precisely can we project onto a thin suspended silk that's wobbling round cos an acrobat is twirling themselves up and down at the bottom? And it's probably spinning a bit too. And quite bunched up.'

'I think you've answered your own question there,' murmured Gareth.

'Can we rig some motion tracking markers on the silks?' asked Tom brightly. 'There's a new Cocoa module that lets us track the orientation of projection surface in real time and do all the physics to work out how to distort the video output to compensate. It could take care of the spinning and the wobbling. Maybe not the bunching though.'

'I didn't understand a word, but we should do what Tom says,' said Geoffrey.

Mel was frowning. 'I love it,' she said solemnly. 'I mean, you know I love it; last year I was all over this stuff in Leicester. But, and this is a big "but", is circus the *heart* of the piece? I'm not saying it's not, but *if* it's not, I don't want it in my way.'

There were nods all round, and a thoughtful silence.

'What do you think, Hattie?' asked Geoffrey, and all eyes turned to her. While she was acutely aware that this was not a conversation to which she felt able to constructively contribute, Hattie had a lifetime's experience of fielding questions like this. She sucked her teeth.

'I'm just here to stage-manage. If you want opinions, that'll cost you extra.'

Geoffrey snorted with laughter. 'If you could teach young Tom here that attitude you'd save us all a lot of time,' he joked. 'But come on, you're not on the clock yet. Do you think that circus is, or can be, the heart of the show?'

Hattie's heart sank. That line normally got her off the hook. Now she'd have to try to come up with something *creative* to say.

'Well...' she began, before realising that the reason she didn't feel qualified to answer the question wasn't *purely* due to a lack of creative imagination on her part. 'Hang on. No one's even told me what the show is yet.'

At this, Geoffrey's eyes widened, his brow furrowed, and he let out an enormous guffaw of laughter. 'You haven't...? Bloody hell, I love Louise more than words can say, but she can sometimes be utterly... Well, we'd better get you a script, then. And I will get an opinion out of you by the time we're done, you know. Hattie's the woman who persuaded me to revive *Roses*, Mel. There's far more to her than meets the eye. Now, it's probably time to get on. Hattie and Mel, you'll want a confab about the batting order, Tom and Gareth you'll be itching to set up your kit, I'm sure, and Maxine, I haven't forgotten about the Klimt, so perhaps we can take a look at that before everything kicks off.'

'Wait, you have a Klimt?' asked Mel.

'Well, technically I have three, but only one is worth getting excited about,' Geoffrey replied.

'If you're showing it off then I bloody want in,' Mel insisted, and in a moment the three of them had swept off. Gareth offered a friendly shrug to Hattie.

'We're in the granary out back. I don't suppose you'd help us unload? Only Tom's back is bad and it'll take me ages to do it by myself.'

'It's the least I can do,' said Hattie reluctantly, not relishing the prospect of a bunch of heavy lifting. 'Sorry Tom, I know you were hoping for someone a bit burlier.'

Tom grinned. 'Would you consider putting on an Italian accent and answering to the name Paolo for the next hour or so? It'd soften the blow.'

Tom brought his car around to the entrance to a large black barn that stood a little way behind the house and they got started unloading its contents. It wasn't so bad in the end: most of the really heavy stuff was on wheels, and Gareth generously insisted on carrying the most awkward pieces. They worked in companionable silence, which Hattie much preferred to the living room conversation earlier.

The barn had been smartly done up inside as a single open space broken up around the edges by a motley selection of crude, period wooden posts that held up various points in the high ceiling, with a hardwood floor, blackout-blinded windows, and a black curtain along one wall that concealed a large stretch of floor-length mirror. An upright piano was off to one side, and sound baffles were suspended at various points, making this a passable venue for a musical recital, a ballet rehearsal, or a theatrical workshop. For anyone other than a theatre impresario it would be an utterly bizarre thing to have installed in rural outbuilding.

As soon as the first bits of kit were inside, Tom went about unpacking and setting things up, which initially meant much poring over a plan of the space and a few short conferences with

Gareth about placement. Then he got to work marking out a few key points on the floor in tape, then laying all manner of cables from point to point, taping them down if they stretched across the floor and running them unobtrusively up the sides of beams and along the bases of walls otherwise. Hattie approved of his technique: her job didn't involve much cable work, but she could appreciate it when it was done well. Goodness knows she'd had to deal with the fallout enough times when it was done badly, including one occasion that had left her with a permanent (albeit small) scar on her temple as a result.

Soon there were three projectors, two small and one big, mounted and pointing at three simple projection screens forming a loose triptych around the central space, all controlled from a desk in one corner where Tom was sitting, itself connected via a few cables to another desk at the back where Gareth's laptop was. While it may have looked to an outsider as though they were both doing the same thing – broadly, poking around on their computers and occasionally causing test cards and grids to appear on the projection screens – Hattie knew that their roles were very different. Gareth was the creative here, tasked with deciding what ultimately should appear on screen; Tom was his technical enabler, in charge of maximising the possible options for what *could* appear.

As all this was coming together, Hattie was trying to make herself useful. Given that Mel had chosen a Klimt viewing over a catch-up, Hattie still had no idea what format the workshop would take, so it was hard to know exactly what would be useful. Big pre-production workshops like this were rare outside the upper echelons of theatre, where the high financial risk and reward made producers keen to hedge their bets before committing to spending a lot of money. The goal was always to assure the production team that the proposed show had the potential to be a hit, and to try to discover where the path to hitdom lay. Normally this was done by rehearsing some or all of the script so that the writers and producers could see what it looked like when performed, allowing plenty of time for experimentation and rewrites and so on. So far, Hattie had no idea how Mel wanted to go about the rehearsal, or in what areas she intended to experiment. But there were some basics she could work on: she got out some chairs and folding tables and set them up tentatively around the room, had a sweep of the central space and fetched and arranged some stationery from her car. After some poking around she managed to find a proper stool for the piano in a cupboard and was just starting to carry it across to its rightful place when a warm male voice behind her called out, 'I can do that!'

She put down the stool, turned, and found herself facing one of the more beautiful men she had ever seen. He was well over six feet tall, but slender, with dark skin and a shaven head that revealed a perfectly shapely skull. He wore a charcoal grey turtleneck, white trousers and shiny black shoes. He had just set down a neat brown satchel and was now striding towards Hattie.

'Oh, thank you very much,' she said. 'Er. I'm Hattie. Stage manager.'

'Calvin,' he replied in a light, pleasant drawl. 'Repetiteur.'

He took the stool easily, sauntered a few steps towards the piano, then stopped and swung back around, a quizzical expression on his face.

'Have we met before?' he asked. 'I recognise your face.'

'I don't think so, but I am terrible with faces I'm afraid.'

'Oh!' he exclaimed, his face momentarily lighting up but quickly transforming into a wince. 'You were at the Revue. The night that, um…'

'Oh. Yes, I was there that night,' said Hattie. She didn't need clarification on which night he was talking about.

'I'm the MD on *The Guilty*. I was supposed to be conducting that night – when the regular conductor's away the musical director steps in. By the time I turned up there were police everywhere.

You were standing with Donna when we were all called together in the auditorium.'

'That's right. I was supposed to be shadowing her. I'm sorry, I don't remember seeing you.'

'I think we were all rather distracted,' said Calvin. 'I was in the corner with Louise. She was a mess, and I wasn't much better.'

A heavy silence hung between them for a moment. Then he smiled again, and said, 'Well, nice to meet you properly, and I'm glad it's in happier circumstances this time. I'm so looking forward to this, aren't you?'

'Well, mostly,' replied Hattie. 'But I don't think I know what I've got myself into yet. No one's even told me what the show is.'

'No? Oh it's a wonderful piece. Adapted from a novel, I think,' said Calvin, before adding a remark that made the floor drop out from under Hattie: 'It's called *The Fall of a Thousand Hopeless Stars.*'

8

Hattie spent the rest of the afternoon sitting in the corner of the granary, reading a copy of the *Fall* script that Calvin lent her, feeling sick.

No one bothered her: it was the most natural thing in the world that a stage manager would want to bone up on the script, and with the heavy lifting done, Tom and Gareth were happy to tinker away with resolution settings and projection angles, while Calvin tinkled whimsically on the piano. As background noise went it was as pleasant and unobtrusive as one could hope for, leaving Hattie free to concentrate on the script.

As a play it seemed… fine. Not Hattie's cup of tea if she was honest about it. It started off as a meditation on living with a terminal illness, then it descended into a protracted road trip featuring the main character and her friends, at least one of whom was apparently imaginary. And then at the two-thirds mark there was a revelation about being a victim of child abuse which felt a little bit forced, as though the author wanted to ratchet up the emotional intensity without really considering what actually fitted with the story that had gone before. But Hattie was prepared to give the piece the benefit of the doubt. If she had been able to concentrate on it then perhaps she would have picked up on all sorts of underlying themes that tied everything together and made it all feel coherent and balanced.

But she couldn't concentrate at all. For the most part she was just confused. Why would Geoffrey be workshopping Eoin and Lel's show? And... *was* it Eoin and Lel's show? There was no mention of any names on the script itself. The front page contained only the name of the play and a paragraph of legalese aggressively forbidding sharing any of the contents with third parties. As Hattie read she tried to recognise Eoin's style in the words. It seemed like the kind of thing he *could* write, but truth be told she couldn't think of anything particularly distinctive in the little work of his she'd come across in the past. And of course, the script didn't contain any music, just lyrics, so there was no way of knowing if Lel had...

Hattie looked up suddenly. Calvin's playing had sounded scattered and random to her when she wasn't paying attention to it. But glancing over, it looked as though he was working his way through a written score; it was just that he was only playing certain passages out loud and skipping the rest. Was that *the* score? It seemed incredible that the thing she was searching for would be right there in front of her so soon after arriving.

As surreptitiously as possible, she stood up and sidled towards the piano to get a closer look. As the details became clearer, her heart sank. There was no composer name on the pages currently laid out on the piano, but the music had very obviously been notated using some sort of software and printed out. That ruled out it being Lel's score: as Eoin had insisted, and as she'd verified when she visited his studio, all his work was handwritten.

'It's delightful, isn't it? He's done the counterpoint *so* well,' Calvin said suddenly.

Hattie was embarrassed. Apparently she hadn't been as surreptitious as she'd thought. 'It's beautiful. Who wrote it?' she asked, as nonchalantly as possible.

'Oh. Um... actually it's not a "he", is it, it's a woman,' replied Calvin. 'How terribly regressive of me. I don't actually have a clue who she is. But I heard something about her joining us next week.

So, I suppose I do have a clue: it's a woman, and it's someone who's alive and well. Sorry. That came out horribly. I was just… thinking about… sorry, never mind.'

The young man turned back abruptly to the piano and resumed playing. Hattie frowned. The bit about it being an alive woman was an odd thing to say in any circumstance, and doubly odd because the implicit converse was that it was *not* written by a dead man, which rather mirrored the thought that had flashed through Hattie's mind.

Mystified, she sat back down and tried to turn her attention back to the script. She was interrupted soon after by a polite cough from the granary door.

'Hello. Excuse me? Hi everyone. Just to say that dinner is ready in the main house, if that's okay?'

The speaker was a small, smartly dressed, very young-looking woman with blonde hair, freckles aplenty and watery blue eyes. She turned her attention to Hattie, and the veneer of professional detachment abruptly crumbled, revealing an earnest, almost cringing apologeticness.

'Hattie, isn't it? Goodness, sorry, hello, I'm Louise, we spoke on the phone last week. I'm so, *so* sorry about the mix-up with the script! Obviously we'd intended for you to get a copy right away.'

'It's no problem,' replied Hattie, shaking Louise's proferred hand. 'I've just been reading Calvin's.'

'That's great! Well done you, but you shouldn't have had to, it was all a big misunderstanding. But anyway, here's a copy for you. Also, Geoffrey wants everyone to have these.'

Along with a script, she handed over two books. One was a paperback copy of *Fall*, and the other was a slim hardback, entitled *Advanced Theatre Practice*, by someone called Jala Senguel, MA. Hattie regarded this last book suspiciously. In her experience, there were very few aspects of theatre that you could meaningfully learn about from reading a book, and more abstract and theoretical works, such as this appeared to be, were good for little more than propping doors open backstage.

Perhaps Louise read the expression on her face, because she added, 'It's okay, I don't think he's expecting you to read it. But the author will be here next week, so I think he thought it would be nice. Anyway, if there's anything else you need just let me know. Honestly, anything.'

Hattie smiled and offered her thanks.

'No problem. But look, leave that here for now, you can pick it up later. In the meantime come get some food,' said Louise, smiling. She was cheery and bubbly, but there was something desperate about her friendliness, Hattie noted. She came across as someone who was doing a very good impression of an extrovert.

She walked with Louise, Calvin, Gareth and Tom back to the main house. A long, narrow table stood in a long, narrow dining room, and at one end Geoffrey, Mel and Maxine were just sitting down to eat. There were four new faces as well, two men and two women.

'Here come the troops!' cried Geoffrey. 'Just in time to meet the twirlies. Now, Gareth you're up here, Calvin you're next to Hera, Louise you're next to Dylan, Hattie you're next to Calvin and Tom you're next to Louise. Sit down, introduce yourselves, and let's dig in and get to know one another.'

Hattie said some hellos and sat down as directed, noting as she did that the seating plan had been determined by role: producer and director at one end, designers next to them, then actors, then 'misc' – Calvin and Louise – after the actors, and the stage manager and the techie last. Perhaps the fact that it had come so naturally to Geoffrey to arrange things in this way said something about his attitude to the role of backstage people, she thought to herself. But equally, perhaps she was ascribing too much forethought to Geoffrey, and all he was really doing was filling up the table from one end to the other in rough order of arrival. Either way, it was fine: Hattie was very happy to sit with anyone, after all.

She allowed Tom to pour her a glass of what looked to be a rather expensive red wine. It certainly tasted like one: drinking it was a bit like drinking a velvet curtain. But it paired very well with the beef wellington and asparagus that was being served. Hattie wondered if this was what Geoffrey counted as 'hardtack and water'.

Tom and Calvin hit it off right away. They were both a little bit camp, but while Tom delighted in being over-the-top and outrageous, Calvin was a little more sedate and demure. He pretended to be horrified by some of the things Tom said, but the twinkle in his eyes gave Tom all the encouragement he needed to carry on. Hattie was more than happy to let the two of them do most of the talking, and she easily took on the role of their appreciative audience, laughing at every joke and placing leading conversation-starter questions into the few lulls in conversation. Louise divided her attention between their end of the table and the actor apparently called Dylan who was sitting next to her. She smiled her brittle smile throughout, and spent much more time listening than talking.

Towards the end of the meal, after the plates had been whisked away by the discreet attendant who had occasionally materialised over the course of the meal and replaced by coffee jugs and a platter of petits fours, Geoffrey dinged his wine glass until everyone fell silent, then leaned forward on his elbows so he could see every face, and began to address the company present:

'So, first of all, we won't do applause because it will only embarrass her, but all of this' – here he gestured vaguely at the tabletop – 'is thanks to the wonderful Tinca who's just disappeared into the kitchen. She lives down the road and she's my catering goddess. She's absolutely marvellous and she'll be taking care of us all week, so if there's anything you need do let her know. But be aware, if you start getting precious and demanding eggless meringues and so on she'll tell you to sod off, and then she'll tell me to sod off. So allergies and special requests only, yes?

'Next, thank you all so much for coming. One of the great delights of working in this business for as long as I have is that every so often an opportunity comes along to do something truly special, and you have the freedom to choose who you do it with, and you can invite people who you trust and love and care about along for the ride. You're all of you very dear to me, I love working with you all, and I am beyond honoured to be able to start this grand new adventure in such wonderful company.

'Finally, the past couple of weeks have been extremely difficult for many of us. We lost, in the most awful possible circumstances, a very dear friend. Lel was… well it goes without saying he was a genius. And he was a consummate professional. But so much more importantly than that, he was a genuinely good soul, he was warm, he was merry, he was kind. We will be feeling his absence for some time. So, while it's a feeble gesture, I hope you don't think it will be crass if I propose a toast: To Lel.'

'To Lel,' everyone mumbled, and Hattie could see painful emotions on the faces of many of the diners. In particular, the actress sitting between Dylan and Gareth was shedding tears freely. Hattie felt a lot of sympathy: Geoffrey's speech had been sensitive and heartfelt – he always had a way with words – and while she hadn't known Lel at all herself, she felt a keen pang of sadness, surrounded here by Lel's friends.

Conversation slowly resumed, and the meal came to a close. Louise began to do a round of the room, explaining to everyone where they were sleeping.

'You're with Delphine in the main house,' she said to Hattie. 'I can show you the way now if you like.'

'That sounds fab,' said Hattie, standing up and hoping not to have to admit that she had no idea who Delphine was.

'Let me just grab Del... Oh, I think she's nipped to the loo. All right, when she gets back I'll take you up.'

Now that she was up it didn't seem worth the bother to sit down again, so Hattie made her way to the other end of the table where Geoffrey was on his feet, opening a new bottle of wine on the sideboard.

'Hattie, my love,' he said in greeting. 'How was the food? I hope it wasn't too plain.'

'It was spectacular, as you're already well aware, Geoffrey,' she replied.

Geoffrey's eyes twinkled. 'Slap bang to rights, you've caught me fishing for compliments without a licence, eh? Well, we all have our insecurities. Ready for tomorrow?'

'Maybe. I'm still playing catch-up. Speaking of which... this show. *Fall*. What is... what *was* Lel's involvement?'

Geoffrey's brow furrowed. 'Minimal,' he replied. 'Oh, I think you might have got the wrong end of the stick, from what I said earlier—'

'It's just that I'd heard Lel was the one who actually had the stage rights to it. With... well, with Eoin.'

Geoffrey shook his head. 'No no, I think you've been misinformed. *I* have the rights. I certainly spoke to Lel about it, and I think he knocked about some ideas with Eoin a while back, but it didn't come to anything. The music was gorgeous of course, but totally misused, and the script was all over the place. I tried to set him up with a better writing partner, but he was stuck in that toxic working relationship with that awful, *awful* man...'

He tailed off for a second, leaving Hattie feeling uncomfortable. She didn't like hearing Eoin spoken of like that. He had always been prickly, sure, and had a tendency to say the wrong thing, but he was never *that* bad. Was he?

Coming back to the here and now, Geoffrey continued. 'Sorry. I don't want to get into all that. He seemed to delight in being rude.

Lel was the only person in the entire world who gave him the time of day – well, him and Louise it turns out, for reasons known only to herself, I'm sure. But you'll meet Jala, our wonderful writer, tomorrow, and Teri, the composer, will be here next week. They're absolutely tiny, barely out of nappies, but my goodness, the *energy*. Now' – his attention snapped away from Hattie and back to Mel and Maxine at the table – 'I want your honest opinion on this one: my agent in Bordeaux assures me it's every inch as chunky as a Lafite, but I can't make up my mind…'

And with that Hattie was forgotten, and she would have found herself dawdling awkwardly had Louise not just then tapped her on the shoulder. Standing next to her was the woman who had been crying at the table, although she now looked much restored. This must be Delphine.

'Shall we go?' asked Louise, and Hattie nodded assent.

They made their way back to the front hall, then up the broad central staircase and along a landing to a large and modern-furnished bedroom. Looking through the doorway Hattie was relieved to note that there were twin beds: she had reached a point in her life when she was still prepared to countenance sharing a room with a stranger, but after decades of bunking up with all comers on the road she felt she'd earned the right to her own mattress.

'I'll leave you to it,' said Louise, already retreating down the landing. 'Sorry about the script. Again.'

'After you,' said Hattie, allowing Delphine to enter the room first and sit down on the bed near the window. Hattie made her way in behind her and hovered by the other.

'Well, this is nice,' she said. It was: ancient timbers protruded along the walls as a reminder of the age of the house, but the room was otherwise modern, with clean cream carpets, high ceilings and a small amount of tasteful furniture. The windows were wooden-framed, lead-latticed and small, but there were plenty of discreet uplights mounted on the walls to make up for the lack of natural light.

Delphine nodded her agreement, but didn't answer. There was an awkward pause, which Hattie eventually filled by saying: 'Hello, I'm Hattie. Stage manager.'

'Hello,' said Delphine. 'Do you not have a bag?'

Hattie hadn't noticed before, but Delphine had brought in with her a tidy black duffle bag.

'Oh,' said Hattie. 'I left my things in my car.'

Delphine nodded again. She didn't seem particularly disposed towards conversation, and Hattie, sensing that she might be trying to secure some time by herself, added, 'I might go and fetch it now.'

She made her way down the stairs and let herself out of the front door, being careful to leave it slightly ajar so she could get back in again when she returned. It was a light summer evening – even though the meal had lasted a long time, they had started early and were done soon after 8 o'clock – so she had no difficulty seeing the way to the field where her car was parked. She retrieved her suitcase and small holdall and started to make her way back towards the house, pausing when she heard two male voices in conversation. The sounds appeared to be coming from the other side of a set of fence panels that marked out a small kitchen garden.

'No, never,' one of them – Hattie recognised the voice as belonging to Calvin – was saying. 'Lel always talked about him like some harmless lost puppy, but if you heard it from anyone else…'

'They said he was an irredeemable arsehole?' suggested his companion. That was Tom, Hattie was sure of it.

'Well, yes, so who knows?' replied Calvin.

There was a huffing sound that Hattie recognised as the exhale of a lungful of cigarette smoke.

'Maybe he was an arsehole. Nothing wrong with arseholes in general. They have their merits in the right context, don't you think?'

'Well, perhaps,' came Calvin's coy reply.

Hattie suspected they had up to this point been talking about Eoin, but it was quite clear the conversation was now taking a more intimate turn and Hattie, not wanting to intrude, quietly made her way back into the house.

By the time she had made it back to the room Delphine was gone. From the sounds emanating from downstairs it sounded like the evening was picking up pace, but Hattie wasn't in much of a mood to socialise. She had no idea what to make of what Geoffrey had told her just now. Did it mean that the script and score for this workshop were nothing to do with Eoin and Lel? Was there a *different* version by Eoin and Lel that was floating around somewhere? And what was all this stuff about who owned the rights?

Hattie would have loved to have rung up Eoin to ask him about all of this, but he had been insistent that she should never call him directly. His plan had been to switch phones every few days anyway, so the number she had for him might be out of date already.

In the end she took a shower and put herself to bed with a book, telling herself that it would all make sense in the morning. She was asleep before Delphine came back to the room.

9

In the morning Hattie woke up early, feeling more alert and resourceful thanks to a night's sleep in the pleasingly comfortable bed. Intrigues aside, she was here first and foremost to stage manage a workshop, she reminded herself, and on that front she had some work to do to get off the back foot. Not least, she needed to set up a working prompt book, and for that she needed her copy of the script, which she'd left in the granary the previous evening. So she pulled on some clothes as quietly as she could, hoping not to disturb the sleeping form in the bed next to her. She slipped out of the room, down the stairs and out of the front door once again. This time when she walked past the kitchen garden there were no sounds of surreptitious flirting.

But there was a large peacock, perched heavily atop a wooden fence panel. At least, the front half looked like a peacock. But it seemed to be missing the fun bit at the back. As she approached it gave out an aggressive shriek and adjusted its plumage boisterously. This gave Hattie pause. She'd never had an audience with a peacock before and had no idea if they were violent creatures. She dimly remembered something about the males using their feathers for territorial displays of some sort. Was this one, lacking a big show-off tail, likely to be more or less aggressive as a result, and was she trespassing on its domain? It looked a similar size to a swan, and everyone knew that a swan could break your arm.

Deciding that there was no shame in a precautionary retreat,

Hattie backed away, only to bump into another creature, this one somewhat larger, greyer, wearing linen trousers and a poncho, and holding a horse blanket.

'Oops, sorry,' said Hattie reflexively.

'Steady there,' said the newcomer, gently. His voice was hoarse and friendly, his accent refined. The peacock gave another shriek, as if in greeting.

'Sorry about this. She's mine. Geoffrey gets absolutely livid when they crap in his garden, but this one's *determined* to nest in his summer house.'

'Oh, she's a girl is she? I don't know the first thing about peacocks. I think I've only ever seen pictures of males.'

'Yes, she's a girl, her name's Fatima. Here's a useful fact about peafowl: they go absolutely dotty for ginger nut biscuits. Could you give me a hand? Just crumble this up and sprinkle it on the ground' – he pressed a biscuit into her hand – 'and we'll see if we can lure her down. That's it, try to make it as obvious as possible what you're doing. Then step back a bit, she'll be a bit wary of you as you're new. I'm Charles, by the way.'

As Hattie brushed the last crumbs off her hands and stepped gingerly away, Charles had his eyes fixed intently on Fatima who, after a moment's consideration, hop-flapped her way down to the ground and started pecking up the chunks of biscuit.

'Good, good,' breathed Charles, edging forward. 'Now...'

He abruptly pounced forward, flinging the blanket on top of the errant peahen and following up swiftly to clamp it down to the ground with his hands, pinning the creature underneath. For a moment Hattie thought he'd trapped the bird, but then saw its head poking out from the far side of the blanket. It hooted in dismay and started to wiggle itself free.

'Quick! Grab it!' Charles commanded. Hattie, not particularly keen to put herself within range of that rather long beak, hesitated, and within a couple of seconds the bird had freed itself and flown straight upwards with a great noisy flapping sound, coming to rest on the roof of the house, where it hooted indignantly once more.

'Bugger,' said Charles, picking himself up.

'Sorry I wasn't more help.'

'Not to worry,' he replied cheerfully. 'That almost never works, but Geoffrey does fuss so, so it's good to show willing. She'll pop back over the hedge when she gets lonely.'

He dusted off the blanket and started to fold it up.

'So. You're here for the big workshop, are you? It's all Geoffrey's been talking about for months.'

'Yes,' said Hattie. Then, feeling that this was perhaps not quite enough by itself, she added, 'It's very exciting.'

'Well then, I won't keep you. If Fatty comes down again, or if Geoffrey kicks up a stink about her, do come and grab me – I'm the next house along on that way.' He gestured vaguely to his left.

'Will do,' said Hattie, and the strange man waggled his finger at the peahen, then sauntered off around the house. Hattie stole one more glance at the temperamental Fatima, then continued on her way to the granary.

She settled down at her desk inside, transferring her new copy of the script, leaf by leaf, into the lever arch file, attaching those circular hole punch hole reinforcement stickers to each sheet of paper as she added it in, and interleaving script pages with blank sheets of paper at the start of each new scene to provide additional room for notes. Then it was time to draw vertical lines on the back of each sheet, so that when the folder was open on any given page, the printed text was on the right hand side and there were three columns on the left hand side into which she would be able to add blocking, technical cues and directorial notes.

Her students complained about the tedium of putting together a prompt copy, and it certainly was repetitive work, but for Hattie there was an undeniable pleasure in the process. It was partly the satisfaction of doing a job carefully and well, partly the fact that it required just enough concentration to keep at bay whatever her other stresses and cares were, and partly a sort of nostalgia: each new folder she put together reminded her of all the other folders, created in various poky little rooms of her past, carted around the world, thumbed and scribbled in and abused and then, for the most part, filed away in boxes under the bed or on the shelves in the office that was really just a walk-in cupboard. It had been a while since she'd last made one – once you move up from Deputy Stage Manager to Stage Manager it stops being your responsibility most of the time – so the memories that this stirred were mostly the older ones, of the wilder days…

In no time at all other people were appearing in the room, clutching their coffee cups and making their preparations, and Hattie realised she'd been off in her own head for ages. Not only had she not quite finished her prompt copy, she'd also missed breakfast. She wasn't worried, though. She felt grounded now, sure of purpose and ready to do the job she was being paid to do.

Calvin was here, warming up on the piano, playfully blending scales and arpeggios with snatches of show tunes, and occasionally sneaking glances over at Tom, who was frowning furiously at the monitors in front of him, while geometric calibration images flashed up on the projection screens around the room. Maxine and Gareth were sitting at the back, slurping drinks and muttering thoughtfully to one another, and the four actors, Hera, Dylan, Delphine and Pip, were wandering in and out, puffing and gurgling unselfconsciously as they warmed up their vocal cords.

Geoffrey and Mel were the last to arrive, accompanied by a young woman who was hugging a laptop to her chest. She had big eyes, a big mouth, a big nose, big cheekbones and big frizzy hair, but the rest of her was tiny, and she wore denim dungarees over a white, long-sleeved T-shirt.

'Good morning everyone!' exclaimed Geoffrey. 'Are we all ready to get started? Now, this is Jala, our wonderful writer.

She's responsible for this glorious script of ours – well, her and Tahmima, who wrote the original novel, of course. Everyone say hello to Jala!'

The name Jala rang a bell and it didn't take Hattie long to place it: this was the woman who'd written that ghastly theatre book. She looked too young to have written a book at all, and, at a first glance at least, too normal to have written something quite so… conceptual. Hattie had tried to dip into it the previous evening, but had given up part way through chapter one, after the fifth use in as many paragraphs of the word 'affordances'.

There was a chorus of hellos, causing Jala to put on a defensive smile and try to duck slightly behind the protective cover of her laptop. If Geoffrey noticed her discomfort he didn't show it, instead steering her to a seat beside him right at the edge of the performance area. Mel sat on his other side, and the actors, by unspoken agreement, sat down on the stage facing them.

'Marvellous,' continued Geoffrey. 'Now, this is Mel's workshop, she's in charge, I'm just here to facilitate. So I'll hand over to her, and she's going to tell us what we're hoping to achieve from this workshop and how we're going to achieve it. All I'll say is this: don't be alarmed, don't be uncomfortable. We're all friends here. We've got a couple of weeks to play with, and in that time we're working to get a feel for how the text stands up on stage, and what elements we can add to tell the story with. We're all dramaturgists here! All ideas are welcome, and particularly bad ones: let's get those out of the way now, as it were. We'll start with a simple read-through, then we'll go scene by scene. So, let's get started, shall we? Let the dog see the rabbit. Hattie, do you want to start us off?'

Hattie was caught off guard, having been expecting to hear from Mel before anything like a read-through started. But she remembered that this was how Geoffrey had always been: an unstoppable juggernaut of energy, who drove his way through every production with good-natured impatience.

'All right,' she said, clearing her throat noisily to buy herself time as she leafed quickly to the front of her script. *The Fall of a Thousand Hopeless Stars. Act one, scene one. A private room in a hospital. Hope is in the bed.*'

There was an awkward pause.

'Er… which one of us is playing Hope?' asked Hera.

From his corner desk, Tom snorted.

Geoffrey frowned for a moment, then let out a big belly laugh.

'Marvellous! Bloody marvellous! Talk about jumping the gun! All right, all right, Mel you'd better step in and sort this all out for us. But let's not get too tied up with who's playing who, it really doesn't matter. For now, Hera why don't you take Hope, Delphine you take Sammy, Dylan you can be Titus, Pip you be St Christopher, and whenever someone else comes on we'll give it to anyone who isn't already in the scene. Does that work? Mel, what do you think? Excellent, then let's crack on. Hera, your line.'

'Okay… It's a song, right?' asked Hera, her brow furrowed. 'Do you want me to just say the words, or I could have a stab at sight reading if you like…?'

'Just read it, my love. Until Teri gets here I've half a mind to ignore the music entirely. Tell you what: Calvin, could you sort of underscore while she's reading? It'll be horrible, I know, out of time, all over the place, it won't fit at all, but don't worry, don't worry, I just want a bit of mood to give us a bit of a semblance, if you see what I'm getting at?'

'Righto, Geoffrey,' said Calvin calmly. 'I'll just sort of vamp on the melodies, shall I?'

'That's the thing. You know what I'm after, so just do that. And Hera, you can do a little bit of "pretend-that-I'm-actually-singing-this" acting. Know what I mean? Right, let's get on, shall we?'

'Right. Well… *There's an image of me/Another version, and she/Stands so purposefully/In defiance and free,*' began Hera, awkwardly at first, but gaining confidence as she continued. '*And this image of me/Is as far as can be/From this crumpled little shadow tied by intravenous tendrils to a cold, hard, metal hospital bed.'*

As she spoke, Calvin began tinkling on the piano, an odd, stilted melody that occasionally soared into big swooping phrases before lurching back into terse staccatos. Hattie wasn't sure if this was a reflection of what the music was actually like or if it was just down to Calvin having to jump around to keep up with where Hera had got to in the lyrics. Either way, it made for unsettling listening, but not necessarily in a bad way.

The song ended, a scene of dialogue between Hope (Hera) and Sammy (Delphine) began, and the read-through started to pick up steam. Whenever a new character entered, Geoffrey would bark out an actor's name to read the lines. Each time there was a song, Calvin would do his thing in the background. Any time anyone stumbled over a line Geoffrey would yell 'Keep going! Keep going!', as though they were all racing against the clock. It was a manic, absurd way to start the workshop… but in its own way it was oddly effective. Everyone was engaged, the energy in the room was high, and not a moment was wasted on pointless pondering or prevarication. This was Geoffrey's knack: he was ruthlessly single-minded in pursuit of what he wanted, but he was charming enough that he brought other people along with him for the ride. For example, Mel had so far not had a chance to get a single word in edgeways in what was supposedly a workshop that she was running, but she was nonetheless smiling and attentive, and occasionally exchanging muttered suggestions and ideas with Geoffrey as each scene unfolded.

A little under two hours later, Calvin plonked out a final chord on the piano, and the read-through was finished.

'Well,' said Geoffrey, beaming. 'That was a glorious mess, wasn't it? Three quarters of the show doesn't exist yet, and of the quarter that does exist, ninety per cent is entirely wrong. BUT – I don't think I'm alone in saying this am I? – there's something there. Isn't there? Yes? Yes? You can feel it Gareth, can't you? And you can too Jala, although you're scared to admit it to yourself. Eh? There's gold in these hills. Bloody brilliant! Now, no talking, let's take a thirty-minute break where discussing the show is *strictly forbidden*, so it has a chance to work its way into our subconscious unadulterated, and then let's come back and discuss. Right? Right!'

And with that he strode out. Hattie couldn't help but smile. Geoffrey delighted in being an eccentric, but everything he had said was true. The show *was* a mess, it didn't remotely hang together, and it wasn't at all obvious to Hattie how to fix all of its problems… but there was something powerful about it. The plot was compelling, even if it did meander around a bit pointlessly in the first half and fizzle out at the end, the characters were fun, albeit inconsistent. And most importantly (to Hattie's mind, at least, and this was one of her private bugbears in musical theatre), with the exception of the inevitable expository opening number the songs were generally placed at points where it made sense on some level for a character to be expressing themselves through something more than just words.

Now, whether thirty minutes of contemplation would actually help anyone in solving the show's various difficulties was another matter, but it also wasn't Hattie's problem. She wasn't there to make *Fall* a success; she was just there to facilitate the process. So she used the pause to stop into the main house for a wee and a cup of tea.

When she came back about half the company were in the room. Calvin was singing a song in a beautiful light tenor voice, accompanying himself on the piano, while Hera listened raptly.

'Lovely,' she said when he finished.

'Glorious,' he agreed. 'And coming right after the courtroom scene, it had them *weeping*, it really did.'

'I can't believe I haven't seen it yet.'

'You must, you must. Of course, the mood has changed entirely now. Even the name, *The Guilty*, makes you think about… And it's just so Lel, you know? Everything about it.'

His fingers had started playing an instrumental version of the chorus he'd just been singing, but the sound was interrupted by a loud sob from Delphine. Hattie looked over and saw the actress, teary-eyed, struggling to her feet.

'Sorry, I need some air,' she blurted, blundering past Hattie in a dash for the door.

'Oh God, I'm such an idiot,' mumbled Calvin.

'What?' asked Hera.

'Delphine was in the original cast, but left soon after it opened. Lel worked very closely with her in rehearsals. His death must still be so raw for her. So crude of me to keep playing his songs and banging on about him.'

'Oh my lovely, you didn't do anything wrong. You weren't being crude.'

'Well… I feel terrible though. I'll just not talk about him or the show again. I mean, not never again, but you know.'

Delphine eventually returned, looking a little wobbly, and Hera wordlessly gave her a big hug. The others eventually reconvened, and the workshop began in earnest. At this stage it was fairly cerebral stuff: finally given an opportunity to make a contribution, Mel put it to the group that a central theme of the piece was the concept of imbalance, and a good hour was spent as the group combed through the script looking for literal and metaphorical examples of this. Then Maxine countered that it seemed to her that the heart of the piece was really that every character, in their own way, is desperate to return home, but ends up further away, and more time was spent trying to find evidence to support or refute this hypothesis. A break for lunch was followed by Jala uncomfortably pointing out that really they shouldn't be looking at her script at all, they should be looking to the original novel, as the decisions she'd made in her adaptation about what to include and what to leave out hadn't been 'validated' yet, and so until that was done, her curatorial choices shouldn't be allowed to limit their thinking. This was pooh-poohed by Geoffrey, who was adamant that she had captured what needed saying admirably, and that the question was rather how to say it. But then Mel asked, 'Well… so what *does* need saying?', and Geoffrey had no answer to that, and there was a thoughtful silence that was eventually broken by Tom who, looking out of the window, remarked, 'Geoffrey, is that a peacock taking a dump on your car?'

10

By the end of the day Hattie was tired, despite having had very little to do. It was all right that she'd had a quiet day. Her job wasn't to be always busy, it was to be always *ready*. And in its own way that was tiring too, even if it had manifested itself in her sitting quietly at a desk while other people waxed lyrical about the elements of dramaturgy and the creative process. But it was the kind of tiredness that wasn't necessarily sated by yet more stillness.

So when they downed scripts at 6 o'clock, Hattie took advantage of the hour's gap between the end of the workshop and the beginning of supper to take herself off for a little potter round the grounds. She explored the flowerbeds and ornaments that broke up the expanse of lawn at the front, peered at the various herbs growing in the kitchen garden, wove her way around the outbuildings and explored the wilder, more secluded parts towards the peripheries, where a swing seat was being subsumed by weeds in a secluded grotto, a noisy pump pushed a thin trickle of water down some rocks poking out of a pond, and a suspiciously clean and new-looking 'ruin' lurked: two stone walls met at right angles, one with an arched window in it, the other with half a doorway, both crumbling away to nothing after a couple of metres.

She returned to her room feeling refreshed. Delphine was there, lying on her bed, giving Hattie a moment to take her in. She was tall and dark-haired, perhaps in her early thirties. Every time

Hattie had seen her, her face had been coated in a thick layer of foundation, with lipstick liberally applied. On Delphine, makeup felt like armour. She was currently reading Jala's *Advanced Theatre Practice*, with every indication of enjoyment, or at the very least of comprehension.

'Hello,' said Hattie.

'Hi,' Delphine replied.

Hattie hesitated. Her few interactions with Delphine so far had been a bit… sticky. The other woman wasn't exactly rude, but she certainly seemed standoffish. Hattie didn't mind that in and of itself, but if they were going to be roommates for the next couple of weeks it would be helpful if things were a bit easier between them. It was probably worth putting a bit of effort in, just to see if she could be persuaded to reciprocate.

'Well done today,' Hattie offered. 'I always think it must be difficult being an actor in a workshop, because you never know what's being asked of you. Especially when you have to keep switching parts. I thought you did well in that scene with all the nurses.'

Delphine looked curiously at Hattie, who wondered for a moment if she'd said something to cause offence. But then she replied, with a seemingly genuine smile, 'Thank you. I've not done much like this before. But it's quite fun.'

Then she went back to her book. Hattie decided to leave it at that. Lines of communication had been opened, at least. And she could work on getting Delphine onside over the next few days. She picked up a cardigan, then went down to dinner.

Geoffrey once again enforced a seating plan, but Hattie was interested to note that she was no longer banished to the far end of the table. This evening she found herself sitting between Maxine the designer and Pip the actor. Delphine, who came down a few minutes later, was opposite, between Mel and Gareth. While he wasn't overt about it, Hattie thought it possible that Geoffrey's intent tonight was to seat everyone *away* from people in the same discipline as them: designers were not placed next to designers, nor actors to actors, nor techies to techies. Louise was not present, and Hattie realised she hadn't seen her all day. Perhaps she had been dismissed back to London now that the workshop was up and running.

The taciturn Tinca brought in a huge tureen of venison stew, and the meal began. Hattie swiftly discovered that Pip had just finished a show at the Tavistock, a pub theatre at which Hattie had stage-managed a chaotic and scandal-ridden production the previous autumn. They quickly bonded over various anecdotes about the venue's peevish and idiosyncratic artistic director. She also found common ground with Maxine in that they both secretly enjoyed being called on to help with a little costume work – sewing, mending and minor alterations – but had both discovered that if they ever admitted to this enjoyment they invariably got an entire costume department's-worth of work dumped on them, causing the pleasure to pall.

With good food, and in pleasant company, Hattie found herself relaxing, and allowed herself to accept Tinca's periodic offer to refill her wine glass. By the end of the meal she felt an enjoyable tingle in her cheeks. Geoffrey made another small speech, this time advising them that while they would all technically be working the following day, which was a Saturday, they wouldn't be in the granary. Instead, he had arranged for them to see a matinee performance of the circus spectacular at the Yarmouth Hippodrome, convinced as he still was that the best way to help tell the story of *Fall* was through the medium of circus arts. This struck Hattie as a delightful idea. She'd heard of the legendary retractable on-stage swimming pool at the Hippodrome and had often been curious to see it. She excused herself to nip to the loo, hoping afterwards to learn more about the trip and the show.

The bubble of her good mood was about to be burst, though: in the loo, she checked her phone and saw she had a missed call and a text message from a new number. The message just said, 'It's me. Are you free to talk?'

Hattie immediately knew the sender must be Eoin, and he must have switched phones. She felt a sudden flood of guilt. She'd hardly thought about him all day and given no mind to the questions around Lel's score. She finished up in the bathroom, then quietly snuck out of the house, avoiding the company, who were slowly making their way in ones and twos from the dining room to the sitting room. Hattie wandered back to the derelict swing seat she'd discovered a couple of hours earlier at the end of the garden and, once she was sure no one else was in earshot, she rang Eoin back.

'Hullo, Hattie,' he said as he picked up. His voice was scratchy, and there seemed to be a lot of noise in the background.

'Hello. Goodness, it's a bad line. Where are y— wait. I probably don't want to know, do I?'

He barked out a short laugh. 'Sorry, it's probably not funny really. It's just that I'm never sure what's a sensible precaution and what's just a result of me having watched too many spy thrillers. But no, I think you're right, best if I don't say, so you don't have to lie.'

'But you're well?' asked Hattie.

'Not really. My head feels like I'm having a stroke, my chest feels like I'm having a heart attack and my stomach feels like I'm having the all-you-can-eat buffet at Song Loon in Chinatown, and all three have been feeling the same way for a week. I'm half out of my mind with stress, and the other half with boredom.'

'I'm so sorry.'

'Don't be. It's nothing I don't deserve I'm sure. But… I don't suppose…'

'I don't have anything on Lel's score directly, but I've learned *something*,' said Hattie, recognising his impatience for an update. She explained about this new version of *Fall*, adapted by Jala and Teri, and how Geoffrey had dismissed Lel and Eoin's version out of hand, making it sound as though it had barely made it past the idea stage.

'But he also said that *he* had the stage rights,' Hattie added. 'He was absolutely adamant.'

'Then he's a lying… well. He's lying. Lel and I went to Tahmima in person, we talked her round, and we got agreement in writing, and all parties signed a contract. Which, if I could trust my bloody agent not to sell me out to the police, I could have in front of you by tomorrow. If you want, you could probably get hold of Tahmima yourself—'

'I believe you,' she assured him. 'And I suppose it wouldn't be so unlike Geoffrey to say what he *wanted* to be true and wait for reality to accommodate itself to his needs.'

'He must be banking on our agreement lapsing at the end of the year, at which point he can swoop in. Vulture!' spat Eoin. 'But what about this other version you're workshopping? What's it like?'

'It's… rough. It's got promise. Good music. Needs a lot of editing. They're thinking of doing something with circus skills for the staging.'

'I can see the thinking,' Eoin replied. 'But… hold on. Can you send me the script?'

'I've only got a paper copy. But I could send you some photos. I think I could get sued for sharing it, but if it gets out that I'm helping you, a lawsuit from Geoffrey is the least of my worries.'

'I don't need the whole thing. I just want… maybe I'm being paranoid, but I just want to be absolutely certain that he's not trying to pass off my work under someone else's name.'

'Makes sense,' said Hattie. 'I'll try to send it to you tonight.'

He rang off soon after that. Hattie quietly snuck back to the house. By the sound of it Calvin had descended on the grand piano, and the household was having a showtunes singalong. An hour earlier Hattie would have gladly joined them, but after her conversation she had lost her appetite for socialising. She snapped a few pages of the script to send to Eoin, then put herself to bed and spent the night, both waking and sleeping, hounded by memories dredged up from a lifetime ago.

It hadn't taken the young Hattie long to begin to suspect that there was something a little unsatisfactory about Eoin's home life. Not so much from what he said as from what he didn't say, not to mention his obvious disinclination to leave the theatre at going-home time, which at the very least raised the possibility that there was nothing he was keen to go home *to*. And her suspicions intensified the first time he turned up to work in a foul mood with an angry red mark across his cheek of the sort that could be caused by – admittedly among other things – being on the receiving end of a vicious drunken backhand.

But he never talked about it. There were several occasions when he appeared in the morning with an unexplained injury, but he just shook his head if asked. He talked about more or less everything *else* – it took him a couple of days to get over his initial shyness, but once he did he almost never shut up, earning him a reputation as a 'gobby little pop-tart', as Jack the stage manager put it. It would have been less surprising in someone older, but he was really still just a child, with no chance to have experienced the real world. Yet Eoin had something to say about *everything*, from the news stories on the radio to the comings and goings of daily life in Knapesfield to the complex web of ever-changing relationships between the staff working at the Tree. He spoke with passion and enthusiasm, and a surprising amount of sense.

Where he *really* got into his stride was on the topic of theatre. Somehow, despite having actually *seen* very little, he knew the plot of almost every play that had been staged in the last twenty years, and plenty that hadn't. He was obsessed with symbolism and took great pleasure in explaining to anyone who would listen how any given scene that appeared at surface level to be about one thing was in fact about something else entirely, if you knew how to look at it.

Not that there were many people at the Tree who *would* listen. At least, not twice. Precociousness does not necessarily equate to abrasiveness, but the sad truth was that there was something a bit abrasive about Eoin. By some measures he probably was more intelligent than many of the adults, but it would perhaps have been wiser of him not to make his own high opinion of his intelligence and low opinion of theirs so obvious.

Thus it was that, despite being generally hard-working (albeit with the occasional tendency to abruptly bunk off for half an hour with no reasons given), quick on the uptake and available to help during a particularly fraught period in the season, Eoin nevertheless found himself bouncing round the backstage departments, being moved on from each rather sooner than he would have preferred, until he eventually landed himself under the supervision of Harriet Fowler as she was then known, who, until Eoin arrived, was at the very bottom of the theatre's pecking order, and therefore had no one else she could foist him on to.

But then again, perhaps Hattie wouldn't have foisted him, even if foist she could. Because, rather to her surprise, she found herself liking Eoin. Yes, he represented the spottiness and self-consciousness of adolescence, a period from which she had only recently escaped, and from which she was keen to distance herself. Yes, he was a little too fond of his own opinions, and sometimes was a little too absorbed in himself when he should have been helping her get on with the job. But he was funny, and silly, and unlike much of the rest of the crew he didn't treat her like a child. He was full of nervous energy, although he always tried to hide it. When he was agitated he'd pick at the skin around his thumbnails with his index fingers, and sometimes this was the only tell he had that something was amiss, but once Hattie noticed it she found herself watching his hands carefully, on the lookout for signs that he needed support or encouragement. She'd never had siblings, but she quickly found herself thinking of him as something akin to a younger brother.

So the two of them fell in together, and she went out of her way to find ways of divvying up her work to share it with him. That was how it went: Jack never assigned any tasks to Eoin directly; instead he just pushed more and more at Hattie, trusting her to pass on bits of it. By the third show, he had earned himself the unofficial title of 'Assistant to the Assistant Stage Manager', and this became widely enough known that he was eventually credited as such in the show programme.

Hattie protected him too, although it was mostly from himself. She was the one who impressed upon him the importance of not offering creative opinions to the designers after he rubbed a few short-tempered people the wrong way during a fit-up. ('It's not our place, y'see. It doesn't matter that you know better than Sherry which way the footlights should be pointing, that sort of opinion shouldn't come from a techie. *She's* the lighting designer, so it's her call. If you just point it where she tells you, and the end result looks rubbish, you'll have done your job better than if you start trying to tell her how she can do *hers* better.') Hattie was also the one to figure out Eoin's secret hiding place, where he liked to go when he needed a break (on a part of the roof reachable from the skylight in the lantern store as it turned out), and while she promised not to reveal his private getaway spot, she did convince him that it might be better for him to only go there at times when he wasn't actively needed in the auditorium.

It lasted longer than it should have done. In a different, less chaotic working environment, Eoin's age and the ill-defined nature of his association with the theatre would have raised some eyebrows earlier on. Had Eoin's family been more attentive (or at least more attentive in a positive way), they might have questioned, upon being notified by his school that it had been several months since he last attended a class, where exactly he was spending his days, and taken steps to get him to return to where he was *supposed* to be. As it was, Eoin kept on turning up, day after day, for the better part of six months, and Hattie found herself growing entirely accustomed to his presence, until one day he didn't turn up. And the next day, he didn't turn up again. And after a week, when it began to seem less and less likely that this was just some temporary blip, Hattie started to ask around only to discover that no one knew where Eoin lived, or who his next of kin were, or how to contact him directly or indirectly (this was, of course, in the days when mobile phones and email addresses were not to be taken for granted). When Hattie, with rising alarm, asked Jack what to do the stage manager just shrugged and said, 'Well, he was never officially here in the first place was he? So I suppose that's that.'

And that was that. Hattie found it unbelievably frustrating that there was nothing she could do… but there was nothing she could do. And so she mourned the loss of her friend for a while, and then got swept up by other changes to her world. Both Jack and Oli, the deck chief, left the Tree in quick succession. Jack moved to a theatre in London and Oli got onto a tour. Hattie, who wanted to do both of those things, hoped that maybe one or t'other would think of her in their new roles, but Jack didn't return her calls and Oli, although he sincerely assured her that he'd love to work with her again and would recommend her name to anyone who would listen, didn't come across any openings for an ASM looking to make her way in the world. So Hattie stayed at the Tree, doing her best to impress her new superiors as they closed out the rest of the season.

And then late one night, after a gruelling fit-up, when Hattie had just got home and was slumped on the grotty sofa her housemates had liberated from a skip, working up the energy to crawl into bed, someone knocked on the door, and kept knocking, louder and louder until Hattie, muttering curses, had stumbled over to it and fumbled the thing open, to reveal Eoin, breathless, tearful and wild-eyed, with no coat on his back, but a half-empty rucksack on his shoulder. It had only been a few weeks since she'd seen him last. He seemed to have grown taller even in that time, but, vulnerable as he was now, he looked somehow younger.

Hattie let him in and sat him down, and it all came tumbling out: about his father, absent for almost his entire childhood, who had a year ago walked back into the house with no explanation and simply picked up where he had left off over a decade earlier. Except that in the intervening time Eoin hadn't exactly turned out the way his father had intended. Eoin told her about being woken up at midnight by his father, tight as a lord, fumbling angrily round his bedroom, pulling down posters and mumbling about not raising 'a fucking fairy'. He told her about the tussles over his books, his clothes, his interests, his friends. About the way that no matter what he said or did he never seemed to live up to his father's expectations, and how, as the evening wore on and his father's blood alcohol level rose, this perceived deficit became a greater and greater source of anger. About the first time he was hit, and the second, and then all the others that blurred into one. About the appeals to his mother that fell on deaf ears. About the mask of benevolence his father wore when he was around extended family, doctors, teachers and priests, about the horror of realising how appealing his father's behaviour could be when he was putting on a show, and the misery of the moments when the guests left, the doors closed, and the mask was abruptly cast aside.

Hattie listened to him talk, and sob, for an hour, an arm around his shoulder, until he had finally let all of it out and he sagged against her, exhausted. She fetched him a pillow and a blanket, and by the time she returned he was already asleep, in all his clothes, on the sofa.

HATTIE STEALS THE SHOW

He was still asleep the next morning when she left for the Tree, and when she returned in the evening he was curled up, still on the sofa, reading one of the few books they had in the flat. He showed no inclination to leave his spot, and Hattie felt no inclination to make him. So he stayed at hers, barely leaving that sofa, for a week.

Eventually, her flatmates began to express a little impatience. They didn't mind Eoin per se, they said, but it was a bit much to have their living room abruptly turned into some stranger's bedroom. This wasn't to become a permanent arrangement, they insisted.

They were right. Eoin was still a child. Staying with her could only be a stop-gap. He should be at home, with his mother. But there was no way he could go back to his father, that much was obvious.

There were no easy answers, so Hattie dithered. She persuaded her flatmates to put up with the boy for a little while longer, she sought advice from her own well-meaning but uncertain parents, and she spent long nights in conversation with Eoin trying to reason through a solution, with no effect. They were in a deadlock.

Eventually Eoin floated the idea of temporarily staying with a school friend of his, to give Hattie's flatmates a break. Hattie encouraged this idea, but when Eoin rang up his friend he was delivered a shock: his father had appeared at the school gates a few days earlier, tearfully begging everyone from Eoin's class for information about Eoin. His son had, he said, gone missing, out of the blue, and he was worried he had been abducted. Of course, as he well knew, it had been so long since Eoin had actually turned up to school that no one there had the first clue where he might be, but once word had got around that he was missing, he had become something of a local *cause célèbre*. Posters had been put up in local shops, letters had been written to the local paper, and half of Knapesfield (particularly the half who didn't spend their entire lives backstage at the theatre) knew about his disappearance. The police were now involved.

It brought tears of frustration to Eoin's eyes that his father, the very reason he had left, was now playing the concerned parent, eliciting sympathy and pity, and roping the general public into his ploy to drag Eoin back to him.

Hattie asked why the man was so keen to get Eoin to return. Wouldn't he be happier now that he was gone? Eoin shook his head and explained that, especially while sober, his father took a great deal of care over appearances. How could he pass himself off as a happy family man, reunited with his adoring wife and child after years of regrettable but unavoidable absence, if his only son had run away from him?

Hattie began to think that there must be a way this could be resolved. If all Eoin's father wanted was a story he could tell, was there a story that might involve Eoin going to live with his grandparents, or family friends, anywhere that was out of his father's direct line of sight? Everyone would be happier then, surely? Eoin was unconvinced, but Eoin wasn't the one who needed convincing. Hattie realised she was forming a plan…

11

In the morning Eoin had already replied:

> Nope, it's not mine. It's also awful. 'In defiance and free' is grammatically rubbish, and irretrievable. It should either be 'In defiance and freedom' (which doesn't rhyme) or 'Defiant and free' (which doesn't scan). C minus, must try harder.

Typical Eoin: he simply couldn't help himself, could he? Hattie permitted herself a slight eye roll, then got up. The household was generally slow to rise, but a breakfast sideboard had been laid out, presumably by the industrious Tinca. Hattie helped herself to coffee and a croissant, then pottered around downstairs until she found a second sitting room with lots of books and some comfy armchairs in it (Hattie knew without having to be told that Geoffrey would refer to this room as 'the library'). A selection of newspapers was laid out, so she settled down to do some cryptic crosswords.

However, when, half an hour later, she had still seen neither hide nor hair of any of the house's other denizens, Hattie realised she had been presented with an opportunity. Tucking a paper under her arm, she got up from her chair and decided to undertake a little quiet snooping.

The house was broadly arranged in an E shape, with the three prongs pointing backwards. The entrance hall and the large sitting room with the grand piano were both in the main spine, the kitchen, dining room and a downstairs loo were in the central prong, and the quasi-library was in the top prong. On the ground floor there were unexplored sections in every part, and the bottom prong was as yet entirely unknown.

Quietly, and doing her best to look nonchalant, Hattie worked her way along the corridors that connected all sections, poking her nose into every door she came across. This wasn't a serious search; this was just getting her bearings. For the most part she found rooms in which she was sure no musical manuscripts would be found: a small and very neglected-looking home gym; a spartan utility room; a coat-and-boot room that appeared to have been claimed by a swarm of flying ants; an extremely well-stocked pantry. But a couple of rooms showed promise: the main sitting room had a lot of miscellaneous papers stuffed onto its bookshelves; there was one room that seemed to be given over entirely to boxes, at least some of which looked as though they contained documents; and the library where she'd started her search had some cupboards that Hattie was itching to explore. But right at the end of her investigation Hattie came across the door to a room that was tucked up at the end of the bottom prong of the E. Hattie had walked past the outside of that part of the house a couple of times but hadn't thought to look in through the windows. She tried the handle, but it didn't open. After a few more hopeful twists and wiggles she concluded it must be locked.

Disappointed, she started to turn away, then was deeply startled to hear a movement inside the room, followed by the sound of a lock clicking. Then the door opened slightly to reveal Geoffrey, wearing a Chinese silk dressing gown and a frown.

'Oh, sorry!' said Hattie reflexively, then, recovering, gestured with her newspaper and continued, 'My pen dried up half way through the crossword, I was looking for another.'

Geoffrey nodded and turned back into the room. He left the door pulled almost to, though. Hattie was pretty clear he wasn't inviting her to follow, so she hovered in the doorway, watching through the crack as Geoffrey walked over to a large writing desk and fumbled in a pen pot. The desk was pushed up against a window, and from Hattie's viewpoint she could make out an array of framed posters mounted on one side, and bookshelves and an armchair to the other. This was clearly Geoffrey's private study. It was surprising to Hattie that Geoffrey, an outgoing and easygoing man, would lock himself in, though.

He returned with a biro in hand. 'I'll swap you a working pen for an interesting clue,' he said.

'All right. Er… *Trounces heads of stage school, suppressing sound of mirth*, ten letters, got a G in the middle.'

'Easy,' replied Geoffrey, handing over the pen. 'Slaughters.'

Hattie smiled. 'That'll do it. Thanks very much.'

Geoffrey nodded at her and closed the door. As Hattie walked away she heard the lock click again in the door.

By lunchtime everyone was up and about, and a minibus had pulled up to the front of the house. A couple of the actors seemed slightly the worse for wear, as though perhaps they'd had slightly *too* much fun the night before, but there already seemed to be an easy familiarity emerging among the group. Hattie suddenly felt guilty for spending her first two evenings not socialising. She wasn't being paid to make friends, but it wouldn't make anyone's life easier if she got a reputation for being too standoffish. She resolved to be a little more sociable from now on.

And in fact, this trip to Great Yarmouth might be just the thing for that. Once they'd eaten, they all piled into the minibus. Hattie found herself sitting next to Dylan, the actor with whom she'd had the least interaction so far. He was ginger and muscly, with a short beard, long eyelashes, and a penchant for board shorts that showed off a collection of calf tattoos. Apparently he'd done some well-received work in a supporting role in a film about the Krays not too long ago, and more recently he'd played a solid Macduff at the Old Vic. He wasn't your typical West End musical theatre actor, but he'd done well in the various parts in *Fall* he'd picked up the day before.

'All right my lovely,' he growled warmly, in what Hattie was *fairly* sure wasn't an affected East End accent. But you never could be quite sure when the performance had stopped with actors.

'All right,' she replied. 'First time going to Yarmouth?'

He nodded. 'You?'

'I've toured there a couple of times. There used to be a lovely little theatre there, a converted church. I think it fell down, though.'

Dylan gave her a cryptic look. 'This is just a hunch, but are you one of those people who's worked in *every* theatre in the world at one time or another?'

Hattie couldn't help but laugh. 'The world? No. I've barely done Asia or South America, never once set foot in Africa. I've done a bit in Europe, but it's patchy. But, well, UK... I mean... I suppose I've got around a bit.'

'Thought so,' said Dylan, nodding sagely. 'You've got the look.'

'The look, do I? What, grey hair?'

'No!' replied Dylan, and suddenly his knowing demeanour was replaced by a look of horror. 'I didn't mean that, sorry, I really didn't want to cause offence, I say such bollocks sometimes. I just meant you looked, you know, *travelled*. Oh God, that sounds worse...'

Hattie didn't have a brilliant ear for accents, but even she picked up that, as his agitation grew, a lot of the Mile End went out of Dylan's accent, and was replaced by something a little bit more home counties. Dylan struck Hattie as someone who was very careful to project a certain image of themselves, and it was interesting to see how quickly the edifice came tumbling down.

'You're all right my love. I've got a lot of years on me but I'm proud of all of them,' Hattie reassured him. He still insisted on apologising a few more times, but once he got over that he started quizzing her on her favourite theatre, her least favourite theatre, her worst tour, her best tour, and a thousand other prompts that had Hattie scrambling to bring to mind a thousand moments from the course of her career. It felt a bit self-indulgent to spend the entire journey talking about herself, but Dylan did seem to be genuinely interested, and it was a pleasant enough way to pass the time.

Meanwhile on the row in front of them, Calvin and Hera were seated together, but Calvin's attention was constantly being diverted by Tom, who was sitting across from them, and had a constant stream of anecdotes and remarks directed squarely at Calvin. By the time they reached Great Yarmouth Hera was beginning to look both left out and put out.

The show at the Hippodrome was a great success: the circus acts were spectacular, the comedy patter was satisfyingly groan-inducing, and the way that the stage converted itself into a pool for the finale was, from Hattie's professional perspective, very interesting. She found herself missing Nick for the first time since she'd arrived: he'd have been absolutely fascinated by it. She could hear him in her head hypothesising at length about the mechanisms involved, and felt only slightly guilty that in her imagination all of his theories were wrong.

Afterwards they all piled into an almost-empty pub not far from the venue. They didn't all fit around one table, so they split across two, and Geoffrey masterminded it so that the creatives sat with him, while the four actors, two techies and Calvin were seated separately. It made sense: ultimately the workshop was *for* the former group, with the latter there to support them. The writer, designers and director were the ones who were supposed to have been inspired by the show they'd just seen and use it to develop ideas for their own project. Everyone else was just along for the ride.

They made the best of it, though, putting away a couple of pints each before Dylan proposed a penny football tournament amid the beer mats and drink spills on the table. Calvin was sceptical, while Tom would only play if they each staked a fiver, and was then thoroughly flabbergasted when Hattie calmly wiped the floor with them all and took the pot. ('In various venues at various points I've had a lot of time to kill,' she said with a sly shrug.)

The conversation, unsurprisingly, remained in the vicinity of circus and circus skills. Hera told a funny story about how she'd once entirely falsely claimed she could ride a unicycle when auditioning for a part in a show in Iceland, and had relied on a series of increasingly elaborate ruses and excuses to get out of being discovered. Pip admitted that he really had had to learn to juggle for a show once, but declined all invitations to show off his abilities, claiming that he required very specific sorts of balls to be able to work his magic. ('Huh. Me too,' sniffed Tom). Then Delphine, who was probably the quietest of the people round the table, got up from her chair, found a space on the floor, lay down on her back with her knees bent, and very slowly, but perfectly smoothly, lifted herself up into a standing bridge pose, with her feet and hands flat on the ground but her legs almost vertical and her stomach, exposed as her top was pulled up towards her ribs, perfectly flat, at the same height as the table.

Equally gracefully she then uncurled herself up to a standing pose, then, as the group burst into rapturous applause, gave a little bow, then sauntered off to the bathroom.

'Bloody hell,' breathed Dylan. 'Now *that's* a woman.'

'Oh aye?' said Tom. 'The breeders have finally noticed each other.'

'I'm sorry, "breeder"?' asked Pip. 'Are we throwing out heterophobic slurs now?'

'It's not a *slur*, it's a term of endearment,' replied Tom. 'I think it's sweet that Dylan has a crush.'

'Okay, first of all,' complained Dylan, 'I don't have a crush. Yet. Second of all, me and Delphine are not the only straight people here. Hera?'

Hera shook her head.

'All right,' said Dylan. 'Then Hattie, how about you? You're—'

'Very happily married, and even happier never to be called a "breeder",' Hattie replied.

'And then Geoffrey,' continued Dylan.

'I think he's above such things,' put in Calvin.

'Oh he's really not,' replied Tom. 'He's just *very* discreet about it. I will concede that Gareth and Mel are both your lot.'

'My ears are burning. What on earth are you all on about?' called across Geoffrey from the other table.

'We're running a sweepstake on who'll be shagging who by the end of the week,' shot back Tom. 'I'm sorry love, no one's bet on you at all.'

'You're a degenerate and a scoundrel. Drink your drink and behave,' was Geoffrey's good-natured riposte.

When Delphine returned, the discussion on proclivities subsided into a steady background level of innuendo. After another half an hour or so, Geoffrey announced that it was time to go. They finished their drinks, and as if by magic the minibus was waiting for them as they emerged from the pub.

With a little alcohol inside them it wasn't long before the drive home descended into another showtune singalong. There was a general preference for Sondheim and Lloyd Webber, although Tom snuck in a request for 'Everyone's a little bit racist', and Dylan was unexpectedly insistent that they sing 'Let it go' from *Frozen*. Hattie noticed that by the end of the drive Tom had his arm casually around Calvin's shoulders.

Supper was waiting for them by the time they got home, and so, to Hattie's surprise, was Louise. She was hovering in the doorway as they walked in, a big bundle of paperwork in one hand and a pen in the other. Hattie saw her awkwardly trying to get Geoffrey's attention without, it seemed, having the guts to interrupt or get in anyone's way. When she eventually caught his eye he dismissed her with a casual wave of his hand without even pausing in his animated discussion with Maxine about the relative influence of Craig and Appia on modern scenography. Hattie watched as Louise deflated back into her corner and, feeling a pang of sympathy for the young woman, went over and offered her a greeting.

'I thought you'd gone back to London?'

'Oh, I have. I did, that is. I just nipped up to get Geoffrey to sign some things, then I'm off again.'

'You nipped up… from London to Norfolk and back again… on a Saturday? Just to get a signature? Is there a lot of that sort of thing in your line of work?'

Louise nodded. 'He has to deal with lots of contracts. There's the venue in Dubai, the American tours and the Vegas show… lots of paperwork.'

'Well, it looks like you've got it well in hand. I'm sure Geoffrey values the effort you put in for him.'

'I…' Louise tailed off and looked abruptly down at the floor, and when she looked up again, Hattie was horrified to realise that the girl looked like she was starting to cry. Somehow Hattie had managed to say something very wrong.

'I'm sorry my love—'

'I'm fine!' Louise blurted, loudly and forcedly enough to make it immediately clear that she wasn't. Hattie and Louise were mostly alone in the hall now, but the last stragglers making their way into the dining room in front of them looked around in confusion at the loud sound of her voice.

'Oh, well… er, I met your intern,' said Hattie, casting around for a way to change the subject. 'Lorna. She seems a nice girl.'

'She's great!' said Louise, her voice still constricted as she worked to regain her composure. 'I'm sure she'll do well in the industry. She just needs to understand that it really is hard work. You have to buckle down.'

Hattie nodded, approvingly. 'A lot of people don't realise that,' she said. 'Just because theatre is fun and glamorous, that doesn't mean it isn't *also* a lot of very hard work. The actors, the creatives, they need some headspace to do their job, and that's fair enough. But people like you and me, we're there to buckle down and get on with it.'

'That's right,' said Louise, looking and sounding almost back to normal now. 'You've got to give the creatives some leeway. Don't you? It's not their job to be nice to us, is it?'

That was a rather odd remark, Hattie thought to herself, but before she could say anything in return, Geoffrey poked his head out from the dining room doorway.

'Come on Hattie, we can't start supper without you. It'd be Hamlet without the prince! Will you eat, Louise? Tinca's made masses.'

'It's all right, Geoffrey, I need to be getting back. What do you want me to do with the Vegas contracts?'

'Oh just chuck them in my study. I'll look at them on Tuesday.'

'I think we need signed copies for the New York office on—'

'Oh, no no no, we're nowhere near ready for New York. I need Finlay to query the non-compete, so I think we're still a week away from signing. Next time check with him. You could have saved yourself a trip.'

'Yes Geoffrey,' said Louise, her face a brittle mask of politeness.

Hattie followed Geoffrey into the dining room and found her allocated seat. As they ate, she kept an eye on the glances Dylan occasionally shot over at Delphine, and the glances she occasionally sent in return. By the end of the meal she was feeling pleasantly muzzy, and was happy to settle down on a sofa in the sitting room and watch and listen as the actors gossiped and bantered and played raucous improv games. So relaxed was she that she was quite taken aback to realise that it was 11 o'clock when Delphine abruptly said, 'Right, bed time.'

'Good point,' said Dylan, getting up equally abruptly. 'Goodnight all.'

He walked elaborately slowly to the doorway, then turned, waiting for Delphine, who hesitated and then, with the tiniest hint of pleading in her eyes, said, 'You coming Hattie?'

Hattie, noticing her cue, nodded and hauled herself up from the depths of the sofa. The three of them walked in silence up the stairs, and Dylan bade them a slightly disappointed goodnight at the women's door.

'Thank you,' said Delphine quietly once they were inside.

'No problem,' said Hattie.

'Dylan's absolutely lovely, but he's started giving me soulful looks and I wanted to avoid an awkward moment.'

'Fair enough,' said Hattie, and then, probably because of the wine that was sitting on top of the beer in her stomach, added nosily, 'Not your type then?'

'Not my type,' Delphine confirmed. 'Don't get me wrong, I like manly, but there's such a thing as *too* manly. And – forgive me, this is awful – I'm not a huge fan of ginger. No, give me slim, tall, clean-shaven, dark-haired for preference.'

'Righto,' said Hattie with a chuckle. 'If I ever find myself with someone like that going spare I'll let you know.'

Delphine smiled in return, and took herself off into the ensuite bathroom. Hattie lay down on her bed and found herself frowning: as Delphine had been describing her ideal man, a memory of a photo had popped into her head. She'd seen the photo in the papers recently, and it matched Delphine's description. It was a photo of Lel.

12

Sunday was quiet. It was an official day off, and no activities had been laid on, optional or otherwise. At breakfast Tom nonchalantly mentioned that he thought he might take a trip to the seaside town of Southwold, and Calvin, equally nonchalantly, offered to join him. Tom readily agreed to this, but appeared not to hear when Jala also expressed an interest in coming. The two men made a swift exit and once they were gone the crestfallen Jala expressed a little bit of unease, rather surprisingly, about being left alone for the day. However, another party was organised by the actors to take a trip to a *different* seaside town – Thorpeness – and she was welcomed to this rival expedition. Gareth and Mel had both got up early to drive back to London to spend the day with their partners and families; Maxine had come down with a cold and announced her intention to spend most of the day in bed, and no one was quite sure where Geoffrey had got to.

Hattie, therefore, was left in large part to her own devices. She felt a pang of guilt for not driving back home to see Nick, but she couldn't quite face two tussles with the A12 in a single day, especially not in the context of having a mild but persistent hangover from the night before. Then she realised, with a little relief, that Nick would be working today anyway. So she treated herself to a lazy morning, relaxing with a book until all the beach-bound detachments had departed.

When they were gone, however, she steeled herself into action.

Her *other* responsibility needed tending to. With Geoffrey's whereabouts unknown she didn't dare try anything to get into his study, and she didn't want to risk being caught poking around in the room full of boxes. But she did feel confident exploring both the library and the sitting room at her leisure, sorting through all the paperwork in search of Lel's errant score.

She found nothing, but at least she was confident by lunchtime that it was because, in those rooms at least, there was nothing of importance to be found. So, satisfied by a sense of progress, she took herself off for lunch in the village pub she'd spotted a couple of minutes' drive from Trevelyan House. It was a small place and busy, but Hattie had turned up early enough that, after a little bit of hesitation, the owner said they'd be happy to serve her if she wouldn't mind eating at the bar.

Hattie ordered the pork platter and a sparkling water, and rang Nick while she waited, hoping to catch him on his lunch break. He didn't pick up, so she left him a voicemail and started to put her phone away. Then she stopped and, on a whim, tried calling Abua again. This time he picked up.

'Hello?'

'Hello there. It's Hattie.'

'Oh! Hi. Er… how are you?' Abua sounded worried, defensive even.

'I'm very well,' Hattie replied in her most soothing voice. 'How are you doing?'

'Yeah… I'm good. Well, I'm… I'm okay.'

Hattie waited for him to elaborate, but he didn't offer anything more, so eventually she prompted him with, 'And the Young Vic?'

She heard him draw in a deep breath.

'I didn't go,' he said.

'Oh?'

'I… haven't been well.'

'I'm sorry to hear that,' said Hattie. 'Nothing too serious, I hope?'

'No, it's… I mean… Look, I… I just…'

Hearing him struggling, Hattie interjected, 'When we spoke, at graduation, I thought maybe you were having a hard time with, shall we say, jitters about the starting work. But it sounds like maybe it's a little bit more than that.'

'Um… yes.'

'I wonder if maybe you've slightly lost confidence in yourself. It's easily done.'

'Well…'

'In which case, perhaps if it's helpful to hear: You're really good at this. You're a stage manager, through and through.'

'I'm really not sure I am…'

'Trust me, Abua. I see it in you. I don't want you to get me wrong, I'm not saying you're God's gift, or that somehow you're better than all the other students. You're too sensible to believe me if I fed you a bunch of hyperbole, so I won't. I just want you to hear me when I say that I know you, and I know you can do this.'

'Okay. Um. Listen, I have to go. Sorry. Is… is that okay?'

'Of course. But hang in there. If you want me to have a word with the Young Vic lot, I can. When you're ready.'

'Uh… okay. Maybe. Um. Goodbye for now.'

He hung up, and Hattie put her phone away. This was uneasy territory for her. Over the course of her career she'd witnessed people crack up in a variety of different ways, and she'd often wanted to help, and had often tried to, but it was seldom that she'd done any good. You can't solve all of other people's problems for them, and there are some sorts of problems you can't even help with. But she still felt compelled to try.

Lunch arrived, and it was delicious. Hattie mulled over the call with Abua while she ate, then mulled over it a little bit more when she had finished. Then, accepting that there was only so much benefit to be had from protracted mulling, she settled the bill and went back to the house. It was still quiet – no one seemed to be back from any of their trips yet – so Hattie spent a little time in the afternoon snooping around the upper storey of the house. Disappointingly, but unsurprisingly, all she found was bedroom after bedroom (including one in which Maxine was snoring congestedly). By the time the others returned, Hattie was clear: if Lel's music was anywhere in the house, it would either be in the room full of boxes, or in Geoffrey's study.

On Monday morning they were all back in the granary first thing, where they were joined by a new face. Teri, the composer, had appeared. She was short and broad, wearing a floral dress and red, thick-framed glasses. If Jala had looked nervous when she arrived, Teri looked *petrified*. The others went round the room introducing themselves, and Hattie did her best to look and sound friendly and unthreatening when it was her turn. But she didn't have a chance to say a proper hello, because Geoffrey packed Teri, Calvin, Hera and Delphine off to the main house straight away to start practising the songs, while the others stayed to explore possible concepts for the *mise-en-scène*.

It was another session without lots for Hattie to do. Inspired by one of the acrobatics routines performed on Saturday's trip, Gareth had some ideas about using projection of pre-recorded footage to give the impression that an actor was dancing with their own ghost. This would apparently complement Hope's monologue in scene four about how she hoped to be remembered after she had died, and how she felt about the remembered version of herself that would outlive her. Geoffrey adored the concept, so they spent several hours tinkering with effects, while a very patient Pip stood still, being blinded by the projection beam. But by 1 o'clock some doubts were beginning to creep in.

'So: on a black background the projection doesn't show up

strongly enough, on a white background the performer doesn't show up strongly enough, and on a grey background it looks drab and ghastly. I'm not sure there's a way forward here,' said Maxine.

'I think there's something we can do,' said Gareth. 'What if we use a white background, but the performer is wearing black? So it's more a silhouette thing?'

'If they're just a silhouette we might as well do the whole thing as video, without a real performer there at all,' grumbled Geoffrey. 'In which case why come to the theatre at all? Why not just watch it on the telly?'

'I wonder if this might be something to return to with fresh eyes later in the week?' suggested Hattie, sensing a squabble brewing. This idea was met with broad approval. They broke for lunch and made their way back to the house, where they were greeted by the sounds of Hera confidently but imperfectly singing the final song from act one. Not wanting to interrupt, they stood and listened outside the sitting room doorway. As the final note on the piano finished, they all clapped, and Geoffrey shouted through: 'Marvellous! Now come get some grub.'

Calvin sat next to Hattie over lunch. 'How's it all been going?' he asked.

'I think we're very definitely in what you might call the "ideation" stage,' replied Hattie tactfully, and Calvin smirked. 'How's the singing?'

'Great,' he said. 'The ladies are both pretty good at reading the dots and sticks, and they're already making some jolly pleasing noises.'

He took a mouthful of Tinca's bruschetta, then added, 'Teri's still finding her feet. I'm sure she's got some strong opinions about how her work should be sung, but understandably she's not sticking her oar in straight away. But the singers do need a bit of direction, so I've been giving it to them. I hope I'm not being too domineering – I want Teri to feel that she *can* speak up and take charge, if she wants to.'

'I'm sure you're being very sensitive about it,' said Hattie. 'And I bet you're right: Teri just needs a little time to settle in.'

Calvin nodded in agreement, but when, after an afternoon's further fruitless 'ideation' in the granary, Hattie returned to the house and, bumping into Calvin on the stairs, enquired as to his progress, he made a pained face and said, quietly, 'Well, I think everyone is as settled as they're going to be, but if I don't keep my hand firmly on the tiller we do tend to drift, as it were.'

He screwed up his face before continuing: 'And look, I don't mind imposing my opinions, but at this stage we should be working to bring out, well, Teri's vision for the music. And I mean it's, it's… It's her music. Isn't it? So she needs to put *her* stamp on it. If she doesn't, then it doesn't really work, does it? But she doesn't *say* anything.'

As he spoke he was getting increasingly worked up, and his voice was getting louder and louder. The agitation apparent in his tone didn't seem to match the careful diplomacy of his words. Hattie, who didn't entirely understand what Calvin was upset about, but who was very aware that Teri was somewhere nearby and quite possibly within earshot, thought she had better say something to try to soothe him.

'Maybe it's just a case of setting some shared expectations about how to work together,' she suggested. 'It might be worth you two having a chat about who's going to be responsible for what, and what you're trying to achieve?'

Calvin smiled. 'You're right. Of course you're right. I think it's just my insecurities showing. I'm very keen to stay in Geoffrey's good books. I've already kicked up enough of a fuss about other things recently. If this workshop turns into something, I'd love to be invited to come along for the ride, you know? It'd be a great gig to have.'

'I know what you mean,' said Hattie.

A bell rang from the dining room, and they both started to descend the stairs in the direction of supper.

'I'll tell you what else has me on edge,' offered Calvin as they walked. 'It's that bird. It spent the whole afternoon on top of the house, squawking every few minutes. It sounds like a falsetto donkey. If you're trying to really *listen* to someone singing a soprano part, a peacock is really quite off-putting.'

'Peacock? *Bastard!*'

Geoffrey had appeared behind them and evidently overheard the last part of their conversation. His face was dark. 'Charles has assured me on numerous occasions that he would keep his bloody birds under control. I don't know whose neck to wring: the peacock's or his.'

'Oh, now, I don't want to get anyone into trouble…' said Calvin, anxiously.

Geoffrey grunted angrily. Then, seemingly collecting himself, he said, 'Tell you what. I'll have a word with Tinca. If she knows a decent recipe for a peacock casserole then we'll solve the problem that way. Either of you a steady shot with a 12-bore?'

The twinkle in his eyes was back, to the evident relief of Calvin. The three of them went in to dinner.

Hattie was curious to get to know the young composer who had riled Calvin up so effectively, and by good luck she found herself seated opposite her at dinner. Opportunities for conversation were limited, however, as Tom was sitting to Teri's left, and Calvin was sitting to Hattie's left, and Tom spent most of the meal in full flight, taking charge of the conversation at their end of the table as he sought to entertain and impress his new friend.

'Oh God, the Apollo?' he said in response to some harmless-seeming story about a previous show at the New Apollo theatre by Pip, who was sitting on Hattie's right. 'Jesus, Murray is *unbearable*, isn't he?'

'Murray Pendleton?' asked Hattie, recognising the name of the New Apollo's technical manager. 'I've worked with him. He's not bad.'

Tom made a face. 'Oh no no no, he's *no bueno*. It's not that he's boring. I mean, he *is* boring, but it's not that. It's the way that you can't do a single thing in his auditorium if you haven't first written it up as a line item on one of his checklists. Want to go up a ladder during fit-up? Not unless your fit-up checklist has "go up a ladder" on it. Want to go *back* up a ladder? Sorry, you've already checked that off, you'll need to create a new list. Want to take a piss? Ooh, better get your pen and paper out. It's pathological.'

Sensing that Tom was more interested in being entertaining than being accurate, Hattie declined to deflate his hyperbole. But it irked her. She liked Murray. And while she couldn't deny that he was not the most socially effervescent character, he was also a kind and loyal man who had over the years won Hattie's unstinting approval. Tom was fun, and funny, no doubt about it. But he was yet to learn that in an industry where everyone knew everyone and some ties ran deep, you had to be careful who you spoke ill of.

Teri didn't participate much in the conversation, whether through diplomacy or shyness Hattie couldn't be sure: she just hunched over her cottage pie and peas. She didn't eat much, Hattie noticed. Her hands were always busy with her knife and fork, but she mostly used them to push little morsels of food around her plate, only very occasionally bringing one of them up to her mouth. On the other hand she did accept several refills of her wine glass.

At the end of the meal, as soon as people started to get up from the table, Teri slipped away with a wordless, apologetic nod to the assembled company, presumably heading up to bed. Hattie expected she wouldn't see her again that evening, intending as she did to stay downstairs with the group for half an hour, as part of her new conscious effort to be more sociable. When she stood up to move into the sitting room, however, she found that her hip was twinging again, so, for the sake of having a chance at sleeping later, she nipped upstairs to take a pill. She was somewhat surprised to see Teri listlessly pacing the landing.

'Are you all right, my love?'

'Oh!' said Teri, awkwardly. 'Sorry. This is stupid, but I'm not sure which my room is. I only came up once this morning and I was a bit distracted, and everywhere looks so similar.'

She smiled apologetically, and Hattie noticed that her eyes were slightly glassy in a way they hadn't seemed earlier in the day: Hattie got the impression that Teri was rather drunk, which would certainly explain her current disorientation.

'Not to worry,' she said cheerfully. 'Let's just go and ask Geoffrey which room you're in.'

'Oh no!' exclaimed Teri, her eyes widening. 'I'm too embarrassed. Please.'

'All right,' replied Hattie, suppressing a sigh. 'Well, perhaps we can work it out. Do you know who you're sharing with?'

'Jala.'

'Ah, okay. I'm not entirely sure which one is hers, but there are three sort of wings up here. She's not in this one, and I think Geoffrey's got the one at the other end all to himself, so shall we take a look in the middle one?'

Teri agreed, and Hattie led her down the appropriate corridor where (helped by what Hattie could remember from her snooping the previous day) they quickly found Jala and Teri's room.

'Thank you,' said Teri. 'Sorry.'

'It's no problem,' said Hattie soothingly. 'I think we've all had a rather long day, haven't we?'

Teri nodded. 'It's been *so* long. I thought it would never end.'

Then she was shaking her head and she continued: 'But it's fine. It's fine, it's all fine.'

'All right,' said Hattie, bemused. 'If you ever want a quiet chat about anything, just let me know. I'm always happy to try and help.'

But Teri didn't seem to be listening, and she was already pushing her bedroom door closed, leaving Hattie standing thoughtfully in the corridor.

13

Hattie didn't have a moment to catch up with Calvin over the next couple of days, so she had no idea whether his working relationship with Teri, and his opinion of her, improved at all. But there were no audible tantrums from either party, which Hattie took as a good sign.

In the meantime, in the granary, they were starting to move on from abstract dramaturgical ideas to a more concrete exploration of the staging of different scenes. Hattie rather suspected that this was largely driven by Geoffrey getting bored of talking theory all day, but this suited her fine: the more time spent with actors standing around delivering lines, the more straightforward Hattie's role in the room became: she was the collective memory of the group, keeping track of every idea that was called out, every nuance of timing and movement, and, most prosaically, where in the room the actors ended up standing in each different part of each different scene.

The fact that they were moving away from theoretical conceptualising didn't mean that they were treating the script as set in stone, though. On the contrary, Jala was constantly rewriting things on her laptop and nipping back to the house to print new pages to hand out. (The printer was in Geoffrey's study, and Hattie noted that while Geoffrey was very happy for Jala to go in there to use it, he did request that she lock the door behind her and return the key to him every time when she was done.)

Hattie watched Jala work with approval: criticism of a script during rehearsals can be quite bruising to a writer's ego, especially when those in the room are not just pointing out problems but also suggesting their own improvements. But Jala was happy to pull anyone's ideas into her script if they improved on what was already there, while not being afraid to push back if she spotted a flaw in any proposed change. Self-confidence without ego, Hattie thought. Exactly what you wanted from a writer in this situation. And very different from what you'd expect from the author of that ghastly pretentious book on theatrical theory.

The only thing that was a little bit strange about her was a noticeably jumpy disposition. She spent a surprising amount of time peering out of the granary windows at nothing Hattie could discern, she twitched at loud noises, and she was clearly very uncomfortable spending any amount of time by herself: whenever she went to print something, she would casually suggest that Teri, or one of the actors who wasn't currently busy, accompany her. No one commented on this, and indeed it wasn't particularly inconvenient or out of the ordinary. But it did seem a little unnecessary: printing a few sheets of paper isn't a two-person job however you cut it up.

More broadly, and more importantly, the group as a whole started to get onto the same wavelength. They were having fun, and what was beginning to emerge resembled something approaching an actual, honest-to-goodness show. There were recurring themes, there were character arcs, there were genuinely funny bits and all. Everyone could feel it. It was exciting.

Where it started to go wrong was on Thursday after lunch. By this point, Calvin and Teri had had three full days of 'note-bashing' with the actors, and Geoffrey was now keen to start giving some creative attention to the songs. So for the afternoon session the full company assembled in the granary, as they turned their attention to the bus station scene in act two. In the book the whole scene took place in the middle of the night in a rainstorm, so Tom and Gareth had tremendous fun pulling up stock video of rain to loop on the screens in the background to set the mood.

The first half hour was fine, with Jala and Mel tinkering merrily with the dialogue as Hera (playing Hope) and Pip (playing St Christopher) traded barbs. But then they got on to the song, a confrontational duet titled 'You promised me'. Pip delivered his line, Calvin played the introduction on the piano (a few rather mournful legato phrases), Hera opened her mouth to sing… and was cut off by Geoffrey who shouted, 'Whoa! Stop! Stop right there!'

Calvin lifted his fingers from the keys and waited expectantly, while both actors squatted down, awaiting further instructions.

'Well, that's not right at all, is it?' Geoffrey said cheerfully. 'That introduction is beautiful, but it stands out like a sore thumb in the context of the scene. Don't you think, Teri?'

'Oh God, sorry!' yelped Teri, who was sitting in the corner near Hattie.

'Oh don't apologise, this is exactly what we're here to learn.'

There was a moment's pause, as Geoffrey looked expectantly at Teri. But Teri simply looked blankly back.

'Well, we can change the intro, can't we?' Calvin prompted. 'That's the easiest thing in the world. Maybe we could do something a bit choppier? Less melodic? Like how we start "It takes me back"?'

'Yes, but "It takes me back" uses the hospital motif, we can't put that here,' murmured Teri.

'Well, no, it doesn't have to be that motif, I just mean that sort of feel. It could be something completely new,' suggested Calvin.

'I suppose so,' said Teri, dubiously, her voice small and her eyes wide with panic. 'I'm just not sure if we introduce a new thing here, whether it'll feel out of place.'

'All right, then is it easier if we just cut the intro entirely and have Hope jump straight in?' asked Calvin brightly, although

Hattie thought that his smile was starting to look a little strained.

'Good idea,' said Mel firmly. 'At least for now. Let's try it again. Hattie?'

'Let's take it from St Christopher's line: "Always with the supplication, can't you give me just a little adoration from time to time?"'

So they did, and after a few lines of dialogue Hera jumped straight into the song, a little shakily at first as she looked to Calvin to check she was singing in the right key, but with increasing confidence as she got through the first verse, and she got half way through the chorus before Geoffrey called another halt.

'Well now that's interesting, isn't it? You know what I mean, don't you Mel?'

'Oh absolutely,' replied Mel. 'Yes, it's completely… well, exactly.'

Hattie entertained the possibility that Mel in fact *didn't* know what Geoffrey meant, but decided that that was a rather cruel interpretation of her answer so chose to give Mel the benefit of the doubt.

'The energy, it just completely drops in the chorus,' Geoffrey elaborated, as Mel nodded furiously. 'We lose that wonderful tension we've been building up in the scene.'

'Is it just how I'm singing it?' asked Hera. 'I could give it a bit of…'

'Welly? Some cheeky razzmatazz?' Geoffrey grinned. 'Oh lovely, let's try it. I'm sure it won't work, I just want to hear what you do with it.'

They took it from the top again, and Hera attacked the chorus with verve, eliciting moans of delight from Geoffrey every time she belted a high note or sprinkled a little growl onto a low one, but as soon as Calvin started on the bridge that would lead the song into verse two, Geoffrey called a halt to proceedings once more.

'Wonderful. Wonderful, wonderful, wonderful, and *utterly* wrong. You hear it, Teri, don't you? It's the same problem as the intro – well, I suppose because it's the same music as the intro, isn't it? – the energy is wrong, and the momentum just dissipates. Let's change it!'

'Um… I suppose I could write a new song in place of this one,' said Teri, uncertainly.

'No no, you can leave the verses exactly as they are, they're perfect. Or at least, they're good enough at the moment. It's just that introduction and the chorus we need to change. Same lyrics, different everything else. I have complete faith in your ability to fix it.'

'Do you think we could fix it with orchestration?' asked Teri, her voice barely more than a whisper. 'I thought maybe some pizzicato strings…'

'Look, if it doesn't work on piano, it won't magically start working if you chuck a violin at it,' said Calvin snippily.

Hattie noticed Teri directing a quick look at Jala, a pleading look on her face. Jala responded with a noncommittal shrug.

'We can't get precious about our work,' said Mel firmly. 'We've all got to give ourselves permission to acknowledge mistakes and make changes. Otherwise what's the point of doing a workshop?'

'It's not that,' said Teri, looking very close to tears, 'I'd be happy to rewrite the song. I just think if I start changing some things and keeping others the same it'll… I mean, maybe if I had a few weeks to get my head around it…'

At the mention of a few weeks Calvin let out an audible snort, and he and Tom shared a look of pure scorn. Geoffrey was quick to suggest a way forward. 'Teri, my dear, I *do* understand how difficult it is to unpick a finished piece of work, especially in the circumstances, but let's not let this derail us. Teri and Jala my love, let's the three of us go and spend a little time coming up with a plan for the music. It's just a case of getting to grips with the creative process, and I'm sure we'll be up and running in no time. In the *meantime*, why don't you lot skip to the end of the song, and look at what happens next, shall we?'

That was it for music for, as it turned out, the rest of the day. Geoffrey took Teri and Jala into his study with a plate of nibbles and locked the door behind them, and they weren't seen again until supper. In their absence Mel started to work through some of the dialogue scenes, but without Geoffrey no one seemed comfortable even proposing new ideas, let alone giving them a yea or nay. At 4 o'clock, with everyone a little bit morose and listless in the granary, Gareth said, 'Look, I've got an idea for how we could make the ghost projection work, but it'll take a little while to set it up. Since we're sort of treading water at the moment, could I use the room to spend some time with Tom and Maxine trying to get it up and running to show to Geoffrey when he reappears?'

No one objected, so everyone Gareth didn't need was dismissed (although Hattie recommended that everyone stay close with their phones on in case they were called to reconvene). Hattie double-checked that Gareth didn't want any help from her, then took herself off to the kitchen in the main house to make a cuppa. Tinca was there, preparing supper. She was a cheerful-looking middle-aged woman, fond of bright clothes and bold lipstick, and her hair, which had streaks of red and pink in it, was tied up into a loose, high ponytail, presumably to keep it out of her way while she worked her magic in the kitchen. Finding herself alone for a few quiet moments with the person responsible for what were genuinely some of the best meals of Hattie's life, she decided to try to get to know her a bit better.

'Hullo!' Hattie said cheerfully, eliciting only a non-committal smile in return. Tinca was standing at a worktop surrounded by mounds of vegetables, so Hattie followed up with: 'Do you need a hand at all? I've got some time.'

'Ooh, maybe,' replied Tinca, her face lighting up. 'Are you any good at chopping onions?'

Hattie thought back with a burst of self-consciousness to the last time she'd tried to prepare a vegetable, and Tinca picked up on her hesitancy, adding: 'Or, if you really want to help me out you could peel these potatoes.'

Hattie gratefully accepted the simpler task, and was soon set up in a corner with a tub of muddy spuds and a peeler. She found even this duty a little daunting at first, being acutely aware that Tinca operated to a very high standard, but quickly got the measure of the tool, and was soon happily spewing peelings into a pile for the compost bin. Once she'd got the hang of the potatoes Hattie felt able to handle conversation as well, so she said: 'So do you cater for Geoffrey a lot, or is it only when he has big house parties?'

'Yes to both,' Tinca replied. 'He brings me in whenever he has a lot of guests, but that's most weeks. There are always people popping up. He'd be better off getting a full-time cook, but he says he doesn't want to have servants because it makes him feel "uncomfortably feudal" as he puts it. So he keeps me on speed-dial, and when I'm not free there's a Polish bloke in the village, and when neither of us is around there's a catering company in Beccles who make a killing.'

'That sounds like it works out quite well for everyone, then?'

'I think so. I do sometimes have to be quite firm with him. He's so used to getting what he wants, but my mum's out near Malaga and I do insist on putting my visits to her first.'

'Quite right,' agreed Hattie.

'It's fun, though,' Tinca continued, and Hattie was pleased that the other woman, who had initially come off as rather reserved, was now offering further contributions to the conversation unprompted. 'He lets me spend what I like within reason, and it means I get to try things I otherwise wouldn't have a chance to cook. And for the most part Geoffrey's not picky about what I put on the table. Some of his guests can be a different story.'

'A bit precious, are they?'

'Oh God yes. Honestly, sometimes I feel like I'm feeding toddlers. They won't eat this, they won't eat that, they *will* eat the other but not the way you've prepared it, and some of them you'd think have never been taught even basic manners.'

She leant forwards conspiratorially to Hattie. 'There was one fellow, a composer or something like that, who was just *awful*. Do you know what he did? He—'

'Goodness,' announced Calvin, walking into the kitchen behind Tinca. 'I think today is very much a day for Hobnobs. Do we have any?'

He started poking around the corner of the counter with the kettle and cafetieres, where Tinca occasionally put out plates of biscuits in the afternoon.

'There should be some in the cupboard by your head,' Tinca replied. 'No, to the left... yes, there.'

'Oh yes, wonderful. Thanks Tinca, you're a lifesaver,' said Calvin, retrieving the packet and fishing out a couple of Hobnobs. Then he spotted Hattie. 'Oh hullo! What a day, eh?'

'Yes,' said Hattie, noncommittally. She had a feeling she knew what was coming, and wanted to tread carefully: you need to make sure you don't accidentally take sides when people fall out in a company. She was also feeling pretty gutted that Calvin had interrupted just as Tinca was gearing up to spill the beans: Hattie couldn't be *sure* which composer Tinca was talking about, but she had a suspicion.

'Honestly, I've never seen the like of it. This morning? I don't think I've ever come across a composer who flat-out refused to change her music. Certainly not before rehearsals have even started. I mean, we're not even in *pre*-production yet! Have you? Ever seen anything like it?'

'I'm sure it's just a case of everyone finding their feet,' Hattie offered cautiously.

'Oh you're so tactful, and you're right, of course, I shouldn't bitch,' said Calvin, nodding furiously. 'But *still*... Oh hello!'

Pip had wandered in as well, and soon he and Calvin were deep in discussion about Teri and her admittedly startling behaviour in the morning. Tinca quietly went back to chopping onions and Hattie got on with her potatoes. Teri's attitude was rather disappointing, but there was something odd about her behaviour, something Hattie couldn't quite put her finger on. Her reticence didn't seem to come from a place of ego and insecurity but rather seemed to Hattie to be something else as yet unidentified.

She finished her peeling and received a warm thanks from Tinca, then decided to make her way to the library for a quiet sit-down. On her way through the hall she bumped into Geoffrey, coming from the direction of his study.

'Aha! Just the person – or at least the sort of person – I was hoping to find. This is well below your pay grade, but Louise isn't here, so I wonder if I could trouble you with a task?'

'Whatever you need, Geoffrey,' said Hattie with a professional smile, her heart quietly sinking as she felt her quiet sit-down slipping away from her.

'There's a recording I need you to dig out. A CD. I'm pretty sure it's got a handwritten label saying "Rough compositions" on it, and it's in a folder – probably green, maybe yellow – marked *Roses*. It'll be in one of the boxes in the yellow room. Do you know the yellow room? It's just round the corner there, I mostly use it for storage. You know the one? On the left. Sorry, I know it's a faff, but I want to play Teri something, one of the early drafts of "Your name", you know, the big eleven o'clock number. Can you do that for me?'

'Of course,' Hattie replied. 'I'll get right on it.'

This time her smile was more genuine, and if anything she felt the need not to betray her full enthusiasm: she'd been looking for an excuse to poke around in the room full of boxes, and now one had been handed to her on a plate!

She went straight to the room and settled down for a good old nosey around. She wanted to be strategic about this. It didn't take long to spot that the boxes on the left hand side of the room seemed to contain neatly packed folders of various colours (including some green and some yellow), while the ones on the other side contained more of a miscellany. To give herself an excuse for spending as long as possible going through as many boxes as possible, Hattie started her search with the boxes on the right hand side. That way, if disturbed, it would be more believable that she was taking so long because she hadn't yet found the thing she'd been sent to look for.

Frustratingly, it soon became clear that these miscellaneous boxes were unlikely to contain any music by Lel. Nothing in them was less than a decade old, and from the dust that had collected in some places, Hattie got the sense that some of the contents were considerably older than that. What she was working her way through was an archive of paperwork from every show Geoffrey had been involved with from the eighties to the noughties, and a lot of it was material that had clearly never been properly sorted: one box was filled entirely with flyers for the 1996 European tour of *Midnight Street*, one contained a few printed out letters sitting on top of several reams of blank printer paper, another one held an assortment of promotional T-shirts and branded sweet packets that had an expiry date of 2003. This wasn't the sort of place you'd find a draft of anything recent.

The boxes with folders in, when she got to them, were at least more ordered: clearly at some point someone had made a start on rationalising all these documents, and each folder was filled with genuinely important-seeming documents for one specific show. Once she'd given up on finding Lel's music, it didn't take her long to track down the box dedicated to *Roses*, and the folder of scripts and scores. Sure enough, there was a CD, labelled as Geoffrey had supposed, which Hattie retrieved. She carried it with her out of the yellow room and along the corridor to Geoffrey's study. Behind the closed door she could hear an animated discussion, which quieted as soon as she knocked. Geoffrey opened the door and beamed when he saw what was in her hand.

'Oh wonderful, that's exactly it! You are utterly indefatigable, aren't you? Excellent. Now, Teri, I want you to listen to this. In fact, I want to lend it to you. Do you have a CD player? No?'

He turned back to the women inside as he was speaking and started to close the door. Over his shoulder Hattie caught a brief glimpse of Jala and Teri. The former was looking tired, the latter utterly miserable. Hattie felt some sympathy for them both. Geoffrey was normally fun to be around, both on the job and off, but this didn't look to have been an enjoyable afternoon in his company. Still, there was nothing she could do about that for now.

She tried once again to take herself off for a quiet sit-down in the library, but once again was interrupted when she got to the hall, this time by the doorbell. As no one else seemed to be rushing to answer it, Hattie did the honours, and found herself looking up into the pallid face of a tall, thickset man in a police uniform. She recognised him: he had been the one to take her statement in the aftermath of discovering Lel's body.

'Good afternoon,' he said. 'Is Geoffrey Dougray in?'

Suppressing her reflexive flinch at coming into close contact with an officer of the law, Hattie smiled politely and said, 'I believe so. What shall I tell him it's about?'

The man sighed, and replied in a surly tone, 'Just tell him a copper's here to talk to him, will you?'

Hattie could feel the smile freezing on her face, so she replied, 'Certainly, I'll be right back,' and closed the door – *not* slamming it, of course, but not being particularly tentative about it either – before the officer could step into the hall. She went and fetched

Geoffrey who, with a mystified look on his face, dismissed Teri and Jala, retrieved the officer from his doorstep and invited him into his study.

News of this latest development spread round the house faster than Hattie would have thought possible, and when at supper Geoffrey had not reappeared, the nature of the policeman's visit was all that anyone was prepared to talk about round the table.

'Well I mean, obviously it's about Lel, isn't it? But what is there left to say?' said Tom.

'Do you think they've caught him? Eoin, I mean?' asked Gareth.

'Maybe. But why would they need to talk to Geoffrey?'

'Perhaps they're putting together the case for prosecution? Obviously Geoffrey's a part of that. Maybe they're prepping him for the witness stand,' suggested Tom.

'But that'll be months off!' pointed out Hera sceptically.

'What if… I mean, don't jump down my throat, but what if something new has come to light? What if it turns out it wasn't Eoin?' said Calvin, immediately provoking a storm of derision and complaints from the others assembled.

'I said *don't* jump down my throat!' he pleaded in response, but the conversation had already flowed on, with Tom theorising that, as Geoffrey had known Eoin for some time, maybe he was being pumped for insights into where the fugitive might be hiding.

Hattie allowed herself to tune out of the increasingly wild spirals of speculation, which would very likely have continued for the entire meal had Geoffrey not finally reappeared, taken his place at the table and, making no acknowledgement of his recent visitor, launched into a spirited anecdote about an actor acquaintance of his who had been lured away from a plum role with the Royal Shakespeare Company by the hollow promise of Hollywood stardom. There was no more talk about the police officer: when Geoffrey changed the subject, it tended to stay changed.

HATTIE STEALS THE SHOW

She didn't sleep well that night. The weather was heavy and muggy, and even with the window open it felt like there was no fresh air in her room. She tossed and turned, irrationally irritated by everything from the feel of the bedsheets to the soft snoring of Delphine in the other bed. She woke up early in the morning and, to clear her head, took herself off for a walk round the grounds while it was still cool. There was the slightest hint of dew on the grass, and fat pigeons were chasing one another from branch to branch in the trees above her head. She picked her way along the path towards the quiet spot with the swing seat but, rounding the corner of the fake ruin, stopped suddenly with a sharp intake of breath: there on the ground in front of her was a mess of feathers, interspersed with spots of blood and chunks of... *something*. It took a few seconds for her to make sense of what she was looking at, and then she realised: these were the brutally dismembered remains of a peahen.

Act Three

14

The apotheosis of twentieth century theatrical discourse was undoubtedly Antonin Artaud's characterisation of theatre as a plague. His seminal depiction of performance as a form of cruelty both embodied and entirely rebutted the postmodern narrative that preceded him. But what are we, children of a new millennium, to draw from this? Only this: that suffering remains as integral as ever, being bound deeply into the medium of performant expression.

– From *Advanced Theatre Practice*
by Jala Senguel, MA

'It was probably a hawk,' surmised Nick sagely.

Hattie frowned. 'I don't think they're very big, are they?'

'Can be. I'm pretty sure they can be.'

'What, bigger than an adult peacock? Peahen, I mean? This thing was the size of a small dog, honestly. I think hawks prefer… sparrows maybe? Nothing bigger than a pigeon, I'm pretty sure.'

'Fox, then.'

'I suppose… it's just, foxes normally eat what they kill, don't they? They're not like cats. And this thing was still… whole. Well, not as in it was all together, but, you know, all the pieces were still there. Just not… connected to each other any more.'

'Could it have been a cat?' Nick suggested

'I don't think a cat would have been able to tear it into such big chunks.'

'Hm. Is Norfolk one of those places with persistent rumours of wild panthers running round? No, that's Surrey isn't it? Oh! Black Shuck!'

'What are you on about?' asked Hattie, bemused.

'It's a… thing. Folklore. Countryside legend. Big giant dog roaming the wilds of East Anglia. Like a persistent ghost story, been sighted off and on for hundreds of years. I saw it on the telly once.'

'So you're saying I should put the mysterious death of the neighbour's peahen down to a centuries-old ghost story?'

'Well… you've rejected all my other suggestions. And what remains, however improbable…'

'Oh get on.'

'Sorry, Cockatoo,' said Nick, with unexpected sincerity. 'I suppose it reminded you of how you found Lel, did it?'

'Er… yes, exactly,' replied Hattie in surprise. She occasionally forgot that her husband was capable of feats such as insight.

But Nick wasn't quite on the money, she realised. His thinking was that finding the peahen's body was upsetting because it brought back a painful memory, namely that of finding Lel's body. But there was more to it for Hattie: a big part of what was shocking about finding Lel's body was the realisation that there was someone who had been physically and psychologically capable of doing that to a person. Someone violent, angry and dangerous. And now, faced with the dismembered body of this poor animal, she couldn't help shake the thought that a plausible explanation of what had happened to it – perhaps the most plausible explanation given the paucity of obvious alternatives – was that it had had an encounter with someone similarly violent, angry and dangerous. And it was hard, once that thought presented itself, to maintain that there might be *two* such people that Hattie had found herself in close proximity to just a few weeks apart. It was a stretch to assume that whoever killed Lel had also killed the peahen. But how *much* of a stretch was it?

No part of this train of thought would occur to Nick. As far as Nick was concerned, Eoin had killed Lel, and wherever Eoin was, it wasn't Trevelyan House. Hattie found herself again feeling a divide opening between herself and her husband, as the magnitude of the secrets she was keeping about Eoin and Lel imposed itself between them.

'On a lighter note – well, sort of – you got a letter,' Nick was saying.

'Oh yeah? Who from?' asked Hattie, forcing herself away from her thoughts and back to the conversation.

'ACDA. Well, someone at ACDA I suppose, but it doesn't have a name at the end. It's not so much a letter as… well, a piece of paper. Honestly, I can't wrap my head around half of it.'

Hattie didn't for a moment question why Nick had opened a letter addressed to her from her employer. All information was fair game in their marriage, and they'd been opening each other's post for decades. She winced again as she thought about the things she'd been withholding from him recently.

'So what's it about, then?'

'Ah, well now, exactly. Let's see, I had it just now… Here it is. *"Notice is hereby given as per section 4 of the Articles of"…* blah blah blah, a bunch of legalese, something something something, and here we go… *"extraordinary meeting of the Board of Governors to discuss the Proposals as submitted in the Memorandum dated Thursday 25 July"*… No mention about what the proposals are, it just says to ask the Secretary, but I'm assuming this is Jolyon's skulduggery, right? Anyway, the *interesting* bit is that among all the gibberish, someone's highlighted this line: *"Representations may be made in writing from all Invested Parties to the Secretary in advance of the meeting for consideration of the Board."* So. What do you make of that?'

'Honestly I'm not sure,' replied Hattie. 'Was there a covering note?'

'I hope you know deep down that I would have mentioned by now if there was,' said Nick, just a tad touchily.

'Sorry,' said Hattie. 'I do occasionally get emails with stuff about board resolutions and meeting minutes from ACDA. I normally ignore it. I don't think I've had a letter before. Was it just that one bit that's highlighted? No other markings on it?'

'Just that one sentence.'

'Bizarre. I suppose it makes sense that they're doing some sort of consultation about it, but they could be a bit clearer.'

'Do you think you might want to make a representation in writing?'

'What would I say? "I like my job, please don't take it away from me"?'

'I suppose.'

'Do you think it would do any good?'

'I dunno. Doubt it.'

'Well then,' said Hattie, uncomfortably.

'Still. Feels funny just ignoring it. Why don't you ask Rod what he thinks?'

'Last time I saw Rod he was in full-on headless chicken mode. I think they all are. No, I'll speak to Mark. He's not quite so bad as the rest of them.'

'He's a headful chicken, is he?'

'Maybe. Or maybe a headless something else. Goat, perhaps.'

'If you say so. Anyhow, I'd best be off. Anoor'll be here any second.'

'Righto. Enjoy the plumbing chat.'

'Bye-bye, Cockatoo.'

'Bye-bye, Cocker One.'

Hattie hung up reluctantly. She was used to not having Nick around, but recently it had been because he'd been the one to be off on tour. Away from her home turf for the first time in over a year, Hattie found herself feeling his absence more keenly.

It didn't help that all day she hadn't felt able to talk to anyone else about the peahen. The natural person to mention it to was Geoffrey, but something inside her warned her off bringing it up with him. And that meant she couldn't tell anyone *else* about it either, because the first thing anyone else would ask would be why she hadn't told Geoffrey about it, and she didn't have a good answer for that.

So she'd left the body where she'd found it and spent the day feeling quietly agitated about the poor creature, while trying to maintain a façade of professionalism as they worked their way through the day's rehearsals. At least *that* was going a bit smoother. After the awkwardness of the previous day, everyone had been a little more wary of proposing musical emendations to Teri, but she, to her credit, had been much more responsive to, and even proactive about, the idea of changing the songs. Evidently Geoffrey's session with her had had the desired effect.

And now it was Friday evening, and with an early supper finished Hattie wasn't in the mood to socialise with the others downstairs, but neither could she quite make herself settle up in her room. She felt stuck.

In the end she took herself off for a walk. She was keen to avoid the far edge of the rear grounds near the ruins, for obvious reasons, so instead she trotted over the front lawn until she reached the drive and then, turning, followed that towards where it branched off from the little lane. In the early evening, in early August, it was still entirely light, and the dappling of the trees that lined the road looked calming and enticing, so she carried on walking, thinking that perhaps she might wander down into the village. It was only when she found herself turning off the road at the next driveway that she realised her legs had tricked her, and she had lured herself away under false pretences. Because the house that she was now walking up to was, according to her best guess, the one that belonged to Charles, the owner of the peahen.

It didn't take long for her guess to be confirmed: strutting across her path was a magnificent and enormous peacock (this one, she was fairly sure, really was a peacock; it had a vast, baroque tail plumage that spoke pretty strongly of male fashion sense), and it seemed hardly likely that Geoffrey had *two* next-door neighbours who kept such birds.

She nearly lost her nerve at the door, but before she had a chance to change her mind it opened anyway, and Charles appeared.

'Oh hullo,' he said with a smile. 'Don't tell me: Fatty's shat on the sundial?'

'I'm afraid not,' replied Hattie, and her tone must have conveyed that something more serious was amiss, because Charles's smile disappeared instantly. She explained how she had found the bird's body in the morning, and explained, as gently as she could, that its end did not appear to have been a peaceful one.

Charles listened, and nodded sadly. 'There's always a danger once they get into the habit of roving,' he said. 'It's happened before. To her mother, in fact. I never was sure what got her. I *suspect* it's a dog that got loose. There are some big ones in the village, and half of them are allowed to roam free, which I've never thought was a good idea. But I've got no proof, and you don't like to accuse your neighbours. Although I'm surprised Geoffrey puts up with dogs in his garden. Somehow it always happens in his bloody garden. Where did you say the body was?"

'Down the back, near that tumbledown folly thing.'

'I'll collect her in the morning. Or at least, whatever's left of her. Oh what a shame. She was a very silly creature, but I had her from a chick. Twenty years, you know, and she could have lived for another twenty. So it goes.'

Hattie offered her deepest condolences and then, when Charles showed no signs of wanting to prolong the conversation, she bade him goodnight and turned away. As she left, she explored how she felt and realised that she was less upset than she had been, but only marginally so: there was still something troubling her about the whole episode. But her feet automatically pointed themselves back to Trevelyan House, so she followed them and ten minutes later was back inside, hovering by the kettle in the kitchen as she made herself a soothing cup of tea while a friendly but unforthcoming Tinca finished the last of the washing up on the other side of the room.

The next day was Saturday, but this time there were no theatre trips planned. Instead, everyone was back in the granary all day, continuing to work through scenes. They were deep into the nitty-gritty now, with the focus on the merits of individual lines and moments rather than the nature of the piece as a whole. This was good, fruitful territory to be in, and everyone could feel it, so spirits were high even though it was intellectually (and for the actors also physically) demanding.

Hattie was grateful for the work. She was finding that, despite everything else that was going on around it, she was enjoying the workshop itself. Of course she was. It let her occupy the exact space she had striven to inhabit throughout her working life: being thorough, organised and above everything else *useful*, all in aid of creating theatre. That was the sweet spot: practicality in service of art, pragmatism as a conduit for creativity. She didn't normally express it in such broad strokes: usually she would just say, when defending her chosen career, 'Well, I like theatre, and I like getting stuff done.' Perhaps, she considered, she was getting a little more reflective as she aged.

At lunchtime she was standing by the spread Tinca had prepared, reflecting in this particular moment on the relative merits of a ham bap versus a chicken sandwich, when her phone rang from an unknown number. She knew what that meant. Guiltily she ducked away and as soon as she could get out of earshot of the dining room, answered.

'Bad time?' asked Eoin.

'No, now's fine. Are you all right? The police came here to interview Geoffrey on Thursday. I was wondering if something had… changed.'

'Really? No, nothing's changed on my end. I'm still here, still lying low. And you?'

'I've made a little bit of progress, in that I've ruled a lot of places out. If it's anywhere in the house it'll be in Geoffrey's study. The thing is… look, I don't want to be the bearer of bad news but I think there's a pretty decent chance it's simply not here. Even if Geoffrey does have it, isn't it more likely it's in his London office?'

'It wouldn't be there,' said Eoin quickly. 'Trust me, I've thought about this a lot. The office is where he does legal stuff, marketing, finance, that sort of thing. Anything creative happens at Trevelyan House. And I mean, come on: if there's one room there that I'd search first, it'd be the study. I'm absolutely not surprised that you haven't found it in the *other* rooms. Can you take a look in the study today?'

'I'm afraid it's not as simple as that. He keeps it locked. I have been trying.'

'Doesn't his assistant have a key?'

'Louise? Maybe, but she's hardly ever here so I don't think that helps. Do you… know her?' Hattie asked, struck suddenly by a memory.

'No, not really.'

'Geoffrey said something about her having a soft spot for you.'

'Oh… well we met a couple of times. Lel got us invited to a couple of Geoffrey's big parties. He spent his time hobnobbing with the great and the good. I'm not any good at that sort of thing. I say the wrong thing as soon as I open my mouth, so I gravitated towards the bottom of the pecking order, where I'm more comfortable. I spent some time chatting to her. We did hit it off, I suppose. And I'm sure Geoffrey's spies will have reported it back to him. I hope she hasn't got into trouble with him by association with me?'

'Not that I've seen. She seems to work very hard for him.'

'She does. I'm sure she does. But that's neither here nor there. Is there *anything* you can do to get your hands on this score?'

Hattie took a deep breath. 'I'll see what I can do. Is there anything about the score that would help me find it quickly? I'm sure Lel put his name on the front, but what if the sheets are all jumbled up? I might not have time for a thorough inspection.'

Eoin let out a thoughtful sigh. 'Well, last I saw it, it was all loose-leaf paper. A3 size. White paper. No, very pale cream I think. Black printed staves, notes and lyrics and all the dots and lines written in pencil. And as the for the music itself… God, I'm no musician, I don't know how to describe it. There was one piece where the tune sounded like "The Marseillaise", if stuff like that helps?'

'The what?'

'You know, the French national anthem? And the Beatles used it as the intro to "All you need is love".'

'That's great, but I can't read music for toffee. I'll just have to look for bits of paper that match your description, and cross my fingers that it's labelled.'

'All right. Good luck. And thank you.' Eoin hung up abruptly.

'Oh… Bugger,' said Hattie to herself. 'How am I going manage this?'

She was still pondering this question in the middle of the afternoon session when they were working on the scene where Hope and Titus crash their car. Gareth and Tom had been having all sorts of fun playing with projection, both to make it look as though the actors were driving and then to evoke the collision itself, but while they and Maxine had deep discussions about the visuals of the scene, Mel and Geoffrey were having discussions of a slightly different flavour.

'I just think it's a little bit underwhelming, you know?' Mel was saying. 'I mean, yes, it's very exciting that they have a little moment of life-and-death drama, but it comes out of nowhere, and then it's over and it's not really referenced again. I mean, this is the emotional climax of the entire piece: Hope gives Titus the wheel, like she's been afraid to do for the whole story. Everything leads up to this moment.'

'Does it, though?' Geoffrey replied. 'I mean, just because it happens two scenes before the end doesn't mean it's the climax. For one thing, Hope giving Titus the wheel isn't really a big deal. It's never been mentioned as an idea before.'

'Yes it is, it's a constant theme.'

'Where?'

'Everywhere!'

'No, I mean... point out one instance where it's actually mentioned in the script. Give me a page number,' said Geoffrey, insistently.

'Well...' Mel tailed off as she thumbed through her script.

'Um... I think that's on me,' called out Jala from her corner at the back. 'It's mentioned a lot in the book, and it *was* in the script at first, in scene one, and scene four, and scene eight and... a couple more. But when we stripped out the bits about car chat – you remember we agreed that it was all getting a bit *Top Gear*? – I think I ended up cutting the stuff about Titus wanting to drive and Hope saying no.'

'There we are then,' said Mel, triumphantly. '*That*'s why it feels so flat when we get here, because we've lost all the lead-in.'

'Marvellous,' beamed Geoffrey. 'What an excellent bit of analytical thinking. Ten points Mel, ten points Jala, zero points to me but that's fine because your success is my success. So, the cut stuff... can we put it back? Without coming over all Jeremy Clarkson?'

'Probably. Do you want to see the old version? I can print it out and we can see if we can cherry-pick which lines we want to put back in?'

And in that moment Hattie saw her chance. Jala was already standing, a USB stick in one hand, her other starting to reach out towards Geoffrey. Hattie launched herself to her feet and announced brightly, 'I can do it!'

'It's no trouble,' Jala said, but Hattie insisted: 'You're in the middle of discussions here, and I'm free. I'll nip across and print out the old version.'

Jala relented and handed over her thumb drive.

'Okay. The backup file from last Monday should have it, and it's only the scenes with Hope and Titus in them that we need. Although we could just look through it on my screen…'

'No, no,' said Geoffrey. 'I can't bear screens, you can only look at one scene at a time. Stuff the environment, let's get it on paper so we can have all the relevant bits laid out in sequence side by side. Here you go Hattie. You can stick the stick straight into the printer.'

And just like that, the key to his study was in her hand. Quickly, before she could betray her rising emotions somehow through her face or actions, Hattie turned and walked out of the granary, then across the drive towards the main house. The timing was perfect: the rest of the company was all together in the barn, so she'd be undisturbed. And the need to print off several scenes gave her a remit to stay in the study for several minutes, certainly enough time for a fairly thorough inspection of the room.

She marched straight through the house to the study, unlocked the door and let herself inside. It was a gorgeous room: a deep pile cream carpet contrasted gently with Venetian red walls, and the wooden bookcases and furniture that filled the room combined elegance with practicality. There were framed posters of some of Geoffrey's greatest successes dotted around, with just enough clutter of books and paperwork to make the space feel cosy without being overwhelming. It was a sanctuary, and Hattie could understand why Geoffrey spent so much time in it.

But she couldn't dawdle: she was here to find a score, not admire the furnishings. First things first, though: she located the printer and, after a couple of false starts, found a port at the side of it that she could plug Jala's USB stick into. The printer's screen burst into life, offering her a bewildering array of options. Good. She could leave things like that for the moment, and if anyone walked in on her she could claim she didn't understand how to choose a file from the stick to print, so was looking for the instruction manual. She was quite pleased with herself for that. *Maybe I missed my calling as a secret agent*, she thought.

Now she could begin her inspection of the room properly. The bottom shelf of each bookcase was given over to stacks of paper, and she attacked these first, looking out for musical notation of any kind. There were a couple of comb bound booklets of music, but these were printed scores, nothing handwritten. In the interests of being thorough, Hattie checked through them in case somehow Lel's original had been transcribed, but drew a blank.

By the time she was done with these a few minutes had passed, so, for the sake of appeasing her conscience, Hattie gave herself a couple of minutes genuinely trying to wrestle with the printer. She managed to make the screen show a list of files on the USB stick and located what she thought was the right file, but held off on hitting print. Then she turned back to the bookcases. At the top of one of them were more papers, larger ones. These looked more promising: Eoin had said Lel worked on A3 sheets. But Hattie quickly found that all these documents were scenic designs and technical drawings, not at all the sort of thing she was looking for.

She turned back to the printer and, after a couple of false starts, persuaded it to begin printing the entire script (Jala had said she only needed certain scenes, but she honestly had no idea how to make the printer do that, and besides, doing the whole thing would buy her more time), and then scanned the room for more places to search. A couple of cupboards in the corner threw up nothing of interest, and the pile of documents under the armchair were all irrelevant (although they did include the printer manual). She was beginning to lose hope when her eyes lit on a filing cabinet tucked right under the writing desk. It was low but broad, with just two drawers. The top one had a label that said 'Scripts', and the bottom one said, to Hattie's delight, 'Scores'.

She yanked open the lower drawer and looked eagerly inside. The contents were divided into green cardboard files, each for a different show. There didn't seem to be any order to them. As it happened, the first file was labelled *The Guilty – Lel Nowak* and Hattie's breath caught in her chest as she opened it and saw, inside, a neat musical score, a photocopy by the looks of it, of an original that had been notated in pencil. There in the corner was Lel's name. Wrong show, but right composer.

This was it, Hattie was sure of it. If Lel's score was anywhere in the house it would be in this filing cabinet. Eagerly she rifled through the files, and in a moment of triumph she spotted it: *The Fall of a Thousand Hopeless Stars – Lel Nowak*. But her triumph dissolved into dismay as she snatched the file out of the cabinet, only to discover it was entirely empty.

She didn't have time to dwell on the significance of this, however, because a sudden knocking sound brought her attention sharply to the window. Standing on the other side of it, in the kitchen garden which the study overlooked, was Tinca. She didn't say anything, didn't gesture, just held Hattie's gaze in a stern, cold stare.

15

'Hattie, don't dash off. I'd like to talk to you.'

Supper had ended, and Hattie had just stood up to excuse herself. After the shock of being discovered snooping by Tinca, Hattie had at first been feeling jumpy (she had forced herself to smile and wave through the window, and point at the printer to explain her presence, and Tinca had eventually nodded coolly and then turned away), but over the course of the afternoon, safe at her desk in the granary, she had managed to calm herself down. She was of course disappointed not to find the score, but her mission was now complete: she had found where it would have been if it was in the house, so confirmed it must be somewhere else entirely. She could tell that to Eoin the next time she spoke, and that would be an end to it, which would be something of a relief.

But now she found her way blocked by Geoffrey, who, though his tone was friendly, had eyes that seemed to Hattie to be frowning slightly. He invited her to follow him, and when she realised he was leading her back to his study, her heart sank and her anxieties began to rise. Had he inspected the room since her visit and found something amiss? Had Tinca told him she'd seen Hattie snooping somewhere she shouldn't? Images of Fatima the peahen appeared unbidden in Hattie's mind. Geoffrey was a large man, a long way overweight but nevertheless powerfully built.

They walked in silence. That too was unusual: Geoffrey liked to fill every pause with the sound of his own voice. He unlocked his study, shepherded her in and gestured for her to sit in the armchair while he took his own seat in the desk chair, which he turned to face her. Behind him, Hattie could see the scripts and scores filing cabinet. She did her best not to look directly at it, lest her gaze confirm her guilt.

'Hattie,' Geoffrey began at length. 'I find myself in something of a pickle as regards you. And in particular as concerns loyalty. Now look, I'm not one for setting up cults of personality. I don't like "yes" men or women and I believe in creativity through conflict. But there are limits. And I can't get very much done if I can't be sure that the people I'm working with aren't, broadly speaking, on my side. Do you follow?'

Hattie nodded cautiously, and Geoffrey continued. 'Now, everyone I work with has flaws. Louise, while she is incredibly hard-working, is hardly the most effective assistant. Tom, although entertaining, sometimes gets so caught up with being catty that he forgets to actually do his job. But the reason I keep them both around is that, at heart, they are fundamentally loyal. Which brings me to you. Now, I like you, I always have, and I hope that you can tolerate me. But it seems to me that we have an increasingly apparent conflict of interest at play, don't we?'

'Do we?'

'Oh you're far too diplomatic, aren't you? We're miles from the nearest theatre but you're still very much the stage manager. Yes, we do have a conflict of interest, and, for the sake of acknowledging the elephant in the room, his name is Eoin. You know that the police came to see me a couple of days ago. They're still looking for him, and they're relatively confident they'll catch him soon, but they're also worried about my safety. There was a little incident a couple of weeks back, I won't bore you with the details, but it appears Eoin hasn't been entirely idle in the wilderness. Now, all of this is by the by, except that they told me a little more about Eoin's past, his known associates and so on. And imagine my surprise at hearing *your* name mentioned.'

Hattie felt herself reddening. The list of names of people who moved in theatre circles who knew the details of her association with Eoin was *very* small. Or at least, it had been until a couple of days ago. But Geoffrey didn't seem to have any interest in making her squirm, because he was immediately talking again.

'Now this suddenly paints our conversation last week in a very new light. The one, you will recall, where you were asking about the rights to *Fall*. I thought you were showing idle curiosity based on hearsay. But now I can't help but wonder whether you had another agenda entirely. So you'll forgive me if I ask you directly: Whose side are you on, here?'

Geoffrey's tone wasn't aggressive, it was solemn. He looked at Hattie with serious eyes, reading her face intently. Hattie felt her heart hammering in her chest, and her lungs felt like they were being squeezed by hands unseen. But she forced herself to meet Geoffrey's gaze and keep her tone measured.

'Geoffrey, to answer your question from earlier, yes I do like you. I like Eoin too. You're right, he and I go way back. What happened to Lel was awful, and I want justice to be done as much as anyone, but that's all out of my hands. What I can do, all I can ever do, is get on with the job. Now, you've given me this job and I'm doing it to the best of my abilities.'

Hattie felt her initial fear transforming into anger. Swallowing, she continued. 'You ask me about taking sides, but I don't see that there are any sides to take. I'd heard that Eoin and Lel had the rights to the show, you've told me that I was wrong, and that you have the rights. If that's true, then there's no conflict, so how can there be sides? There'd only be sides to take if, for example, you *didn't* have the rights, and Eoin had them, and you wanted them. But if that was the case it would mean that last week you lied to me, right to my face. And I'm sure you see the question that would then interest me would be not so much about whether you can trust me, but whether I can trust you.'

There was a pause. *This is it*, thought Hattie. *If he's the one who killed Lel, and killed the peahen, then this will be where he does the same to me. He'll stand up, grab me, and snap my neck like a KitKat...*

But Geoffrey stayed seated, and after a while he nodded. 'How right you are. I'm used to getting my own way, and I sometimes find it helps to assert what I want and wait for the universe to bend itself to my will. Which sounds hugely pompous and hubristic, and of course it is, but it's also very effective. But it does mean that sometimes I talk about things as they will be instead of as they are. The rights being a case in point. I want the rights, but I only *need* them from next year, and by the end of the year I shall have the rights, so from my perspective that's functionally the same as having them already. But when you asked me about it, I glossed over it, and a statement of intent crossed the boundary into being a lie. Which was, as you say, a breach of trust, and one for which I apologise. I will try to regain your trust by being honest with you now.

'Lel and Eoin went to Tahmima Ortlauf and persuaded her to give them an option on the rights to a stage adaptation of her book, an option that would expire if they hadn't opened a production within five years. That was nearly five years ago. In the interim they knocked around some ideas, but I don't think it was anything serious. Certainly what they showed me was in a very embryonic form. It's a shame, because the book is begging for a stage version, and as you know I have – or had – a very high regard for Lel. But, and you'll forgive me if I don't spare your feelings in this regard, Eoin is a hack, and worse than that he's no fun to work with. Since the only way I could initially do it was to do it with him, I decided to pass, and thought no more about it until a few months ago. I recently asked Lel what he wanted to work on after *The Guilty*, and he tossed out a few ideas, with *Fall* conspicuous by its absence. I checked in with Tahmima, and sure enough she'd heard nothing about a stage version, so it became apparent that they were going to let the option lapse. Well, I immediately got her to agree to give me the rights when it did – like I say, it's begging for a stage adaptation. It would have been awkward with Lel, but that's the price of doing business. I had half a mind to ask him to come on board for my version, but I knew he'd refuse out of loyalty to Eoin. Loyalty, of course, that Eoin repaid with murder. But that's it. That's where we are now. Except that, as I say, Eoin has been engaging in a little light skulduggery that makes me wonder whether he has caught wind of this workshop, hence the seeds of suspicion that started to be sown in my mind.'

'And that's the whole truth, is it?' asked Hattie. She knew she was pushing her luck being this assertive, but she doubted she'd ever have another chance to get Geoffrey to be so candid.

'Whole truth? There's no such thing. But I think that's everything that's relevant for now. I wonder, then, if you would be prepared to be candid with me. What's Eoin up to?'

Hattie found herself suddenly on the back foot again, and she didn't like it. Geoffrey's story had the ring of truth about it, but she didn't have time right now to untangle what that meant with respect to Eoin. For now, it would be best to be cautious. However, she didn't feel she could lie.

'Eoin got in touch with me,' she explained. 'After Lel... well, afterwards. He's adamant he had nothing to do with... that. And he wants to stage *Fall*. He says he'd been trying to convince Lel for a while, and now he wants to put it on to honour his memory. He says it was their last collaboration. I've no idea how he'd manage it, what with the police and all. But he did say' – Hattie found herself plunging on despite being unsure if it was wise to do so – 'that he didn't have a copy of Lel's score. He said you were the last person to have it.'

'Did he now?' mused Geoffrey. 'Well if you speak to him again, you can tell him to leave me alone. I gave it back to Lel years ago.'

Hattie caught herself glancing involuntarily back at the filing cabinet. The score had been there, it wasn't there any more. She had no reason to suspect Geoffrey was lying.

'Well,' he continued, 'I think we understand one another a little better now. Thank you, Hattie.'

He stood up, and she did the same, but before he opened the door for her he added, 'A word of advice, though: leave Eoin well alone. I know he's your friend, and I have some sense of the source of the bond you two have, and what you owe each other. But he's a murderer. A violent, bitter and quite possibly deranged man. Don't let your loyalty slip into gullibility.'

The next day was Sunday again, and this one started off much like the one before it, with various members of the company appearing downstairs at staggered intervals. Louise had also reappeared, although she seemed preoccupied with errands for Geoffrey, and was constantly coming and going between different corners of the house, clutching different bundles of paperwork every time Hattie saw her.

Things moved more slowly in the dining room where, over the course of a drawn-out breakfast, various plans were made for outings and activities. Delphine expressed a desire to drive to Blakeney Point to see the seal colony, and the other actors signalled their interest (Hattie thought that Dylan maybe agreed a little too readily, and she wondered whether more work was needed to dampen any amorous intentions he had in that direction). Calvin said he'd like to go up to Norwich for a potter round the apparently very attractive Elm Hill district, and Maxine, Jala and Teri offered to come, too. Hattie was glad that Teri and Calvin seemed to be getting on better, but she did note with mild surprise that Tom kept his head down and his eyes glued to his phone while that plan was being mooted, as though keen to avoid being invited along. If that was his motivation, he certainly got his wish: by late morning both expeditions were getting ready to depart, and with Gareth and Mel both in London for the day again, and Geoffrey once more in parts unknown, it looked like Hattie, Louise and Tom would be left alone in the house.

'Are you sure you don't want to come with us, Hattie?' asked Delphine, back in the bedroom, as she gathered her sunglasses and handbag.

Hattie wasn't sure at all. In fact, now she came to think of it, she thought she might well enjoy seeing some seal pups. It was just that, she realised, no one had directly invited her at breakfast, and she hadn't felt it was her place to butt in on other people's plans – stage managers are supposed to be generally unobtrusive after all – and somehow until now it had been quietly assumed by all parties that she would be fending for herself. But now that the offer was there, she found herself losing her nerve about accepting.

'I don't think there's room in the car, is there?'

'There will be if we squish. So long as Dylan goes in the front there'll be room for everyone else in the back. Or you could drive yourself and meet us there?'

'Oh, no, I'm not a fan of Norfolk roads, thank you. I'd just get lost.'

Hera popped her head round the door. 'You ready?' she asked Delphine brightly.

'Yup, I'm just trying to convince Hattie to come too. Do you think Pip would mind driving as well? That way we can take two cars.'

'I'll ask him,' said Hera, disappearing down the corridor again, and Hattie was suddenly aware that a fuss was being made over her that she'd not asked for. Worst of all, she wasn't sure that either saying she did want to come along or that she didn't would lead to a dissipation of the fuss. In the end she went simply because by the time the rumour chain had reached Pip it seemed that everyone had already decided she would come, so she chose to go along with it.

The drive up was uneventful. Hera went in Pip's car, Dylan in Delphine's, and Hattie diplomatically accepted Delphine's enthusiastic invitation to join her party, avoiding catching Dylan's eye as she did. Delphine's professed lack of romantic interest in Dylan didn't seem to stop her getting on with him in a more general sense. The two actors chatted merrily as they drove northward along a series of increasingly small and winding country roads en route to the coast, first about Jala's book, which they both seemed to take tremendously seriously despite not being able to articulate any actual concrete insight or advice from it, and then more generally about acting and their own experiences of the industry. The two of them clearly had a lot in common. They had both been to drama school at a similar time and both, through luck of the draw, had been given parts in their student showcase productions that didn't play to their strengths, meaning that at the point they graduated neither had an agent, and had to watch as their more successful classmates stepped straight onto West End stages and Hollywood film sets. Both had doggedly worked and networked their way up, determined to make up for their slow starts, and over a period of years both had seen their efforts begin to pay off. Hattie delighted in hearing their successes. Too many actors never managed to get their careers going and languished in the bottom tier of semi-professional productions before eventually losing hope and giving up.

They finally arrived at a place that an app assured them was Blakeney Point, but that seemed to Hattie to be a deserted moorland, devoid of any sign of seals, sea or civilisation. They got out of the car, and Dylan sprinted off to scout the surroundings while Delphine got on the phone to Hera to try to work out where she and Pip had got to. Hattie was left alone for a brief moment before her phone rang and to her surprise she saw that Mark, her boss at ACDA, was calling.

'Hullo,' she answered. 'How are you?'

'Surviving. Or rather, I'm working towards surviving. Did you get my letter?'

'No, sorry, I've not been at home. Wait. I did get something from ACDA. Something about a meeting of the Governors. Was that you?'

'Yes, that's the one. Have you had a chance to work on it yet?'

'I'm not sure I follow. Work on what?'

She heard Mark taking a breath. He was, by and large, a patient man, but in times of stress his patience did seem to come at a personal cost.

'The situation is as follows,' he replied brightly. 'I need all the tutors to submit statements in support of the technical department. The mission statement of the ACDA governing body is to promote excellence and professionalism in the British performing arts through education and training. Regardless of what Jolyon keeps incorrectly spouting in his memos, it doesn't say anything about *who* is to be trained, or in what. It's not just about performers. If we can put together a strong enough case that our course promotes excellence and professionalism in the industry, we can show that axing it is fundamentally incompatible with the mission that the body is duty-bound to pursue. I've been reaching out to the unions, the theatres and all our old alumni to get them to help make our case, and if I was allowed to present that case in the meeting on Thursday week it'd be a cakewalk. The problem is, the only mechanism we have for influencing proceedings is for ACDA staff to submit written statements. Jolyon's invoking whole slews of archaic procedures to try to make sure we don't get a look in. The long and the short of it is I need a couple of paragraphs from you on the vital importance of the work you do, the impact the training has on students, how the industry couldn't function without institutions like us churning out sensible, skilled techies to keep the lights on, that sort of thing. If you can have something for me in the next week, that gives us plenty of time to submit it via the proper channels. Clear?'

'I… I don't know. I'm not sure what I can say.'

'I think I've just told you, haven't I? Obviously you'll want to put it in your own words.'

'Yes, but—'

'Look, you can just mull it for a while if you like. Shall I call you back on Thursday and we can get down to the specifics?'

The tone of Mark's voice made it clear that only a very limited range of responses to this question would be acceptable.

'Okay Mark, I'll see what I can do.'

'That's the spirit. Must dash, I have a lot of calls to make. Enjoy the weekend.'

He rang off, leaving Hattie feeling uneasy and perplexed.

'You all right?' asked Dylan, startling her. He had reappeared at some point while she was on the phone, looking enthusiastic and slightly out of breath.

'Oh yes, fine thanks. Did you see any signs of seals?'

'Not directly, but there's a footpath heading off that way. It's sort of going parallel to the shoreline, so maybe it gets closer to it the further along you go. I thought we could try that.'

'Hera says we've gone the wrong way,' said Delphine, reappearing. 'We want to drive back into Blakeney, then through it to the next village along, following signs for the beach. There's a car park there.'

'We could probably walk round and meet them if we—' Dylan began, but Hattie and Delphine were already getting back into the car and he, after a second's consideration, followed suit.

'Who were you on the phone to?' Delphine asked Hattie.

'My boss at ACDA. I've been tutoring there. He says he needs me to write a statement about how the stage management course helps promote excellence in the performing arts.'

'Ugh,' said Delphine, pulling a face. 'I hate that kind of thing. You have to keep "proving value" and "evidencing outcomes" if you want to get any funding for anything. Why can't we just make art because it's art, without having to justify ourselves?'

'Still, it must be easier for stage management,' suggested Dylan. 'I mean that's a job that needs doing, and you need people who know how to do it, right? Can't have theatre without the crew, can't have a crew without training.'

'That's the thing, though,' said Hattie, awkwardly. 'I didn't train. I just turned up and made myself useful. Half the job is just common sense, and the other half you learn best by actually doing it. I mean, don't get me wrong, I'm not *averse* to people doing a course first, but I don't think it's exactly essential.'

'Ohhh, well that's easily solved then: just lie,' offered Dylan. 'Lie through your teeth. Don't you think, Del?'

'Oh yeah,' agreed Delphine. 'I mean, if your boss wants you to write a statement saying the earth is flat and two plus two equals a mince pie, you do what he says and get on with your day.'

'I suppose so,' said Hattie uncomfortably. 'I'd just rather I didn't get sucked into all this mess.'

'Trust me: life is too short to give it a second thought,' said Dylan. 'Worry about the things that matter, don't give any space in your head to things that don't. Honestly. We all only have a limited amount of time available to us.'

He settled back into his seat as he expounded on his theme. 'I've been thinking about this a lot recently. I don't know why. Maybe it's all this talk about Lel, you know? I've just been thinking: what's all the stuff that he left undone, right? I mean, there's a man with all this creativity, this potential, this track record of great work, who's in a unique position to create new things and have them heard, I mean, like, really *heard*, and he must have had a thousand projects in mind, a thousand ideas ranging from fully written shows playing in his head that he hasn't written down yet to the most early-stage, un-fleshed-out concepts that he knows he'll get to one day… but there is no 'one day', because all of a sudden – pfft – he's gone. It's over. Think about what he had to offer, what he lost, you know? And maybe there was a way of avoiding that end, that early exit. I don't know because I didn't know him or the details, but if there *wasn't*, if somehow it was inevitable that he'd go when he did, you have to think: what could he have done differently? What choices could he have made within that, you know, boundary? Given the choice, do you think he'd have spent all that time doing, I don't know, tax returns? Laundry? Or would he have squeezed every moment out of his life, to let him create one more little bit of art, and write one more song? I know what I'd choose.'

Delphine was frowning. 'Not to be mundane but I think there are good arguments against skipping doing your laundry just for the sake of fitting in a bit more theatre,' she said, her tone abrupt and snappish. 'And in my experience tax returns take up more of your time if you *don't* do them than if you do.'

'Oh sure, sure, I'm not talking about those specifics, I just mean in general. Like, you've got to make the most of the time you have available, especially us artists. I think Lel—'

'I mean, yeah, I take the point about time being precious, of course, but I'm not entirely sure that applies to creative people more than anyone else. I think it's more about what you do to be happy while you're alive than what you leave behind. Especially in theatre, where there *is* nothing left behind,' objected Delphine irritably.

'Yeah, yeah, sure, but I mean that's my point. Use the time for whatever matters to you, don't waste it on things that don't matter. I'm sure Lel would say that—'

'Oh for God's sake, will you PLEASE shut up about Lel!' yelled Delphine suddenly. 'I'm sorry, but you didn't know the first bloody thing about him. You don't know who he was or what he wanted. You don't even know how he spent his life…'

There was a pause.

'I'm sorry,' mumbled Dylan uncomfortably. 'You're right. I didn't know him. You did. I'll shut up now.'

They spent the rest of the car journey in awkward silence, and when they arrived in the car park Delphine got straight out of the car and made a beeline for Hera, and the two of them strode quickly away in the direction of the beach, leaving Pip, Dylan and Hattie to follow along awkwardly. Dylan was morose, and Pip quickly picked up that something was amiss, although he expressed it in characteristically laconic style, simply raising a quizzical eyebrow at Hattie behind Dylan's back.

Thankfully the awkwardness didn't last long. Time, it has been often remarked, is a great healer, but it turns out that in a pinch, a beach full of newly birthed seal pups and their mothers will also get the job done. All the actors went immediately gooey at the sight, and even Hattie, for whom maternal soppiness was not a natural sensation, found her heartstrings being tugged at. They couldn't get very close, as there was a lot of protective fencing in the way, which was perhaps for the best, as by the time Hattie, Pip and Dylan caught up with Hera and Delphine, the two actresses were already making semi-serious plans to kidnap one of the pups and bring it back with them.

'They just look so *soft*!' Hera exclaimed. 'I could have one in my flat. In the daytime it could play in the bath and at night it could be my hot water bottle.'

It took a little persuading, but eventually it was grudgingly agreed by all that seals belonged on beaches and not in bathtubs. By the time they made it back to the car park the air was largely cleared, but nonetheless Hera casually asked if she could swap with Dylan for the ride back home, and Dylan accepted with crestfallen grace. Hattie wondered, again, what the history between Delphine and Lel was. This wasn't the first time she had become uncharacteristically upset at the mention of the dead composer. Although, it had to be said, her response to Dylan's crass philosophising hadn't been entirely unreasonable.

On the drive home, Hattie had a thought. Listening to Dylan and Delphine talk about their experiences making their way in the world post drama school had reminded her of Abua. It made her sad to think of him, sitting at home, quietly unravelling. He lived in south London, she knew. If she was in town she probably wouldn't be able to resist paying him a visit. She was aware that he'd become something of a mission of hers, and she was worrying about him far more than any of her other students, but there was something unbearably vulnerable about him. Maybe he reminded her of the young Eoin.

Either way, it seemed to Hattie that Abua was at a critical juncture, and if his resolve was failing, and he needed a nudge that Hattie couldn't currently give, then perhaps the best thing would be to find a way of getting him to nudge *himself*. If he could only re-establish the quiet confidence and determination he'd shown as a student, that would be enough to propel him forward. If he was back in undergraduate mode, Hattie was sure he'd find his feet again. And Hattie had a notion of what she could do to get him back into a student frame of mind. She pulled out her phone and composed a text:

> Hi Abua, I thought you should know: ACDA's technical department will be closing down. I think you should pop into the building to say your goodbye to it and pay your respects. The door codes haven't yet changed since last term.

It was a little bit of a lie, in that the closure wasn't certain yet, but to Hattie's mind it was all in a good cause. If he set foot back into the building and took some time to reflect on everything positive about his experiences there, surely he'd be inspired to move forward. If that didn't get him going, nothing would.

HATTIE STEALS THE SHOW

They made it back to the road past Trevelyan House, but instead of pulling straight into the driveway Delphine carried on down the hill into the village.

'I thought we could stop in at the pub for a late lunch?' she suggested, and Hattie, remembering the delectable pork selection from the week before, agreed readily. It was only when they sat down at a table (available at short notice only because the lunchtime rush had passed, the landlord explained) and started looking through the menus that she remembered, with a sinking feeling, that, like many female performers whose entire career involves intense scrutiny of their physical appearance and the application of rather unenlightened standards of beauty by casting directors and audiences alike, both the actresses seemed to have learned to subsist primarily on sunlight and water. When Delphine ordered just a starter, and Hera opted for *some olives*, Hattie felt a little self-conscious about ordering a platter that advertised itself as being suitable for 'two people, or one hungry one'. So she wimped out and ordered a falafel and halloumi wrap instead, and gazed forlornly at the more substantial dishes that were deposited on the tables to either side of her.

All considerations of food fled from her mind, however, when she directed her gaze slightly further across the room and caught sight of a face that was jarringly familiar. In the corner, hunched over a bowl of soup, with a newspaper spread out on the table in front of him, sat Eoin.

16

Hattie felt her stomach lurch. What on earth was Eoin doing here? Had he been in Norfolk this entire time? She was acutely aware of the presence of Delphine and Hera next to her and knew just how badly things would go if they saw Eoin. And things would go even worse if they got wind of any connection between him and Hattie. But she couldn't just ignore him. Could she?

It slowly dawned on her that not only could she ignore him, she *should* and possibly *must* do so. She would eventually speak to him and get to the bottom of what he was doing here, but not now. In the meantime, excruciatingly, she tore her gaze away from him and spent the next agonising hour trying, as naturalistically as possible, not to look in his direction, and hold up her end of the conversation as if nothing at all was amiss. She nodded sympathetically when Delphine complained that Dylan kept not very subtly mooning over her despite her best efforts to dissuade him, and laughed appreciatively at a funny story Hera told about a wardrobe malfunction in a Bikram yoga class. She shared, when prompted, a little bit more detail about her tutoring role at ACDA, and when on two occasions the conversation veered in the direction of *The Guilty*, and Lel, she steered it away again, while taking pains not to be too obvious about it. She made it right the way to the end of the meal doing a passable impression of a normal person having a normal Sunday afternoon, and it was as they were leaving that in a moment of weakness her eyes flicked across once more at the table in the corner, and she found them looking straight into Eoin's as he coolly stared back at her. She felt her cheeks flushing, and the little remark she was making about the reasonableness of the bill (ill-judged anyway, as it drew attention to how little the others had ordered) died in her throat.

She covered for herself with a cough, and thankfully Hera didn't seem to have been listening anyway, because she cut in almost immediately with an unrelated observation about the décor. Hattie quickly drew herself up and strode out of the pub, noticing as she did that her reaction to Eoin's presence wasn't just surprise, or guilt, or embarrassment: there was, from somewhere, a not insubstantial dose of fear as well.

They went back to Trevelyan House and Hattie spent the rest of the afternoon puttering around in a state of minor agitation. Calvin's expedition was yet to return, and the house was unexpectedly quiet and devoid of distractions. She considered going outside, but her hip was giving her grief after all the walking at Blakeney, so she thought better of it. But she couldn't settle, and found herself hovering round the house, going from room to room in a way that was neither soothing nor doing anything to rest her leg. So in the end she went outside anyway.

She found Dylan and Pip on the lawn practising stage combat with a couple of canes standing in for rapiers. They looked to be putting together a little routine. First they would work through a short exchange of blows, acting it out in exaggeratedly slow motion as they talked it through, then they would repeat it over and over again, each time getting a little faster, then they would practise transitioning into it from the *previous* exchange they'd worked on, then they'd run their entire sequence of exchanges from the start, and when they were satisfied they'd move on to designing the next exchange. By the time Hattie arrived they already had a good minute's worth of fight worked out, and they showed no sign of being done.

They made a good duo. Pip, slender and supple, moved in fluid twists and sinuous poses, while Dylan, who was broader and heavier, was more sudden and chaotic-seeming in his movements (although, watching him repeat the same sequences over and over again, Hattie was struck by how uniform his movements were across repetitions – he was more in control than he looked). The result was exciting to watch, even at half speed.

At one point Dylan, sweating freely in the sunshine, took a break to pull his shirt off.

'Now we're talking,' called a voice from the other side of a bush.

Craning her neck round, Hattie saw that Tom was sprawled on the grass, watching the rehearsal. She wandered across to him.

'Enjoying your day?' she asked.

'Well, it started off poorly, but in the past hour things are looking up,' he replied, then called out to Pip: 'It really is rather hot. I think Dylan's got the right idea!'

Pip rolled his eyes and carried on practising his footwork.

'I *think* I've got to know these two well enough that this doesn't count as sexual harassment, but we'll see,' Tom murmured. 'How were the seals?'

'Fluffy,' Hattie replied. 'On balance we decided not to adopt one.'

'Well, that's nice. Different strokes for different folks. Baby anythings aren't really my cup of tea.'

'And you didn't fancy a wander round Norwich?'

Tom pulled a face. 'Perhaps another time. In different company.'

Hattie decided not to press. She didn't have an immediate sense of who it was in particular Tom was referring to, and she wasn't entirely sure she wanted to know: there were enough personal dramas going on already. So she nodded noncommittally, and they watched the fight in silence for a while, until Dylan, huffing and red in the face, threw himself down on the ground and declared he needed a break.

The afternoon drew to a close, and Tinca eventually rang the bell for supper. Hattie ate a half-hearted meal and didn't pay much attention to the conversation around her. She knew what was coming, and she realised she was dreading it. It was strange: even though nothing had passed between them, it was entirely clear to her what was to happen next. Perhaps that was just a sign of how well they knew each other. Perhaps it was the obvious thing to do. Either way, she did it. At the end of supper she cleared away her plate, quietly let herself out of the house and made her way to the end of the drive where, as she knew he would be, Eoin was waiting for her.

'Hello,' he said, cagily.

'Hello,' she replied, also cagily.

'So, er... fancy seeing you h—'

'What the bloody hell is going on, Eoin?' Hattie said, her anxiousness giving way to a burst of irritation.

'Well it's a bit complicated.'

'Is it? You're supposed to be on the run, keeping a low profile, and yet for some reason here you are, swanning round in a pub in the village that just happens to be where Geoffrey Dougray lives. Is that complicated, Eoin?'

'I wanted to collect the score. Okay? It sounded like either you'd have it by now, in which case I could pick it up from you, say my goodbyes and be out of your life forever, or you'd have *not* got it, in which case I'd still say my goodbyes and be out of your life forever. But I couldn't just sit there in a tumbledown shed on the other side of the country any longer. So, not to put too fine a point on it... do you have it?'

'No. I found the filing cabinet where he kept it once, but it's not there. I even spoke to him about it, and he says he gave it back to Lel years ago.'

'Well that's nonsense for starters. Lel told me, when I saw him backstage at the Revue, that Geoffrey had it.'

'I... no he didn't.'

'What?'

'When you came to me, a week after that meeting, you told

me that the score was at Lel's studio. You bloody sent me over there. Remember? You had me lie my way past that Kuznetsova woman to look in the studio. It was only *after* that that you decided Geoffrey still had it.'

'No, look, I wanted to be sure. Okay? It was a complicated situation, I didn't want to burden you with all the details. I thought if there was any chance the music, or even a copy of it, was at Lel's studio, I could just get that and not have to find a way of looking for it here. I didn't know that by some miracle you'd end up working here, did I? So I crossed my fingers and sent you to Lel's studio. And now you know, as well as I do, that Lel didn't have it.'

Hattie looked suspiciously at Eoin. She was sure she'd caught him in a lie. And if he was lying about this, who knew what else he had lied to her about?

There was something else, too. Another lie, buried in all of this, that she couldn't identify just now. The back of her mind was insistent that it was there, but refusing to divulge the details. Unbidden, Geoffrey's parting words popped into her mind. *Don't let your loyalty slip into gullibility.* She increasingly had the feeling she was being played for a fool.

'What if Lel did have it, and he just put it somewhere else? What if he was lying to you?'

'No,' said Eoin. 'Lel was a deeply flawed man. He was broken in ways that I'm only now beginning to understand, and I'm still coming to terms with. But he wouldn't lie to me about our show. He took our work too seriously.'

'All right, Eoin. Lel didn't have the score. But it's not here either. I've helped you as much as I can, but there's nothing more I can do. I'm sorry.'

'I understand,' he said. 'I'm sorry too. Thanks for your help.'

He turned and started to walk away.

'Eoin… when did you come to Norfolk?'

'Yesterday afternoon. After we spoke last.'

'So you weren't here on Thursday night? Or Friday morning?'
'Well, no. Why?'
Just checking in case you were the one to rend a peahen called Fatima limb from limb in a murderous rage, thought Hattie. But what she said was, 'Nothing. Goodbye Eoin. Good luck.'

After a troubled sleep on Sunday night, Monday morning felt like a fresh start. Yes, the workshop was nearly over, with only two more days left to it, but Hattie's role in relation to it had just changed significantly. Up until this point she had, effectively, been a mole pretending to be a stage manager for the purposes of infiltrating Geoffrey's household. Now she was, much less complicatedly, an actual stage manager. She had a simplicity of purpose, and she took real comfort in that. She relaxed into the work and was pleased to be reassured that it was going well. Jala's script had evolved into something much more coherent and punchy. Teri had settled down and was making regular, measured changes to the music in response to feedback from the rehearsal room. Gareth and Maxine had developed a shared vision for the visual language of the piece that seemed to lend itself to a combination of physical scenery and projected imagery (and, because it involved a smattering of circus-inspired motifs, Geoffrey seemed helpfully enthusiastic about what they had come up with). Overall, this was feeling more and more like a production-in-waiting, which was the ideal outcome of a workshop process like the one they'd been going through. And at the centre of it all, Hattie was the efficient facilitator, noting things down, bringing up details that others had missed, communicating across disciplines when people weren't all in the same place at the same time, and, most importantly, ensuring that everyone took adequate tea breaks.

So when, on Monday just before the lunch break, Geoffrey announced that they were finally ready to take on the challenging final scene, Hattie was delighted. It meant they were on track, and she was sure that the rest of the company felt just as up to the test as she did. She felt a spring in her step as she walked back to the main house for lunch, and her enthusiasm must have been writ large across her features because Calvin, falling in beside her, said, 'Well. You seem full of the joys of life today.'

'I think I am, yes. Happy to be working, happy to be making progress.'

'Well, I'm glad at least someone's happy,' he sniffed.

Hattie shot him a sideways glance. Something was obviously bothering him and, just as obviously, he wanted to ask her about it. She didn't hugely want to have to be a shoulder to cry on, but he was so obviously looking for sympathy that it would be almost rude *not* to offer it.

'Oh? What's on your mind?'

He sighed. 'Nothing a little mope and a less little G and T won't fix, I'm sure.'

'Well that doesn't sound so bad,' said Hattie, vaguely hoping that if she didn't press for details Calvin wouldn't offer them. No such luck.

'I suppose it's my own fault. I should know better by now than to get my hopes up before I've truly got to know someone. And anyway, I should have sworn off office romances years ago.'

'Things didn't work out with Tom then?'

'Apparently not. I thought they were going well, but as soon as I started to open up I got the cold shoulder. Why is it that gay men can be *interesting* or they can be *nice*, but never both? And, as a follow-up, why, when all I really want is the latter, am I always attracted to the former?'

'Well, it's easily done, isn't it? A new place, new people, it's all very exciting, and it's easy to get swept off your feet. I wonder if what you had maybe had less in common with an office romance and more with a holiday fling. It's just that… well, it's not quite a holiday, is it? Once your fling is flung, you've still got to turn up in the rehearsal room. Still, it's only until end of play tomorrow.'

'You're right,' said Calvin, sighing again. 'Just a couple more days and then I can put this behind me and move on. And in the meantime…'

'A little mope and a less little G and T?'

'Exactly.'

They were in the house now, making their way into the dining room where a tray of Vietnamese banh mi sandwiches was laid out on the sideboard. They were the first to arrive, and the house was quiet. Hattie was about to ask Calvin what, if anything, he had lined up after the workshop was done, but just as she was opening her mouth to speak he suddenly said, 'Do you find yourself thinking about Lel at all?'

'Well, yes,' replied Hattie, caught off guard. 'I mean, it's going to be hard to forget what happened.'

When moaning about Tom, Calvin's tone had been a little bit campy, slightly performative. But now it took on a sincerity that Hattie hadn't heard from him before.

'Quite,' he said. 'I keep thinking back to that night at the Revue. Obviously I wasn't the one who, you know, found him. I was with Louise, but I was still *there*. And it's like… One minute he's walking around, making plans, revelling in the work he's created, the next… poof. I wish I'd… I don't know. He's just in my thoughts a lot. I feel his presence constantly, in the rehearsal room. It's like I'm being haunted by his ghost. Does that make any sense?'

'I think so,' said Hattie gently. 'It's difficult, when we lose people.'

'Yeah, and it doesn't help that I'm still spending all my time playing his music.'

'Are you?'

'Oh. I mean, for *The Guilty*,' Calvin explained. 'We're putting together the tour, so the show needs re-scoring for a smaller orchestra. It's what I'm doing with my evenings."

'Oh.'

'And I'm so used to working with him. It would be easier if…

HATTIE STEALS THE SHOW

I just wasn't even sure that Lel even *liked* me. I think I got on his nerves, and over time he grew more and more withdrawn. I don't *think* it was anything I did, but he was so *off* with me the last time I— Oh hullo, Tinca! I've just been having a maudlin moment, but these baguettes look like if anything can lift me out of it, it's them. What's in them?'

'Pork on the left, seitan on the right,' said Tinca, who had appeared clutching a small bowl. 'They've both got coriander, and if you like heat, here's some chopped chillies you can sprinkle in.'

'Wonderful! A perfect cure for some Monday morning heartache,' said Calvin. He looked across at Tinca expectantly as he said this, but she didn't say anything. He continued: 'It's a double whammy, in fact, that and just feeling particularly sad about Lel. Did you ever meet him?'

Tinca nodded. 'He came up once or twice over the last few months,' she said.

Calvin gave another little sigh. 'Such a tragedy. He was a truly wonderful man.'

Tinca didn't reply, but Hattie noticed just the tiniest purse of her lips, as though she was biting back the urge to say something in reply. But there was no chance to investigate what this unspoken thought might be, because at that point the rest of the company started to filter in, and Tinca used their entrance as cover to make her own exit.

The conversation did give Hattie pause for thought, though. She was surprised to learn that, recently, Lel had had at least one meeting with Geoffrey here, in the place where Geoffrey worked on creative projects. Perhaps it was due to Calvin's insistence that he could feel Lel's presence here now, but Hattie thought this detail must mean something, even if she couldn't yet say *what* it was supposed to mean.

Lunch ended (the banh mi turned out to taste just as delicious as they looked, and while Hattie quietly ensured she didn't sit next to

Calvin to eat hers she saw from across the room that by the time he was done with his food his spirits seemed entirely restored), and once they'd congregated back in the rehearsal room Geoffrey called them to order and announced it was time to start on the final scene.

'Let's just barrel through it, eh? We've got the words, we've got the music, I think we all know what this has to achieve, so let's just give it a go and see how close we get. Look, we've got Louise for once' – he gestured to a corner, and Hattie was surprised to see that his assistant was indeed there, sitting so quietly and inconspicuously that Hattie hadn't even noticed her when she walked in – 'so let's see if we can prove to her that this whole fortnight hasn't just been windmill-tilting. Hattie, do you want to count us off?'

'*Act two, scene sixteen. A private room in a hospital. Hope is in the bed. Enter Titus,*' Hattie read.

Dylan launched into his lines as Titus, Hera into hers as Hope. A page or so of dialogue later, and Calvin struck a chord on the piano, introducing the final song. It was an oddly strident piece, almost a military march. It made sense in the context of the scene, but it sounded like it wouldn't be out of place in the second half of *Les Misérables*. Hera sang a bit, then Dylan sang a bit, then towards the end they came together in a duet, but one of them somehow got a bar out of time with the other, and they ended up singing out of sync in a way that put both of them off so much they both fell awkwardly silent, and Calvin, with a shrug, stopped playing too.

'Not to worry!' bellowed Geoffrey gleefully. 'Do we know what went wrong? Can we go again?'

Hera and Dylan formed a huddle round the piano with Calvin. As they tried to understand who had gone wrong where, Gareth murmured quietly to Maxine, 'Funny little song, isn't it?'

Maxine smiled back, but her reply made Hattie's blood run cold: 'Is it just me, or does the tune borrow a lot from the French national anthem? You know the one? "The Marseillaise"?'

17

Hattie's head flicked up. 'What did you say?' she snapped, entirely involuntarily.

'I'm not being daft, am I? *Ta-tum-ta dum-dum dum-dum DUM-de-dum*, right?'

'Ooh, that awkward moment when you realise your finale is plagiarised,' cooed Tom wickedly.

'Oh it's not plagiarism,' said Maxine, hurriedly. 'It's a reference. Right?'

'I'm not sure I get *why*, though,' said Gareth, his brows creased. 'Seems an odd thing to chuck in right at the end.'

'Well let's ask Teri,' suggested Mel.

'Hmm?' asked Teri, who had been listening in to Calvin, Hera and Dylan's discussion around the piano.

'This song has little snippets of "The Marseillaise" in it, right? We were just wondering why.'

'Oh… well Hope talks about being a revolutionary, so I thought it would make sense to evoke, you know, the idea of the French Revolution to support that,' the composer replied.

'Ye-es, but I think she's talking about the change in the relationship being revolutionary, rather than either of them being *a* revol—' Maxine began, but Geoffrey cut her off.

'Well the point is surely that, crucially in this scene, we're dissecting the idea that "all you need is love". So it's *more* a reference to the Beatles song. Isn't that right, Teri?'

'Oh. Yes, exactly,' said Teri, gratefully, and in that moment Hattie finally understood what was going on:

Teri didn't write this music. Lel did.

Lel was supposed to have been doing this workshop. That was why Teri joined late, and was so awkward at first about making changes to 'her' work. That was why Lel had been coming up to the house earlier in the year, and Geoffrey had met him to talk about the workshop at the Revue. That was why Calvin had been complaining about spending all his time still working with Lel's music. He must have realised as he said it that he'd nearly let the secret slip, and tried to cover his mistake by claiming that he was talking about working on *The Guilty* in the evenings. But even at the time that hadn't made sense to Hattie, as she'd seen him while away almost every evening having singalongs in Geoffrey's sitting room.

It all fitted into place: Lel had written an adaptation with Eoin, but they couldn't get it staged. Geoffrey was happy to stage the show and wanted Lel's music but not Eoin's script. So he'd had Jala write an alternative script, reusing Lel's music. All they had to do was wait for Lel and Eoin's original option on the rights to lapse and they'd be in the clear. Or at least, they'd be clear of Eoin. But what about Lel? How was Geoffrey planning on getting him on board with the idea? Did he really think he could convince Lel to betray his old friend like that? It didn't seem likely to Hattie. And presumably if Lel had put his foot down that would have kiboshed the whole project. In which case… in which case was it in fact rather convenient that Lel died just before the workshop, which he would surely have forbidden, was scheduled to take place? Allowing Teri to be rushed in and masqueraded as the composer?

This was murky territory, and Hattie didn't know what to believe, but one thing she knew for certain was that Geoffrey was still lying to her. He had lied from the outset; when she had caught him in a lie he had lied his way out of it, and he was ruthlessly and coldheartedly trampling on Lel's legacy for his own convenience. All the suspicion that Hattie had built up around Eoin evaporated in an instant. She needed to trust her gut.

'Hattie?'

Hattie's eyes blinked back into focus. It was Geoffrey who had spoken, and all eyes in the room were on her.

'Er...' she said.

'Lead us in, please.'

'Oh. Right. *Act two, scene—*'

'No no, from just before the song.'

'Oh. Sorry.' She winced to hear herself reflexively apologise to Geoffrey. She owed him no such niceties. 'Let's take it from Hope's line, "Don't call me that."'

The scene re-started, the song began again, and now that she knew what to listen for, Hattie could hear the melody from 'La Marseillaise' as clear as day. There was no way it could be a coincidence: two composers couldn't possibly decide, independently, to reference the same piece of music in a song. Especially not given that when asked Teri couldn't even produce a decent answer to *why* she'd referenced it.

Hattie felt completely adrift. She didn't know if she wanted to stand up and denounce Geoffrey, or contact Eoin straight away, or run away and never come back, or all three. She certainly was in no position to pay attention to the rehearsal around her. She sat for a few minutes, her heart pounding and head spinning, until she could take it no longer, and with wobbly arms she pushed herself to her feet.

'You all right?' whispered Maxine to her.

'No,' she murmured. 'I need to... go...'

'What's wrong?' asked Mel.

'I don't think she's feeling well,' Maxine replied for her. 'Do you want me to come with you?'

'No, I'll just go... lie down,' said Hattie, and stumbled out of the rehearsal room as quickly as possible to avoid any further questions. She was grateful to hear no sounds of anyone following her as she walked out of the granary. She didn't know what to do or where to go. She started off down the drive with half a mind to walk into the village to see if she could find Eoin. But she didn't know where he was staying, and even if he hadn't left the area, the chances of him sitting waiting for her in the pub seemed slim. She didn't want to go back into Geoffrey's house either. So she took herself back to the field where the Astra was parked and got in. She couldn't think of anywhere that she actually wanted to drive, so she just sat in the driver's seat, gripping the steering wheel and frowning.

After five minutes she began to feel a little silly, so for the sake of something else to do she got out her phone and sent a message to the last number Eoin had contacted her from, saying simply:

> I'm sorry I didn't trust you. You were right about everything. I think I can prove it.

Then she called Nick. He didn't answer, and the call went to voicemail.

'Hullo, it's Cockatoo,' said Hattie, her voice shaking. 'I'm a bit het up...' She tailed off, unable to think what else to say. She wanted to tell him how she was feeling, but the truth was she wasn't entirely sure how she was feeling. For someone who'd built an entire career out of being level-headed, practical and pragmatic, these were unfamiliar emotions coursing through her.

'I think I'm feeling overwhelmed,' she continued, after a pause. 'It was all a bit complicated for a while, but then I thought I'd got through that and everything was simple again, but now it's got even more complicated and I wasn't ready for it. And it's hard because I've not been telling you everything and I don't like secrets. I just don't know what to do. So... well, call me back, Cocker One. When you get a minute. Okay. Bye.'

She hung up, feeling embarrassed about the incoherent ramble she'd just produced. But her thoughts on the message she'd left didn't have a chance to develop further because they were interrupted by a gentle knock on the passenger side car window. Looking across, she saw Delphine standing outside, stooping to see her.

'Can I come in?' she said.

Hattie nodded, and Delphine opened the door and sat down in the passenger seat.

'They don't need me in the scene, so Pip suggested I should go and check on you. But you weren't in our room, so I've been trying to track you down. Seeing you here makes me think maybe you're not ill. Maybe it's something else?'

'You're right about that,' Hattie said, cautiously.

'Want to talk about it?' Delphine asked.

Hattie was touched that Delphine would offer, but she very much didn't want to tell her what was on her mind. Neither did she hugely like lying, so she searched around for a fudge that would deter further questioning.

'It was the music for that song. It... it reminded me of a piece by Lel. And I got upset. But I don't want to burden you with it – I know that's a sore topic for you too.'

Delphine smiled sadly. 'You're right. I've found it really hard to listen to everyone keep talking about him. But I'm getting over it now. Can I tell you a secret?'

Hattie nodded, relieved to shift the conversation away from herself, and Delphine continued, conspiratorially: 'I hated him. And I've felt so incredibly guilty even thinking that, given what happened. Every time someone says "Oh poor Lel, he was so wonderful", I think to myself, "No he wasn't, he was awful", and then I catch myself thinking that and it makes me loathe myself, and then I get upset. But the simple truth is, he was horrible. He sucked up tremendously to everyone above him, but he treated everyone below him like... well, like they were below him. I saw him slap one of the sound engineers once on *The Guilty*. I couldn't believe it. All she did was bump into him and he hit her, right as she was in the middle of apologising. I tried to get her to press charges, or at least lodge a complaint, but she didn't dare. Of course, he hadn't done it when any of the producers were around. She said that Lel would just deny it, and even though I said I'd back her up she wouldn't risk it. She said it wasn't worth throwing away her career.'

'That's awful,' said Hattie.

'I know. And that's just the start. He was rude, he touched people inappropriately, he yelled at people, but somehow he only ever did it when no one important was watching. And I don't want to sound like I've got a chip on my shoulder, but he was horrible to me personally. He was devious and manipulative, and when it counted he really screwed me over.'

'What happened?' asked Hattie, curious despite herself.

'So I was in the original West End cast of *The Guilty*, you know that, right? I was one of the few who hadn't been part of *Airportland!* at some point, so I stood out like a sore thumb from the get-go, and Lel always acted a bit suspicious of me. It wasn't a big part, but I got a bit of solo singing, and so in the early stages I spent a bit of time with Lel. He had lots of opinions about how his music should be performed, of course, and that's fine and normal, but once we got into rehearsals, the director didn't like something Lel had got me to do. It was nothing really, just a note about which words to sing and which to speak-sing. But anyway, Lel had got me to try it one way, and the director listened to it and decided to do it another way. Fair enough, totally normal.

'And then, just as we were starting previews, Lel came and told me that the director had changed his mind and wanted me to go back to doing it Lel's way. And I'm not going to lie, I was already a bit suspicious of Lel at that point – just a few small things during rehearsals – so I went and checked with the director, and lo and behold he'd said no such thing. Lel had just straight up lied to me. And look, I didn't drop Lel in it, I just said, "Oh, sorry, I think there was a little miscommunication" and left it at that. But Lel completely blanked me from that point on, and then three weeks into the show I sprain my ankle and need to take a couple of days out – which is fine, because we've *got* an understudy all sorted – and twenty-four hours later I find out I've been re-cast!

'If I hadn't spent the *entire* rehearsal process palling up with Geoffrey, that would have been it, my entire West End career killed off. As it was I had to spend three weeks buttering him up just to get him to confirm that Lel had been the one who pushed to give me the boot. When I managed to convince him of *why* I'd been shafted, he promised to find a way to work with me again on something, to make it up to me, which is why I'm here.'

Delphine let out a big sigh. 'But now he's dead and you can't speak ill of the dead, can you?' she added with a shrug.

'Sorry, my love,' said Hattie. 'That sounds pretty grim.'

Delphine let out a sudden bark of laughter. 'Oh God, I came here to talk about *your* problems, and I've just dumped all mine onto you.'

'Oh, I don't know. There's nothing like someone else's issues to put your own ones into some perspective. I feel a bit better already,' Hattie lied.

'I think death is just one of those things that jumbles us all up in different ways. I hope your jumbling isn't too intense or too long-lasting.'

'You're very kind. I think I'm going to be fine.'

'So what do you want to do now? Shall we go back into the room?'

While every fibre of her being was screaming 'No', Hattie couldn't see a way out of it.

'Let's go,' she said, with a weak smile.

The two of them walked back to the granary and slipped into the back. There was a heated discussion going on about whether the Hope/Titus reconciliation that was made explicit in the book made for a stronger ending if it was only implied, and so no one paid them much attention, allowing Hattie to slide gratefully back into her chair. She was so angry with Geoffrey that she didn't trust herself to look at him without scowling, so she decided to pay close attention to Teri, the other party to the subterfuge. But was she the *only* one? Thinking about it, anyone who'd been involved with the production for a while would have to have known that the music was Lel's, wouldn't they? Certainly Jala, who would have had access to the music for months while she wrote her own lyrics to it, and Calvin evidently knew. And it didn't seem unlikely that Mel would have known as well. Geoffrey was famously secretive about his projects, so details of who was involved might not have filtered through to the actors… but what about the designers? Gareth and Maxine would have been on board for a while, wouldn't they? Surely they'd know?

Hattie looked round the room suspiciously. How many of these people had Geoffrey convinced to go along with his lies? And what threats must he have made to ensure it stayed a secret despite so many people knowing? Was it fear of legal reprisals that was keeping his co-conspirators in line? Or something worse?

She made herself take a breath. Her mind was spiralling and she'd been indulging it for too long. It was time to get a grip. Right now she was the stage manager in an ongoing rehearsal. Everything else could wait until the rehearsal ended. She forcibly put all other thoughts from her mind and got back to the script.

They made it through to the end of the day, and the consensus was that while the final scene wasn't yet working, they had at least elucidated the questions that needed answering, even if they hadn't managed to find the answers themselves yet.

'This feels like the perfect moment to go and think about something else entirely, have a good meal and a good night's sleep, and come back fresh in the morning,' said Geoffrey. 'And, by some happy chance, it's six o'clock, so that's exactly what's about to happen!'

Scripts were shuffled, water bottles rescued from corners of the room, and the company started to disperse. Hattie tried to engineer it so that she left at the same time as Teri, with the thought of finding a way to corner her about the musical plagiarism that she had apparently signed up for, but just as she was about to make her carefully timed exit, Tom called out, 'Hattie, can you help me hump around some projectors? Gareth wants to try something for tomorrow.'

As much as Hattie wanted to say no, her professional pride rendered her constitutionally incapable of doing so, so she watched forlornly as Teri made her exit, before turning her attention to the task assigned to her. Tom wanted to re-orient the projectors so that one of the large ones was at a much more oblique angle to its target screen than the other, and then suspend the small one so that it pointed directly down onto the floor. Neither of these was particularly complicated in and of itself, but pulling up all the cables that needed moving without disturbing the ones that didn't, and then re-taping the moved cables into their new positions and finding neat ways of accommodating the excess coils was the sort of job that was done most easily with two pairs of hands. They worked slowly and methodically, and by the time they were half way done the room was empty, as everyone else had made their way back to the house.

'You all right?' asked Tom as they worked.

'I'm fine,' replied Hattie. 'I felt a little peculiar earlier, but it passed.'

Tom didn't strike her as the sort of person she would be particularly keen to entrust with any sort of confidence.

'Well good,' said Tom. 'Hopefully you'll get some rest soon. We're nearly at the end anyway, thank goodness. I'm looking forward to signing off, packing up and getting the hell away from here.'

'Oh?' said Hattie, only half listening, as she worked her way patiently along the edge of the floor, neatly taping down a pair of HDMI cables.

'Oh it's been fine,' continued Tom, as he climbed up the ladder in the middle of the room again. 'Mostly. But I don't like to dwell on my mistakes. And bloody hell did I make a mistake.'

'Is this your Calvin thing?' Hattie asked before she could stop herself.

'That's the one. I've always thought you don't really know someone until you know them in the biblical sense. And lo and behold: sweetness and light on the outside, and on the inside a bloody scorpion's nest. And look, I'm adventurous, certainly, but— bugger, I'm out of LX tape, could you pass me some? There should be a roll on the desk... Thanks! But I'm not psychotic. I'll be glad to have got away with just a couple of bruises. Does that look straight to you?'

'Your downstage left corner is more downstage than your downstage right.'

'Don't worry about downstage; I'll fix that with keystoning. I just need the upstage edge to be level with the wall. From here it looks off.'

'I think it's all right.'

'Well, that'll do for now. No matter how good I get it, I guarantee Gareth will ask me to tidge it in the morning, so I might as well leave it as it is. All right, I think that'll do us for today. Thanks very much.'

He flashed her a very brief smile, then dumped himself back down at his desk where he busied himself with some video software on his laptop. The message was clear: the conversation was over. Hattie, aware that she had been a reluctant participant in the first place, nevertheless found herself a little disappointed. The salacious hints Tom had started dropping about his bust-up with Calvin had managed to get Hattie's full curiosity. *Stop being nosy*, she told herself. *You've got enough of your own business to mind; don't get wrapped up in any more of other people's.*

She said 'See you in a bit', and made her way back to the house, hopeful again that she might be able to corner Teri. However, by the time she arrived, Teri was already sitting down to dinner, with people all around her, and Hattie couldn't get close. Then after the meal ended Geoffrey pulled Teri away for a chat, and Hattie didn't see her again. Disconsolate, she gave up and took herself off for a walk outside.

She did a loop of the garden, deep in thought, and was just crossing the gravel on the way back to the house when she met Louise coming the other way. Geoffrey's assistant was looking worried and harassed, and Hattie was beginning to suspect that this was her normal state of being. She was, equally typically, labouring under the weight of a large armful of paperwork and, when she caught sight of Hattie and tried to wave to greet her, the top half of the pile slithered and fell, splaying onto the ground.

'Oh no!' she yelped, and Hattie lurched forward to help retrieve the errant papers before the evening breeze made off with them. Between the two of them they managed to round up what seemed like everything, and gather it back into a pile that Louise clamped firmly to her chest.

'Thank you,' she said.

'More contracts?' enquired Hattie.

'Mostly. Some scripts as well, and lots of tax documents. The usual. Oops!'

The pile was threatening to tumble again.

'Give some to me,' said Hattie, and Louise gratefully did so. 'Where are we going?'

'Just to my car,' said Louise.

The two set off in the direction of the field-cum-car park. Perhaps inevitably, given everything on her mind, Hattie found herself saying, before she could stop herself, 'So I heard you got on with Eoin Norell when you met him?'

'Oh. Well. Sort of,' replied Louise cagily, and Hattie realised just how crass her question had been: no one wants to be outed as an ally of a presumed murderer.

'Sorry, all I mean is… Eoin was a friend of mine, although we lost touch a long time ago.'

'Oh,' said Louise.

An uneasy silence descended between them, and Hattie felt herself turning red.

'I just mean, it must have been hard for you, all of this. Er… you were at the Revue that night, weren't you? You were there with Calvin when it happened?'

'No,' snapped Louise. 'I wasn't there. I only met up with Calvin afterwards.'

'Right. Sorry,' Hattie mumbled. 'I shouldn't have brought it up.'

'No, it's… I did like him,' said Louise. 'When we first met I was having… a bad day. And he was very kind to me. And we stayed in touch for a little bit after that. Everyone said he was rude, but he was just… clumsy with words. I suppose that's ironic for a writer. There are a lot of people in the industry who are only nice when it helps them, and normally the only times people are nice to me is when they think it'll help them suck up to Geoffrey. Eoin was sort of the opposite.'

'I agree,' said Hattie.

'But then he killed someone,' said Louise, her tone brittle and her expression pained, as if the words were causing her discomfort as they came out. 'So I must have been wrong about him.'

'Maybe,' said Hattie.

'It's not a maybe. When I turned up at the theatre there was a dead body in it. He murdered Lel.'

Her voice was flat, but in that flatness Hattie could hear a lot of emotion. Understandably.

They fell back into silence, and when they arrived at Louise's car Hattie handed over her half of the papers and wished her a safe drive.

Walking back towards the house, Hattie found herself oddly reassured. With everyone around her condemning Eoin, it was good to know that she wasn't alone in seeing something better in him. That perhaps she had been right not to write him off immediately.

It was all, finally, falling into place. Her trust in Eoin had wavered, it was true, but never fully broken, and now it was being rewarded: she now knew that *Geoffrey* was the one who was lying, which meant Eoin was the one telling the truth. He was innocent, and Hattie had a chance to clear his name, to save him like she hadn't been able to save him before.

Now all she needed was to not bugger it all up…

18

Eoin had never told her his home address, but he *had* once mentioned the name of his father's local boozer. It was a little way across town, and Hattie was reliant on the bus, and she couldn't get moving until twenty minutes after the final curtain at the Tree at the earliest, but with a little hustle she managed to make it a bit before closing time on a Thursday night.

It was obvious who he was as soon as she walked in: he had Eoin's eyes, his long nose, his curly hair. He was propping up the bar, part of a line of half a dozen men of a similar age, all just starting on their next pints of bitter. They were chatting, laughing, looking like the friendliest bunch of gaffers and geezers in the world. Hattie had a moment of doubt: was this really the man who had been responsible for all the cuts and bruises?

But she understood well enough that what defines a predator is not how they behave when they're *not* hunting. Swallowing her anxiety, she walked up to the bar and forced herself to say, slowly and calmly, 'Mr Norell? Can I have a word?'

He looked round, surprised, then gestured broadly. 'By all means.'

'In private, please. It's about your son.'

The other fellows at the bar hushed, and Mr Norell's eyes widened momentarily. Then he nodded, and walked wordlessly over to the back of the pub, to an empty table. Hattie followed him, and they both sat down.

'Do you know where he is?' Norell asked, earnestly. His face was full of concern, and his eyes were slightly welling up.

Hattie nodded.

'Well?'

'He's safe,' she assured him, 'but I'm not going to tell you where he is.'

Norell's face clouded immediately. 'What is this?' he demanded. 'You bring my boy home, you hear me? Right now.'

'He'll come home when he wants to come home,' said Hattie, struggling to keep her voice level and her breath from catching in her chest under the angry gaze of Eoin's father. He wasn't broad or muscled, but his posture spoke of strength, and violence. 'But he isn't going to come home at all unless there are some changes. That's why I'm here. To see if we can come to an arrangement that works for everyone.'

'What are you talking about?'

'He hates you. He hates you because of the way you treat him and the way you hurt him, and he won't put up with it any more. He's not going to stay under the same roof as you again any time soon, but maybe there's another way. Maybe there's relatives? Or friends? Maybe there's a way you can do right by him and provide for him without you two having to be around each other, but if you do right by him maybe he'll help you keep up your pretence of happy families and no one needs to know—'

'Are you blackmailing me?' he suddenly snarled.

'No! I don't want anything.'

'Fuck off! Get the fuck out of here, right now! Go on, before I lose my temper!'

His voice was raised, his eyes were dark, and Hattie was suddenly aware of how small was the little table separating him from her. She stood up abruptly and backed away.

'And you tell my boy to come home,' he continued, standing and taking a menacing step towards her, 'cos if he's not back by the end of the week then I swear to God when I do see him he'll wish he'd never been born!'

Norell was yelling now, his face purple, specks of spittle erupting from him. Under the gaze of the shocked patrons at the bar Hattie's nerve went entirely, and she turned and bolted out of the pub, and she didn't stop running until she was several streets away and certain that no one was following her.

Too jittery to wait at a bus stop, Hattie walked the whole way home, ruminating as she did on her total failure to negotiate a solution to her problem. Eoin was still up when she got back, and he must have read the dismay on her face because he immediately asked, concerned, 'What's going on?'

Reluctantly Hattie explained to him the plan she had concocted, and just how badly it had gone. Eoin put his head in his hands as he listened, and when she was done he sat in silence for a long while.

'It's no use,' he said, eventually. 'I can't escape him. He'll find me whatever I do. I can't stop him. Maybe I should just go back. He'll beat me to a pulp, but maybe the longer I leave it the worse it'll be.'

'Can't you say you'll tell everyone if he hurts you again? If he wants to keep it a secret so much, can you use that?'

'That's not how he thinks. If I say something like that he'll say I'm blackmailing him, and that's another reason to hit me. He knows that he's in control of the narrative. His friends and family will believe whatever he says. And even if they don't, they won't dare admit it. He's surrounded by terrified courtiers.'

'Then you know what?' said Hattie, suddenly certain of the way forward. 'We go to the police. He's not allowed to just hit you with impunity.'

'He's my dad,' said Eoin, 'He's allowed to smack me.'

'Smacking is one thing, but this is grievous bodily harm.'

'No it isn't. You need bone fractures, substantial loss of blood or visible disfigurement. I've read up on all of this. You might be able to call it "Actual Bodily Harm", because he's given me extensive bruising, but I don't have scars or anything, so it's my word against his.'

'You've got witnesses! Everyone at the Tree, your schoolmates, your teachers. Your *mum*, surely.'

'Are you envisioning a *trial*, Harriet? You think somehow my dad's going to end up sitting quietly in the dock while a friendly old judge listens to everyone own up to everything they know, add it all together and then send my daddy away somewhere he can't get to me any more? It doesn't *work* like that. The police won't do anything.'

'I don't believe that!' retorted Hattie. Eoin winced, and she realised she was shouting. She hadn't meant to, she was just agitated and frustrated, and still feeling the emotional after-effects of her confrontation with Eoin's father.

She continued: 'It's their job to keep people safe. I don't *know* what they can do, all right? I don't know anything about it. But I know they can do *something*. So let's talk to them.'

Eoin took a lot of persuading. For three days he said no, and his nervous tic with his fingers intensified so much that he scratched his thumbs raw and had to put bandages on them. But Hattie persisted, and eventually she wore him down and he relented. He wouldn't go with her, he said, but if she wanted to go to a police station and talk to them about his situation, he couldn't stop her.

So on the Monday afternoon, in her lunch break, that's exactly what Hattie did. It took a little while to communicate enough of what she wanted to discuss for the front counter officer to be able to decide who she should talk to, but eventually she was seen by a sergeant, a serious-looking woman who took her off to a slightly threateningly austere room and calmly invited Hattie to tell the whole story. She nodded sympathetically as Hattie spoke, interrupting only to ask for clarifications and particulars. Hattie had vaguely thought she might have the initial conversation in general terms, avoiding specifics, but under this woman's prompting soon found herself divulging names and places, which the sergeant wrote down. Hattie wasn't too worried: she wanted action, not just advice, and she didn't give a fig if it became known to the police at the earliest possible juncture that Mr Norell was an abuser rather than a victim.

When she had finished her story the sergeant nodded thoughtfully and explained that, as Hattie had herself admitted, this was a tricky issue that needed to be handled sensitively. She invited Hattie to wait while she consulted with a senior colleague. Hattie politely declined: she needed to get back to the Tree, as she'd already severely overrun her lunch break. The sergeant then asked to take her details so she could get back in contact, and Hattie, having done so, left the station feeling a weight lifted from her shoulders. The police understood now. The police would handle it.

And handle it they did: the very next morning two officers appeared at Harriet's front door. One of them calmly informed Hattie that details of the case, including her statement from the previous day, had been passed to the Crown Prosecution Service with a view to prosecuting her for child kidnapping.

The other one, equally calmly, insisted that Eoin accompany him back to the police station to give a statement, after which he would be returned to his parents' house. Eoin, hearing them from the sitting room, made a break for the back door, but the officers, seeing him, barged past Hattie and grabbed him before he could make good his escape. They ignored his protestations, deaf to his cries of 'He'll kill me!', and frog-marched him out of the house. Hattie, frozen in shock, unable to believe that everything was unravelling so quickly, caught a last glimpse of his face as they pushed him into their car, fear and misery written all over it. And the next time Hattie saw him was in a hospital ward.

19

The first thing she needed to do was to reassure Nick. He'd evidently got her voicemail when he'd got home from work, because from 7 o'clock onwards she'd had a missed call from him roughly once every fifteen minutes. So she rang him back and he picked up immediately.

'Are you all right?' he asked, his voice catching as he spoke, in a most un-Nick-like way.

'I'm fine,' she said, trying to sound as reassuring as she could.

'You sure? The way you sounded on the phone, I've never heard you speak like that before. I've been worried sick.'

'Oh my love, you didn't need to worry.'

'I've had chest pains. For a moment I thought I was on the way out, but I think it was panic. I don't like it when you're upset,' he persisted.

'Well I'm sorry to have caused you so much suffering,' she said, unable to keep the frustration out of her voice.

Nick sighed. 'No, I'm sorry. This is about you, not me. What's going on?'

Hattie closed her eyes. This was going to be hard. But at this point, probably no harder than not doing it.

'So... all right. There's this show. Well, it's a book. *The Fall of a Thousand Hopeless Stars*. Eoin and Lel had been working on a stage adaptation. But Geoffrey wanted to do the stage adaptation with Lel and without Eoin. And this workshop, it turns out, is for that show. With Lel's music, and someone else's words. Only they're pretending it's someone else's music. It's all a big lie, with Geoffrey in the middle of it. And I only know about it because… well, because of Eoin. That's what he wanted to talk to me about the night he came to see me. And I've kept talking to him about it, and it's only now that I've pieced it all together. And I've not been telling you anything about it because I know you didn't approve, because you didn't want me mixing with Eoin, not with him being accused of murder. But he didn't kill Lel. I'm *sure* of it. I just… I know him. He *is* a liar, but still, I know this isn't something he'd do. I'm sorry, my love. I know I'm not making loads of sense. But I'm right in the middle of this, and I need someone on my side.'

There was a pause, and Hattie could hear Nick's huffy anxious breathing on the other end of the line.

'Well I am on your side,' he said eventually. 'But I don't understand what you're saying. You don't think *Geoffrey* killed Lel, do you?'

'I don't know. It's hard to imagine it, but… well, Geoffrey has ended up getting what he wanted. And I don't think he would have got it if Lel was still alive or if Eoin wasn't on the run. They were the only two people who were in his way.'

'And how about you? Are you in his way?' asked Nick.

'I'm just a stage manager,' replied Hattie. 'I'm not in his way yet. And believe me, I don't want to get in his way. But I want to get to the bottom of this.'

'I wouldn't. I'd just get out of there as soon as I could. It's murky stuff. I don't think you should have any part of it.'

'But what if I can keep Eoin out of prison?'

'Tell the police what you know. Let them deal with it.'

'I think they'd do me for aiding and abetting if they did anything at all. Besides, all I've got comes down to one snippet of music sounding a bit like a Beatles song. I don't think it stands up.'

'Then what are you going to do?'

'I dunno. Just ask some more questions,' said Hattie, uncertainly.

'And what should I do?'

'I dunno. Just tell me everything will be all right.'

'Will it?' Nick asked hopefully.

'I dunno.'

'I have to say, this isn't one of my all-time favourite phone calls.'

'Sorry, my love.'

'Don't be sorry, Cockatoo. Just be careful.'

'I will, Cocker One. I promise.'

'You're a stage manager, not a private eye.'

'I know,' said Hattie. Everything Nick was saying was making sense, but she wasn't getting the comfort she had hoped from this call. 'Listen, I should go,' she continued. 'Can I call you tomorrow?'

'Of course.'

'All right then. Love you.'

'Love you.'

She hung up. Then she immediately called Eoin. She was fully aware of their agreement that he would always be the one to call her, but she reckoned that if ever there was a time to sod the rules it was now. So she called him, but he didn't pick up. The call didn't even go to voicemail. It just kept ringing and ringing, until eventually she gave up.

She wished she could speak to him. She'd spent the last few weeks getting more and more suspicious of him, more and more convinced that this was some sort of wild goose chase, and if she was honest, less and less confident that he *hadn't* been the one to kill Lel. Largely because of everything Geoffrey kept telling her, all of which was so effortlessly convincing, and all of which turned out to be a steaming pile of cow crap, shat out as a distraction from his unscrupulous, deeply immoral and almost certainly illegal plans. She felt such a fool. She'd got drunk with the man a few times twenty years ago, and thought she had the measure of him. She'd been so delighted and flattered to have been offered work by no less a personage than Sir Geoffrey Dougray that it had blinded her to the truth that he was a liar and a manipulator who had only reached his position of prestige through the most ruthless cheating.

Hattie's heart jumped as she realised her phone was buzzing in her bag, and, feeling flustered, she fumbled it out, sausage-fingered, only for the ringing to stop by the time the phone was in her hand. She was deeply surprised to see that the person who had tried to contact her was not Eoin, by any old or new number, but, unexpectedly, Abua. She rang him back, but the call went straight to voicemail.

Hattie frowned. How unexpected. And now she couldn't help but feel rather guilty. She'd meant to check in with him, but then had forgotten all about it straight away afterwards, as her own problems crowded out any consideration of others'. She had no idea if he'd taken her advice and gone back to ACDA, or whether that had inspired him to try again at the Young Vic.

It wouldn't do. She'd try to call him again later, and she'd keep trying until she spoke to him. Whatever it was he'd been trying to reach her about, she'd make sure she found out what it was, and if there was any help he needed that she could give, she'd give it.

She rang him one more time straight away for good measure, but it went to voicemail again. With a sigh, she put her phone away.

Now what? Her feet had led her to the swing seat at the bottom of the garden, so she sat down on it and took stock. She needed to speak to Eoin, but he wasn't picking up his phone. She needed to speak to Abua too, but he wasn't either. There was nothing she could do about those. What she could do, by herself, was try to get some answers.

Hattie strode back to the house, in through the door and marched across the hall to the living room. Inside, a raucous improvisation was going on. Pip and Hera were standing in the middle of the room, foreheads pressed together. She was uttering a series of cartoonishly extreme threats of violence against him in an extremely overdone Scottish accent, and he was roaring back in an extremely overdone French accent, only his replies seemed to be individual steps from some sort of baking recipe. Every time either of them spoke, Jala, Calvin and Delphine, who were sprawled around them on the floor, squealed in delight, while behind them Maxine, Teri, Tom and Geoffrey dissolved in fits of laughter on the sofa.

Ignoring whatever the game was (Hattie had learned long ago that when actors got stuck into something like this it was impossible to get them to rewind and explain how they had got into it – no explanation of why they were doing what they were doing ever made any kind of sense), she crossed over to the end of the sofa where Teri was sitting, squatted beside her and said, quietly but firmly, 'Can I have a word?'

'One sec, one sec, this is *brilliant*,' replied Teri, not looking round.

'I'd like to speak to you now, please,' Hattie insisted.

She had spoken this during one of the very few quieter moments and, hearing her, Geoffrey looked round.

'Everything all right, Hattie?' he asked.

'Yes thank you. I just need to talk to Teri about something.'

'Oh,' said Geoffrey, frowning. 'You know, Hattie, I think we're overdue a chat too. How about you and I go and catch up and let Teri enjoy the revels first, then you can talk to her later.'

His voice had seemed to grow more assertive with each word, and now he started to prise himself off the sofa, but Hattie would not be deterred. She raised a hand to stop him.

'I'd love to catch up, Geoffrey, but I'm going to talk to Teri *first*.'

To emphasise her point she put her other hand on the top of Teri's back, and gently started applying forwards pressure.

'Now, Hattie—' Geoffrey began, but Teri, responding to Hattie's touch, was already standing and Hattie, her iciest professional smile applied to her lips, led her briskly away before Geoffrey had a chance to enforce a countermand.

He knows I know, she thought to herself. *I dunno how, but he's already bloody figured it out. This isn't good.*

She took Teri across to the yellow room, the one filled with all the boxes. It was safely out of earshot of the living room and its environs, and Hattie was pleased to note just how squeaky the floorboards were outside it. Any would-be eavesdropper would have a hard time getting close undetected.

Once the door was shut behind them, Hattie said, without preamble, 'I know what you're doing.'

Teri frowned. 'What do you mean?'

Hattie didn't reply. She just treated Teri to a level stare. Teri began to look a little anxious. 'I'm sorry,' she replied again, 'but I really don't know what you're talking about.'

Again, Hattie didn't reply. She was, she realised, feeling *extremely* angry. She didn't like being taken for a fool, and she couldn't think of anything to say to the composer that wouldn't come out as a yell. So she just stared.

Teri, apparently out of things to say herself, stared back. But her gaze was no match for Hattie's, and her smile began to falter, as a range of half-expressions danced across her face, resolving at last into a singularly worried countenance, as her shoulders raised and she began to lean ever so slightly backwards as if bracing herself for Hattie to pounce.

'Oh God,' she said in a small voice, and Hattie, knowing she'd made her point, finally broke her stare.

'Tell me what happened,' she said, in a gentler voice.

'He told me everything I wanted to hear,' Teri explained. 'He said that he'd been watching my career, he said he loved my work, he said he was starting work on his next big project, a new musical, and it was going to be my name on the billboards. He told me what the show was, showed me a few snippets of Jala's script, and

I got so excited. I even... I feel so stupid, I even went home and wrote a bunch of music that night and sent it to him. I told him I'd felt inspired by the conversation, and he said that he'd love to get into it all with me and scheduled a follow-up meeting... and that was when he sat me down and told me that the music was already written. God, he made it sound so *normal*, like this was just how the West End worked, that when there's a conflict of interest clause this is just what you do. He just kept talking about how great it would be for my career and made me sign the contract there and then. By the time I got home the money was already in my bank account and that was that. I haven't even been allowed to tell anyone about it.'

'Who else knows? Who else was involved with the project before you came along?'

'Well, Jala. And I mean, presumably there are lots of people at the production company. Louise and so on. And then Andrew, of course.'

'Andrew?'

'Well yes, it's his music so... Oh. No. I mustn't say.'

'Teri, are you saying you think the score was written by someone called Andrew?'

Teri's eyes widened. 'No! I don't know. I genuinely don't know, Geoffrey never actually said the name. I was just wildly speculating, based on who might have a conflict of interest clause.'

'You mentioned that before. What is this clause?'

'Well it's... it's what this is all about. If a composer has a contract with one West End theatre, and it prevents them from putting their name on a show that runs in a competing West End theatre then... well, there's a workaround. Saps like me. But it's not illegal. And I didn't tell you, right? You knew about it before you talked to me. I haven't done anything wrong.' There was a pleading note in Teri's voice. The young woman was very, very anxious about getting in trouble, that much was clear.

Hattie paused for a moment, and then said, 'Well, I've got some good news and I've got some bad news. The good news is that no, I'm sure you've not done anything to breach your contract. But the bad news is that Geoffrey has been lying to you, because what he's done is very illegal indeed. I don't know which Andrew you're thinking of, but he didn't write the music you've been passing off as your own. Lel Nowak did.'

Teri's eyebrows rose and fell a couple of times in quick succession as they described a five-act drama of surprise, doubt, realisation, anger and anguish.

'Oh' she said eventually. 'Of course he did. Now that you've said it, I know that it's true. It's his music, it's got his ideas woven into every part of it. And the timing of it, just days after his death. I just wanted to believe so badly that what I was doing was okay, and to justify it I made up this silly little narrative – absurd now I come to think about it – that the whole thing was a last hurrah project written by Andrew… oh never mind. I honestly convinced myself that this was above board. Despite the fact he had me lying to the whole company about it. I feel like such an idiot.'

'My love, that makes two of us.'

'Jala too. Or at least… would she know? We never spoke about who really wrote it. Geoffrey told us it wouldn't be creatively helpful to dwell on the intentions of the original composer, so he banned us from talking about it even in private. He said I should take ownership of the music, full creative control, and treat the originals as just the starting point. And Jala went along with it, even when I tried to talk to her about it. I thought she was just doing what Geoffrey had suggested, creatively but… what if she knew it was Lel's music, and was covering up for him?'

'I don't know what Jala knows,' said Hattie. 'I'm rather inclined to ask her.'

'Yes. But… oh God, I don't think I could face that. No, no, I'm sorry, I can't. I'll just… I'll just say I quit and… I'll leave tonight and I'll give back the money, and… but he's still got the contract, and this is my only… oh God I can't do this, I can't, I can't, I can't…'

Teri had started pacing awkwardly to and fro, her head bent down, her shoulders hunched absurdly high. In an odd way, Hattie found it rather calming: when she had been by herself, her panicked worries and paranoid thoughts started spiralling and threatening to get the better of her. But now that someone *else* was doing the spiralling, she found it easier to fall into the opposite role, of the calm, collected reasoning one.

'Let's not be hasty,' Hattie said. 'We owe it to ourselves to get to the bottom of this. We owe it to Lel too, let's not forget.'

A thought suddenly occurred to Hattie and she continued. 'And on that point, do you actually have the original manuscript?'

'You mean the files? I've got a copy on my laptop.'

Hattie shook her head. 'No, I mean the *original* manuscript. Lel wrote his music by hand. That's the thing that will prove it's his music originally.'

'Oh I see. No, I've only ever seen digital versions. Geoffrey emailed them over to me.'

'Ah well. It was a long shot.'

'Oh!' said Teri suddenly.

'What?'

'Jala did say something about the handwriting once. For the opening number, one of her lyrics had an extra syllable that didn't fit, she said she hadn't been sure if it was a quaver or a rest. I thought she just wasn't sure about how the notation worked, but that didn't make total sense because she seemed to understand everything else. But if she'd seen a handwritten version…'

'That might explain it. Well, it adds to the things we can ask Jala about.'

'I just don't want to cause a confrontation.'

'You're not causing anything, my love. I want some answers,

and there's no point asking Geoffrey. He'll happily lie all the way from here to Sunday. But we can ask Jala what she knows. If you want me to do the talking I happily will. I think you've been rattled enough for one day. But remember: it's Jala, not some monster. Worst case scenario, she's mixed up in this murky business, but that doesn't mean she's going to grow an extra head and start baying for blood if we just go and talk to her, will she?'

Teri shook her head, but didn't reply.

'Well then, let's give it a go.'

'Now?'

'I don't see why we should wait any longer than we have to.'

'A-all right…'

Teri seemed rooted to the spot, and Hattie bit back a grunt of frustration.

'Tell you what,' she said. 'You just wait here. I'll go and fetch her, and let's have it out, shall we?'

Without waiting for a reply Hattie stole from the room and headed for the other side of the house, from which the sounds of wild laughter were still emanating. She had nearly reached the living room when—

'Hattie, it's time for our little talk,' said Geoffrey, looming up suddenly from the darkness behind her.

'Oh!' said Hattie, involuntarily.

'Come on,' he said firmly, putting a hand on her back and propelling her in the direction of his study. 'We won't get a chance otherwise.'

Hattie went where she was led. She wasn't sure if it was politeness, obedience, or a sense of fear about what would happen if she tried to break away from him. His hand felt heavy and strong. Before she knew it she was in his study, and he was closing the door behind her.

'Take a seat,' said Geoffrey. He remained standing for a moment, his neck bent, poking at his phone with meaty fingers. Then he slid it back into his pocket, sat down opposite her and treated her to a warm and enthusiastic smile.

'So,' he began, 'the first battle draws to a close. But the war is young, and there are plenty more fights to be had in this campaign. I think it's gone rather well. Don't you?'

Hattie nodded cautiously, but Geoffrey didn't wait for her to detail her thoughts. Instead he continued. 'And it's been a great pleasure to work with you again. You are very, very good at your job, as I know you know. Whether it's instinct or cunning, you somehow manage to pre-empt the needs of the room, in a way that's very attractive in a stage manager. But it hasn't all been plain sailing, has it?'

This time he paused, inspecting Hattie's face carefully, waiting for a response.

'No, I suppose not,' she said.

'There was the unfortunate misapprehension around rights and dare I say it, a certain reticence to engage fully with the company. I won't call it standoffishness but certainly a little less *bonhomie* than perhaps I remember or have come to expect from my team… and then today seems to have been a difficult day for you. I detect a certain agitation that's not quite in line with what I need. *Unflappable*, that's the quality I'm after in a stage manager. We've talked about sides, and what I need from the people who are on my side. Do you still have it, Hattie? Speaking as candidly as I can, can I rely on you, or is it time for you to retire?'

'Well I'm not planning on giving up any time yet,' said Hattie. She wished he'd just be straight with her. All this ominous but vague talk was giving her a headache.

'Hmm,' he said, slowly. 'Truth be told, I don't know how much comfort I take from that.'

Hattie had had enough. She stood up abruptly – or as abruptly as her hip would allow.

'Are we done?' she said, jutting her chin out.

'I suppose so,' Geoffrey replied. He stood slowly, crossed to the door, unlocked it, carefully opened it and Hattie wordlessly took her leave.

Angrily, she stomped back to the sitting room, determined that if Geoffrey still wanted to get in the way of her finding the truth he'd have to physically restrain her. But Geoffrey didn't follow her, or at least not at any kind of proximity. She made it to the sitting room, shoved open the door, marched inside... and found the writer conspicuous by her absence.

'Where's Jala?' she demanded of the room in general.

'Do *you* know what's going on?' Delphine replied.

'I'm going to bloody well find out. Where's Jala?' Hattie repeated.

'We don't know. She just upped and left. She got a message about something, and just said, "Oh tits" and walked out. She looked *gutted*.'

Hattie's mind flashed back to a few minutes earlier, when Geoffrey had been sending a message on his phone just as he ushered her into his study.

'Oh the slimy little bugger. He was stalling while he got her away from me,' she snarled.

'Who?' asked Delphine.

Hattie's head snapped up.

'Right!' she barked. 'We're finding Jala. Delphine and Hera, look upstairs. Calvin and Maxine, look downstairs. Tom and Pip, check the grounds. Chop chop!'

A stage manager doesn't have much official authority. In the hierarchy of the theatre producers and production managers are at the top, then directors, then designers. Below them, performers and technicians are uneasily adjacent, and stage managers weave their way below and around everyone else, normally only exerting power when they borrow it from others. But over time, if you went for long enough doing the job properly without making an arse of yourself, you could build up a general perception that you knew what you were talking about, broadly speaking, and that when you said something should be done, it was because it did genuinely need doing. And in times of crisis this perception is occasionally helpful.

The inhabitants of the sitting room leapt wordlessly into action, hurrying away to do as Hattie had instructed. Left to her own devices, the rational part of Hattie's brain immediately started to ask awkward questions such as quite how she was going to explain herself when the initial feeling of urgency wore off, and what she was going to do about Geoffrey's presence in the near vicinity. Rather than give these questions enough mental space to get a foothold, she hurried off to look in the granary while the others searched elsewhere.

The building was dark and empty, and none of the places she could see en route – the kitchen garden, the cart lodge, the front lawn – bore signs of life either. She went back to the house. Within a few minutes the four who had been searching the house reconvened in the hall, having drawn a blank, and Pip returned swiftly too, shaking his head apologetically.

'Is she all right?' asked Hera.

'Yes, what is going on?' piped in Calvin. 'Geoffrey's in his study – should I fetch him? Also, Teri's in the other room looking a little off colour. Is this something to do with her?'

'Er…' hesitated Hattie. Was this a good time to lay out the truth about Lel's music? It didn't feel like it.

She was saved from having to decide by the return of Tom, who said, without preamble, 'Her car's gone.'

Hattie swore. 'Does anyone have her number?' she asked, but was met with blank faces.

'I've got her email,' Maxine said. 'Geoffrey will have her phone number, won't he?'

'Where on earth is she going?' asked Hera.

'Jala has gone to take care of something,' came Geoffrey's voice from the corridor leading down to his study. He emerged into the hall, continuing, 'But it's private. I'm sure you all understand.'

Hattie didn't even pause. She marched immediately up the stairs to her room, grabbed her coat and bag, then marched straight back down again, past the assembled company, and out of the front door, not stopping until she reached her own car. There was only one road out of here, the one back towards London. Jala would be headed in that direction. There was every chance Hattie could catch up to her on the way.

An hour later, Hattie, frustrated beyond measure, pulled into a layby and took out her phone. She was beginning to have to admit to herself that she'd gone off half-cocked. As soon as she'd made it onto the A140 she'd got stuck behind a slow-moving lorry, and remembered that most of the road was not wide enough to permit overtaking, at least not unless you were prepared to take your life into your hands. When the lorry had finally turned off she had sped up and soon encountered another car, a small white Peugeot, at which point the fact that she had no idea what car Jala drove became the foremost thought in her mind. Then that car turned off, and the next car, a rather battered Polo, sparked half a memory in Hattie's mind. Could that be Jala? Peering through the rear window at the driver's seat she couldn't see anything to confirm or disprove it. So she followed it, all the way to the bottom of the A140 onto the A12 towards London. But then she lost sight of it on the dual carriageway, and to make matter worse a few minutes later she spotted a sign that revealed she wasn't on the A12 at all, but rather had somehow ended up on the A14 towards Felixstowe.

So now, feeling thoroughly stupid, and disappointed, and *lost*, she needed to get her bearings in more ways than one. She had half a mind to give up and slink back to Trevelyan House with her tail between her legs. It would be awkward as anything, but maybe she could smooth things over.

But no: she needed to speak to Jala. Until she got to the bottom of this she wanted nothing more to do with Geoffrey and his deceitful plans. She *probably* was heading to London. There didn't seem anywhere else she could feasibly go. So if Hattie made it back to London, she'd just have to find another way to track her down. It couldn't be too hard. Surely she knew someone who knew Jala – the theatre world was small, after all, and Jala had several productions to her name – and she'd be able to dig up an address or a phone number. So now all Hattie needed to do was find out where on earth she was and how on earth to get back.

The satnav app on her phone stubbornly refused to give up its secrets. Wherever she was, Hattie didn't have enough phone signal for it to load a local map. What she did have, though, was another missed call from Nick, accompanied by a message. It just said: *Check the news. Did you know?*

Frowning, Hattie opened up her browser and loaded up the BBC website. It took a painfully long time, and none of the top stories seemed anything other than the usual: global humanitarian catastrophes, political crises, dire warnings about the environment, nothing out of the ordinary. She was about to give up and ring Nick to ask for an explanation, when she saw it, tucked down at the bottom next to an article about a celebrity spotted in the Highlands:

**Missing playwright arrested over
'gruesome' theatre murder**

Act Four

20

The fundamental question we must ask ourselves is not 'How can I get the most from theatre, or performance, or art?' but rather, 'What is the most that I can bear to <u>give</u> to my art?'. For whatever the limit – and there will be a limit – we must make our peace with it. While we surrender much of ourselves, put ourselves through much and endure much, the notion of total self-sacrifice in the name of theatre is a romantic fiction. To our shame, there is always something we hold back.

– From Advanced Theatre Practice
by Jala Senguel, MA

Hattie's phone rang for the fifth time: Delphine again. Seeing the name flash up on her screen, Hattie felt herself going red with embarrassment once more.

Well Cockatoo, you've really stuffed it up this time.

It was the morning after her departure from Trevelyan House, and she was back in London. She wanted to say it was an act of principle: that, having discovered the rotten foundation on which the edifice of Sir Geoffrey's production was built, she was having no more to do with it, and was effectively boycotting the final day of the workshop. But the truth was that after her dramatic storming around the evening before, ordering the actors about and hurling accusations at her employer, she couldn't bear the idea of facing them again. Goodness knows what conversations they'd had about her after her departure. Geoffrey would have had an entire evening to promote his own spin on events, and whatever he'd told them she could be sure it wouldn't reflect well on her. They must all think she was a proper nutter by now.

What she *should* be doing, of course, was finding Jala. That was, after all, why she'd left in the first place. Jala was the only person who offered Hattie a hope in hell of getting to the bottom of what was going on and actually *proving* that Geoffrey had been engaging in creative skulduggery. The stakes couldn't be higher either: with Eoin in police custody, it seemed as though his conviction for Lel's murder was almost a certainty at this point. The established narrative was that Eoin, aggrieved at being left behind by Lel's upward career trajectory, had killed him in a fit of rage. The only thing that could upset that narrative would be to present this alternate one: that Geoffrey was determined to stage *Fall* with Lel's music, and when Lel had refused… he killed him, and brought in Teri to pass off the music as her own.

There it was. Up until this point, she'd shied away from even thinking it, but it had to be acknowledged: the signs pointed very clearly to Geoffrey being the murderer. Even a week ago she'd have thought the notion preposterous, but everything was now falling into place.

So, Jala had to be found. The problem was, Hattie had no idea how to go about it. On a proper production, contact details would have been distributed at the start, so everyone could contact everyone, but for the workshop, secretive as it was, this hadn't happened. Geoffrey would have her details, as would everyone at Geoffrey Dougray Productions, but Hattie couldn't exactly ask them.

A quick bit of Googling revealed Jala's website, but the only contact option it offered was the email address of her agent. Hattie wasn't sure she'd be able to convince a third party why it was important that she be put in touch with the writer, but she sent a vaguely worded message anyway, just in case.

Jala's website also listed her professional CV, and Hattie had a go at digging up the crew lists for all her previous shows, in the hope of spotting a name she recognised. But Jala hadn't *done* much, and Hattie's list of theatre contacts had been diminishing recently. She got through several lists of names until she finally spotted one that rang a bell: in January, Jala had a writing credit for a rehearsed reading of a one-act play in a studio theatre in Guildford. A tiny thing, with a cast of four and no credited technicians. The first time Hattie looked at the details she dismissed it instantly. But, out of desperation, she found herself going back over every show, and the second time round she noticed that one of the actors was called Jodie Turrell, and *that* was a name Hattie recognised. Jodie had graduated from the three-year undergraduate acting course at ACDA a year earlier. As Hattie had only started tutoring there part way through the summer term, and as there were few moments that brought acting students and technical tutors into direct contact with one another, she'd never had anything to do with Jodie directly, but she'd seen her perform in the showcase shows that her own students stage-managed, and had remembered her. Jodie had excellent comic timing, and had brought the house down with a particularly well-delivered line in the final scene.

Hattie didn't have Jodie's contact details, but Jodie would most likely have Jala's, and she was reasonably confident she knew how to get hold of Jodie's. She picked up her phone and called Donna Fletcher.

'Hattie! How nice to hear from you,' Donna greeted her. 'How are you holding up?'

'Well enough, I suppose,' said Hattie.

'Still shaken up about Lel? I know I am. I'm still having nightmares about it.'

'It's not been easy,' agreed Hattie.

'I suppose you want to talk about the news,' said Donna. 'I should warn you, I'm not prepared to gloat. I'm glad justice can be done, but I'm not going to harp on about it just because they've arrested him. I don't think it's tasteful.'

Hattie felt as though she was being rebuked, and had to bite back the urge to apologise, reminding herself that she *hadn't* rung up to gloat about Eoin's arrest.

'I agree,' she said. 'I actually wanted to talk to you about something unrel— well, something different. Towards the end of your time at ACDA did you come across an actor called Jodie Turrell?'

'Jodie Turrell... Yes. Did the three-year course. Would have graduated in '23.'

'That's the one. Er... do you have her phone number?'

There was a disapproving pause on the other end of the line.

'I shredded all my paperwork from ACDA as soon as I didn't need it any more,' replied Donna primly. 'Each time a show finished I got rid of anything with any personal information on it. Had to: it'd be a data protection violation otherwise. *Especially* if I'd kept any of this after I left. I hope you're keeping up to date with your shredding, Hattie? You wouldn't want to be in possession of a bunch of students' phone numbers. It'd be unprofessional.'

'No, no, of course not... No, I was just wondering on the off-chance. I know some students like to keep in touch after they graduate, and it'd be different then, wouldn't it...?'

Another pause, then Donna said, 'Well, no, to answer your question, I don't have Jodie's details. Was there anything else?'

'No,' said Hattie despondently.

'All right, well, lovely to hear from you, and speak to you later. Bye!'

Donna hung up, leaving Hattie feeling disappointed and chastised. Of course Donna would have shredded all her paperwork. That would be the *responsible* thing to do. Hattie thought guiltily about the pile of printouts in the cardboard box under her desk at ACDA, all the things that she'd been meaning to sort through, to preserve some stuff for the archive and recycle the rest.

Then she thought about the pile of paperwork again. Was there a chance…? Yes, there was. She stood up and went in search of her handbag.

ACDA was deserted, as she'd expected, and the push-button combination lock door on the side of the building still hadn't been padlocked for the summer, as she'd hoped. She let herself in and started to make her way to the stage management office… then stopped, when she heard a banging noise from the stairwell leading down to the sound basement.

Déjà vu, she thought. *Don't tell me Rod is still tinkering round with his bloody door?*

Her curiosity piqued, she couldn't resist popping down to take a look. She wouldn't mind seeing a friendly face. This time the door to the sound basement was closed, and there was no sign of Rod… but the banging persisted. It was, Hattie noted, more of a muffled thud, more like the sound of someone knocking on a door with their fist than someone hitting a doorknob with a hammer, and it was coming from inside the sound studio. The door had a little round window in it, and Hattie stood herself up on tiptoe and peered in.

The lights were on inside, but she couldn't make out the source of the noise, or see any sign of an inhabitant. There was a coat strewn across the desk in the middle – not Rod's coat, Hattie was pretty sure. He only had one, and he'd had it since 2007, and Hattie would be able to recognise it from twenty paces by both look and smell. This was a black parka that looked far too clean and hole-free to be Rod's.

'Hello?' said Hattie experimentally.

The thumping stopped. Hattie heard a shuffling noise from inside, and a second later a figure appeared on the other side of the window, and Hattie was thoroughly taken aback to find herself looking into the wan face of one of her former students.

'Abua?'

'How did you know I was here?' he asked. His voice was very muffled (the sound studio was partially sound-proofed), but even so, Hattie could hear a lot of strain in it.

'I didn't. I just popped into the building and heard the thumping.'

'I didn't think anyone would come.'

'Why? How long have you been here?'

'Since last night. The door's not working.'

'Wait, so you're stuck in there?'

He nodded.

Hattie tried the door handle. Sure enough, it wouldn't budge.

'Bloody Rod and his bloody DIY,' she breathed, then, addressing Abua, 'So what on earth are you doing in Rod's studio?'

'You told me to come.'

'Not to the basement.'

'No but... You told me to come and pay my respects. I'd already looked around upstairs. I didn't know what I was supposed to be doing. I tried to call you but you didn't pick up, so I came down here just to have a look in. And then the door got stuck. And I don't have any phone signal in here. I think all the wiring and sound insulation is blocking it. Can you get me out please?'

'Of course!' said Hattie, thinking guiltily back to the missed call she'd had from Abua the afternoon before. 'You poor thing, you've been stuck here... is there a toilet in there?'

'No. Do you think you can fix the door handle from out there?'

'Yes. Well, not me personally, I wouldn't know how to start, but I'm sure it can be done. I just need to get... well, I don't know if there's anyone else around. Er...'

Hattie realised she was dithering in part because she was embarrassed. Abua was stuck only because he'd come here when he shouldn't have, and he'd done that only because she'd insisted on it, and she'd done that only because… well, it had seemed like a good idea at the time, but now…

'Hattie *please*,' said Abua. 'Isn't there someone who can come?'

Hattie thought for a moment, then called Rod.

'Oi, you,' she began without preamble. 'I need to get into your room at ACDA, but you've buggered up the door.'

'Hello to you too, flower of my heart. I have not buggered up the door. All I did was to change the locks. But that's neither here nor there, because it's not actually locked at the moment. It'll just open.'

'No it won't. It did. Once. And let someone in. But now it won't let them out again. The door handle won't budge.'

'Oh,' Rod replied thoughtfully. 'Sounds like I may have buggered up the door, then. May I ask who's trapped inside?'

'Doesn't matter,' said Hattie quickly. 'Look, you're not in trouble with anyone except me. But I need you to come on down here and sort it out.'

'That could be a problem. I'm in Doncaster. There's a motor show here; I'm trying to get some clean recordings of some engine noises.'

'Engine noises? Why not walk down literally any street in London?'

'These are very specific engine noises of very specific vehicles. I'm working on a sound poem and—'

'Rod, my love, I care about you very deeply, but the very last thing I want right now is for you to tell me about one of your bleeding sound poems. How can I open this sodding door?'

'Hmm. Well, first of all you're going to need a screwdriver…'

Rod gave Hattie a list of tools she'd need, and she trotted over to the construction workshop on the other side of the building to pick up everything up. Then he talked her through unscrewing the faceplate of the door handle and, with the gubbins inside exposed, finding the bit of the mechanism that had seized up and 'fixing' it. It turned out that Rod's idea of fixing it was, first of all, hitting it a few times with a hammer, and then, when that didn't work, using the claw end of the hammer to try to lever it out. Finally, he told her to put a flat-headed screwdriver into the middle of things and 'just give it a wiggle'. Incredulous, but lacking other options, Hattie followed his instructions and after a little while there was a clonk, and suddenly the door handle turned freely.

'That's done it,' confirmed Hattie.

'You're welcome,' replied Rod.

'Nope. You don't get to "you're welcome" me, not after you were the one to cause this mess in the first place,' said Hattie, acutely aware that her anger with Rod was really just a deflection of her own shame at being the architect of Abua's misfortune.

'Just make sure my mystery guest leaves my room as he found it, will you?'

Rod may have had more to say, but Hattie hung up. Now that she could get to him, her only concern was for Abua. She opened the door and, being careful to prop it ajar with her handbag, stepped inside.

Abua was sitting on the floor, looking melancholy.

'All right, my love. Out you come,' prompted Hattie gently.

He looked up at her. 'Thank you,' he said, in a quiet voice. 'I'm sorry to have caused such a fuss.'

It was enough to make Hattie want to burst into tears. 'Abua, my love, you haven't caused a fuss at all. I was the one who got you down here, all based on my daft notion that... well, it doesn't matter. The point is, I'm sorry. Truly. I just wanted to help you get started in the industry.'

'Yes, but... I mean, thank you, I appreciate you trying to help, but the thing is... actually, do you mind if I go to the toilet? I haven't been since yesterday.'

'Of course! Goodness. Yes, I'll wait.'

After a brief comfort break for Abua, during which time Hattie dawdled awkwardly in the corridor, he returned, looking slightly calmer but still rather pale.

'Are you hungry, my love? I think I've got an Alpen bar in my bag.'

'I'm all right just at the moment, thanks. Look, what I wanted to say... what I've been trying to say for a while now... is that... I don't actually *want* to be a stage manager.'

He looked awkwardly up at Hattie with a little shrug and added, 'Sorry.'

'Oh,' said Hattie. 'Well that's... that's fine, of course. You always seemed to enjoy it, and you're good at it, so I just assumed you'd want to carry on.'

'I know... I mean, thank you, but... it's just a bit much sometimes.'

'Well if it's about coping with the pressure—'

'No, I don't mean the pressure. I mean, it is pressured, but not so much more than other jobs. I mean, it's all so over-the-top, and everyone's so earnest, and you have to give up all your evenings and weekends. And I mean, I like theatre. But maybe it's not where I want to be. But after two years of training I sort of feel like I'm letting everyone down by not carrying on with it. That's what I was trying to say to you after graduation. I was sort of hoping...'

'You were hoping I'd give you my blessing for you to go your own way,' said Hattie, realisation finally dawning. 'You just wanted me to tell you it was okay. And instead I started pushing you in the opposite direction entirely. Oh I'm such a fool.'

'No—' began Abua, but Hattie cut him off.

'I am. I'm an idiot. Because Abua, *of course* it's okay. It's not for me to tell you what you should do with your life. If your heart's not in the theatre then that's all there is to it. Oh I've made everything so much worse...'

Hattie realised that, quite uncharacteristically, she was in danger of bursting into tears. Abua evidently realised it too, because he started shuffling and fidgeting even more than normal, and mumbling, 'Oh... now... uh...'

Pulling herself together, Hattie took a deep breath and said, 'Right, this won't do at all. I've wasted too much of your time already, and I won't waste any more. Abua, your future isn't to be found in a basement in ACDA, it's out there in the real world. So I'm going to let you go and do whatever it is you see fit, and I want you to know that it's none of my business what you do next, but whatever it is you have my blessing, and I'm tremendously proud of you whatever you do. I *hope* that your new adventure starts with a decent meal and possibly a nap in a real bed after the night you've just had, but either way, get out of here and start enjoying your life. I can only say again that I am so, *so* sorry for getting you trapped.'

'It's okay,' said Abua, with a small smile. 'And it makes for *quite* a funny story when you think about it.'

They made their way back up the stairs towards the exit.

'Is ACDA *really* closing the technical course?' Abua asked.

'Maybe. I hope not, but it's a definite possibility. Now... the other day did you say you were thinking about a career in *recruitment*?'

'Maybe. My friend's doing it, she's making really good money and she seems to be having a laugh. I thought I'd give it a go.'

They said a brief, awkward goodbye at the side door, and Abua took his leave. Hattie watched him go, and tutted to herself.

'Hattie, you daft old bat,' she muttered. 'What on earth got into you?'

But she realised she knew what had got into her. She'd been trying to save him. She'd had Eoin on her mind, and, pained by the memory of a young man at the beginning of a promising career in the theatre who had needed her help and whom she had let down, she had lighted on *another* young man at the beginning of a promising career in theatre, and had been so determined *not* to let him down she had completely missed the fact that this one didn't actually need her help in the slightest. And all she'd done was bugger him about.

What a mess. Hattie knew with awful certainty that she'd be cringing with embarrassment every time the memory of Abua popped into her head for years to come. It wasn't a pleasant prospect. Although, she thought to herself, a little recurring shame was no less than she deserved, considering. But there was nothing to be done about that now. And in the meantime, Hattie had a job to do.

She made her way across to the SM office and spent ten minutes rooting through her 'To File' pile, until she dug up a contact sheet for the showcase show from a year ago, and found Jodie Turrell's number. She called it straight away, and found herself explaining to a very confused actress (who didn't remember Hattie *at all*, it turned out) how she needed to get hold of Jala, and hoped that she had her number. By a stroke of luck Jodie did, and she forwarded it to Hattie by text as soon as their call ended. Not wanting to waste any more time (it was 1 o'clock – Hattie had lost the first half of the day already), Hattie rang Jala straight away.

'Hello?' came Jala's voice, after three rings.

'Jala! It's Hattie. I need to speak to you. Er, urgently. Where are you?'

'I'm in the dining room.'

'Which dining room?'

'Well… the dining room. You know. In Trevelyan House. Where are *you*?'

21

Hattie was now deeply confused. What on earth was Jala doing back at Trevelyan House?

'I... thought you'd gone...' she said awkwardly.

'Last night? I went to the village shop to get tampons.'

'But they said you got up and went so abruptly.'

'Only because I wanted to get there before it closed. I didn't know what the opening hours were, and Geoffrey had disappeared off with you somewhere. I sent him a message to ask him, and he replied saying I only had about fifteen minutes, so I legged it to my car. Listen, are you okay? Everyone's been talking about how *you* got up and went so abruptly.'

'I think I've made a bit of a fool of myself,' Hattie conceded. 'But that doesn't change the fact I still need to talk to you. It's really important. I'd prefer to talk in person, but... can you go somewhere private?'

'Not really... we're just snarfing a quick lunch here then we're back into the room for the final scene. Look, where are you? We could really use you here, to be honest.'

'I'm in London,' said Hattie.

'Oh,' said Jala. She sounded deeply weirded out by the whole conversation, and Hattie couldn't blame her. But she seemed a kind woman, and evidently her desire to be helpful overrode her inclination to steer clear of the crazy lady, because she continued. 'Well, look, I've got to drive back to London as soon as we finish this afternoon. I've got to jump onto a plane tomorrow. Um… mostly I'm going to be packing and doing laundry this evening. If you're in town… do you want to pop by? I'm in Clapham.'

'Yes please. That would be great. Thank you.'

And so Hattie found herself awkwardly counting down the hours until Jala returned to London. She went back to the flat and paced around aimlessly for a while. At 6 o'clock she made herself supper, thinking, *that's it, they'll be downing tools and wrapping up at the moment in the granary.* At 7 o'clock she sat down and tried to read a book (*Jala will have said her goodbyes and should be in the car by now*). At 8 o'clock she couldn't take it any more, and set off for Clapham, despite knowing she'd get to the area well before Jala did.

She got off the tube at Clapham Common and pottered around in Venn Street for a bit. They were showing some films at the Picturehouse that Hattie had never heard of. When was the last time she'd been to the cinema? Thinking about it, it had actually been here, hadn't it? And afterwards they'd got a meal at… at a restaurant that was long gone, replaced by a burger bar. She always liked the cinema, but there was never the time. Well, maybe that wasn't true any more. She increasingly had time, these days. She was just out of the habit. Maybe there were more things like that: pleasures and indulgences she'd written off years ago when she was always busy, always travelling, but that now she could start to appreciate. If only she could remember what they were…

Hattie was interrupted from her reflections by a hard tap on the shoulder. She turned and found herself face to face with two extremely glamorous women, perhaps in their early fifties. One of them, tall and thin and wearing a smart blazer, she didn't recognise at all. The other one, shorter and broader and inexplicably wearing a fur coat in the middle of the summer evening heat, had a face she couldn't place… until she opened up her mouth and out spewed a torrent of eastern European-sounding consonants.

'My friend says she knows you. She says you came to her house,' said the tall woman, in a Slavic-tinged accent. Hattie nodded mutely, astonished. The last time she'd seen Madame Kuznetsova she'd given the impression of someone who hadn't left their home in years. But here she was, dressed up to the nines, looking animated and sharp.

Kuznetsova kept talking, and her friend kept translating.

'She says you knew her friend Lel. The one who died.'

Hattie nodded again.

'Did you also know her friend Eoin?'

'Yes.'

'Did you know they have arrested him?'

'Yes.'

'Do you know why?'

'Because they think Eoin killed Lel.'

The tall woman translated this back to Madame Kuznetsova, provoking a torrent of what was presumably Georgian in response. Her friend listened carefully, then said to Hattie, 'Was Eoin driving the car?'

'What car?'

'The car that hit Lel.'

'I don't... I'm sorry, I think there may be a misunderstanding. Lel wasn't hit by a car. He was killed in a theatre.'

The two women again conferred, and Madame Kuznetsova frowned deeply and her voice took on a more frustrated inflection. Eventually the friend said, 'Are you sure? Because when Eoin came to bring the news he said he was hit by a car.'

'Yes I'm sure. Maybe he was trying to spare your feelings. But I was the one who found the body.'

This, when translated, made Madame Kuznetsova's face shift entirely. Her mouth turned into an 'o', her eyebrows raised, and she rushed forwards and grabbed Hattie's face in her hands, cooing unintelligibly.

'And Eoin was the one who did it?' the friend asked, once Kuznetsova's burbling had subsided enough to be heard over the top.

'No. I mean, I'm sure it wasn't him, but I seem to be the only one. I'm trying to work out what happened myself,' said Hattie, uncomfortably.

'Please... tell me... you know, you tell me,' insisted Kuznetsova when she had been told what Hattie had said, and Hattie nodded. Madame Kuznetsova dug out a scrap of paper from her handbag and wrote down her phone number, and then the two women took their leave, walking back in the direction of the common. *Of course*, Hattie realised, *she lives just round the corner from here.*

That meant Lel's studio was just round the corner too. It felt as though she was forever treading round the edges of his shadow. It made her feel uncomfortable. Although that wasn't the only thing that made her feel uncomfortable. It sounded as though Eoin had been to see Madame Kuznetsova after Lel died, but he'd not mentioned anything about that when he sent Hattie round to look for the score. He'd only said that she loathed him and was unlikely to speak to him... and yet Madame Kuznetsova's translator had referred to him as her friend. What was Hattie to make of that?

As she mulled this over, she got a message on her phone from Jala, saying, *'I'm back now.'*

'I'll be right there,' Hattie replied, and she set off up Clapham High Street in the direction of the address Jala had given her.

She found the place easily, knocked on the door, and was greeted by a look of surprise when Jala opened it. The writer was wearing fleece pyjamas and was looking frazzled.

'Oh hello. I didn't think you'd be here this soon.'

'I was in the area,' Hattie said awkwardly. 'Sorry. I can go away and come back if you like?'

'No, no it's quite all right. I was just getting myself a glass of wine. Do you want one?'

'That would be lovely,' said Hattie gratefully, and Jala led her into the flat, through an untidy sitting room into a tiny, cramped kitchen.

'I have to be honest, my head is all over the place. This afternoon was a mad rush. Typically, all the big creative ideas only started cropping up right at the end of the process, and I was desperately trying to get everything down while it was fresh. I could have spent hours just sitting and writing, but I had to rush back here to pack, my editor is chasing me about the second edition of *Advanced Theatre Practice,* and I'm off to Cologne first thing for this whole other thing that I really should have prepped for, so mentally I'm all over the place. Here you go.'

She handed Hattie a fishbowl-sized glass of white.

'I'm sorry,' said Hattie, 'that sounds like a lot. I'll try not to take up much of your time.'

'No, it's absolutely fine, I promise. Cologne is just a bit of fun really, and the book's only there to help me try to land a lecturer gig that's… well, that's another story. But look, I don't know the first thing about what's going on. Did you have a falling out with Geoffrey or something?'

'Sort of. Er… did Teri speak to you at all today?'

'Teri? No. Thinking about it, she was being a bit quiet. Why? Did you have a falling out with *her*?'

'No, not at all. No, it's just that… well… just to come out and say it, I know that she didn't write the music. And I know that you know that too.'

Jala frowned. 'Oh. Right. *That.* God, shall we sit down?'

They went back into the sitting room, where Jala pushed some piles of paper, a hat, a packet of cigarettes and a well-thumbed magazine onto the floor to make room on the sofa for them to sit.

'Yes. So this awful thing where we had to lie to everyone about who wrote the music, including you. It's a horrible thing about this industry, the way it works sometimes, and I really wish it was different, but ultimately I'm not going to say sorry, or that I regret it, because I made a conscious choice that I would make again. I am sad that it meant lying to you.' Jala frowned for a second, then nodded to herself, as if mentally reviewing what she'd just said and confirming she was happy with it. Clearly the wording was important to her. She was a writer, after all.

'I understand what you're saying,' said Hattie, 'and I'm not here just because I'm upset about being lied to. What I want to know is if you know who *actually* wrote the music. Because Teri didn't, and it changed things for her when she found out it was—'

'Lel, yes, I know. I didn't like lying to Teri about that on top of the lie to everyone else, but given the circumstances, and given Teri, she'd have reacted very badly to learning the truth right away, and it would have scuppered the whole thing.'

'You sound like you're very comfortable with this whole arrangement,' said Hattie awkwardly.

'I've made my peace with it,' Jala replied with a shrug. 'I know it's what Lel wanted. He'd been working on this project for years, from long before I came along. He would have wanted to get the piece staged.'

This wasn't the first time someone had confidently told Hattie how Lel thought and what he wanted, and she was very suspicious whenever someone told her that what the dead man wanted just happened to be the thing that most benefited them, too.

'Did you know him? I mean, did you work with him closely on this project?' she asked, trying to keep her tone light.

'No… not really. After Geoffrey passed on his score I spoke to him a little bit about the project, but he didn't get super involved. But that was just because of the rights complications with him and Eoin.'

'So you knew about that?'

'Well, yes.'

'And you don't think it's all a bit suspicious?' asked Hattie, incredulous.

'Think *what* is a bit suspicious?' asked Jala, looking confused.

Hattie let out a sigh of frustration before elaborating. 'So Eoin and Lel have the rights to the show, and have put together a script and score. Geoffrey wants to put on the show with Lel's music, but he legally cannot because of the rights issue. Regardless, he gets you to write an alternative script, which, as you just said, Lel doesn't take much interest in, presumably because as far as he's concerned he already has a script he's happy with. Eoin's script. Geoffrey's attempt to talk Lel round to abandoning Eoin fails, and next thing you know Lel is dead and Eoin is wanted by the police, conveniently removing the only obstacles to Geoffrey staging his show. You rush on regardless, drafting Teri in days after Lel dies to take his place and pretend to be the composer, and everyone is sworn to solemn secrecy about the whole thing. You don't think *that's* suspicious?'

Hattie realised that as she had been talking she had been getting more and more agitated, and was now flailing her arms around wildly enough to risk splashing wine on the sofa. She forced herself to lower her hands and finished in a more restrained tone of voice. 'All I mean is that, given that the only person standing in Geoffrey's way was *murdered*, you seem to be awfully calm about the cloak and dagger stuff you've been participating in at Geoffrey's request.'

Hattie locked eyes with Jala, searching for any indication that her words had had an impact. But the young writer just took a sip of wine and after a pause replied calmly, 'You're right. Lel was murdered. And that's awful. But he wasn't standing in Geoffrey's way. He wanted to do the show, with Geoffrey, and *without* Eoin.'

'No,' said Hattie. 'He—'

'*Yes*,' insisted Jala. 'He told me that, personally, and explicitly. He was done with Eoin. He wanted to do the show with a different writer. I wouldn't have got involved otherwise. The point is, because Eoin was being completely inflexible about the rights, if we wanted to move ahead with the project we had to do it without Lel being seen to have any involvement, not until the end of the year when the rights expired and Eoin lost his claim to it. But we couldn't just sit on the show, because after Eoin had sat on the show for five years, there's no way Tahmima Ortlauf would have given *anyone* the rights without some very solid evidence of concrete intention to stage a production. Lel's involvement was *always* going to be a secret, at least until the rights expired. He was going to have a stand-in in the workshop. Initially it was just going to be Calvin, I think, but then they decided they wanted someone else, and they'd just settled on Teri when Eoin killed Lel. The point is that everything I've done, I did it with Lel's blessing. Including the lies.'

'Hold on,' said Hattie. Her mind reeling. Not so long ago she'd believed that Lel and Eoin's version was nothing to do with Jala and Teri's version. Then she'd learned that Teri's version *was* Lel's version, and she had just about been able to make sense of that on the assumption that Lel knew nothing about his music being appropriated to fit to Jala's script. Now she was being told that Lel actually *wanted* to work with Jala. But that raised a thousand other questions…

'So you're saying that if Lel was alive, you'd still have done the workshop without him? With Teri pretending to be the composer?'

'Pretty much. Lel had this idea that while the rights belonged to him and Eoin, he couldn't be actively participating in the development of an alternative version of the show, without Eoin's script. He desperately wanted it to happen, but he didn't feel he could be involved. I think that was quite noble of him. It would have been a betrayal, he said. He wanted to be in a place where at the end of the year, when his obligation to Eoin was discharged, there just happened to be a script that happened to fit with the music he'd written to tell the story that Geoffrey happened to have picked up the rights for. Then he could step in at that point and start working on the show again.'

'But what would have happened to Teri?'

'Well, she'd be credited with any changes that she made that he ended up keeping, and she'd probably go on to do the orchestration, since she knew the score so well at that point, which would still have been a great outcome for her. That was why it was originally going to be Calvin – because he's worked as musical director for Lel before so he'd be a natural fit. But then something happened to change that. I'm guessing Lel decided to go with someone else for some reason, and he suggested Teri instead. Which, given what then happened is actually quite handy, because it stopped being about someone to act as a stand-in and ended up being about finding a composer who could take over from Lel to finish the show. To give her credit, Teri's ended up being really great at that. Calvin… I don't know, I think he's more an MD than a composer. So it all turned out for the best.'

'So it was quite *convenient* that Lel died, is that what you're saying?' asked Hattie. She wasn't even sure at this moment what point she was making, she was just trying to find something to grasp at amid this sea of new information.

'No, it wasn't, actually. It was bloody awful. I've been crying about it at least once a day since it happened, and I can't tell you the number of times that I've wanted to give up and run away. I've hated lying about it, and I've *hated* how completely ruthless Geoffrey is about the whole thing. He comes across as cuddly and fun, but once you get to know him he's *terrifying*. Calvin too. But at the end of the day he's right: this is how we can pay our respects to Lel. By finishing his show.'

Both women had drained their wine glasses by now. Hattie was beginning to regret finishing hers so quickly. She was feeling light-headed and befuddled, and utterly wrong-footed by the brutal matter-of-factness of this woman, and the trove of new information she had just unloaded. Hattie couldn't think of a thing to say. Jala looked at her with something resembling sympathy.

'I understand why you got all caught up in this idea of Geoffrey being the one to kill Lel – that's what you were getting at, right? Faced with something like a murder it's easy for us all to get carried away. It feels so unreal, like something made up, and then you think, well, if that really happened, what other made-up things could happen? It took me down a whole paranoid fantasy that Eoin was coming for all of us, not just Lel, that he would track down and kill anyone involved in *Fall*. I was scared to be outside after dark at Geoffrey's house. And from what I know of Eoin, I know that makes no sense – I mean, I've not *met* him, but I'm sure what happened to Lel wasn't premeditated in any way – but still, that dark imagining kept happening in the background, to the extent that I can't pretend that I won't sleep easier now that he's been arrested.'

'But that's just it,' said Hattie. 'If you know Eoin *at all* you know it makes no sense. I can't believe he would have killed Lel.'

'Maybe not,' said Jala. 'But it wasn't Geoffrey either.'

22

Hattie made her way back home in a daze. She had been completely blindsided by the revelation that Lel had given his blessing to Geoffrey using his music without Eoin's script. If that was true, it made a nonsense of her idea that Geoffrey needed to kill Lel to further his own aims. Unless Jala had somehow misunderstood the entire situation? Her version of events didn't ring entirely true. For one thing, this idea that Lel wanting not to be actively involved in the development of the show until the rights lapsed was somehow him being 'noble': it sounded more like cowardice to Hattie. As though he wanted to stab Eoin in the back, but didn't want his fingerprints on the knife. It also didn't make sense of how and why Lel died. Unless maybe Jala was lying about the whole thing. Or maybe Lel had wanted to screw over Eoin, but then on the night of his death had had a change of heart after meeting him, and tried to back out of it? Causing Geoffrey to take matters into his own hands? But the more Hattie thought about it, the more she came to recognise that in her heart of hearts she believed Geoffrey hadn't killed Lel. She had been on stage when she heard the scuffle on the fly floor, and mere minutes later there had Geoffrey been, front of house, nonchalantly leaning against the plasterwork. It had seemed credible when she first thought about it, but after having spent some time in his company it was less believable. He was a big man, out of shape and getting on in years. He wheezed when walking between the granary and the dining room at Trevelyan House. The exertion of *killing* someone, manhandling the body and then rushing down a flight of stairs would have taken a toll, wouldn't it? *Something* would have seemed out of place. He was an accomplished liar, but still…

If Geoffrey didn't kill Lel, there were vanishingly few options that made sense. There was something nagging at Hattie, but she couldn't put her finger on it. It sat there, at the back of her brain, taunting her, refusing to reveal itself, as she let herself through the door and greeted her husband, and it was still there over supper. Nick had news: his new tour contract had been brought forward by a fortnight, so he'd be finishing at the warehouse over the next few days and then setting off for Birmingham the following week. This was a very positive thing, both for Nick's wellbeing (he much preferred being on the road) and for their household finances, given the generous per diem he'd be receiving. But Hattie couldn't bring herself to focus on this development. She found herself repeatedly tuning out as Nick explained the details, and the smile she tried to fix onto her face kept fading as her mind kept turning back to secret arrangements and missing scores and a body on the fly floor of the Revue theatre…

Nick, perhaps noticing that Hattie wasn't doing a great job of holding up her end of the conversation, quite quickly suggested that they cut the chat and watch a bit of telly, and Hattie absentmindedly agreed. So they watched a few episodes of some saccharine American comedy, and went to bed. But sleep simply wouldn't come. Hattie lay there, her mind flicking between the constant grumbling of her hip and the events of the last few weeks. A series of faces kept flicking through her mind, those present at the workshop and those present in the Revue on the night Lel was killed, and with each of them, Hattie found herself wondering: who was Lel to them? How did this whole sordid, secretive arrangement around the rights to that one little book involve them? What was it she was missing?

HATTIE STEALS THE SHOW

Gradually, she found some of those faces fading away and some returning more and more frequently to the foreground of her mind. One face in particular kept flashing up, until it became a permanent fixture in her consciousness. And slowly, with awful dawning clarity, some thoughts began to fall into place.

Sleep was a distant memory now. As the sky began to lighten Hattie, still lying motionless in bed, found herself hurtling again and again through a thought process that was exhilarating, exhausting and terrifying. Everything was finally beginning to make sense. And she knew what she needed to do next.

By the time Nick woke up Hattie was already showered and dressed. He asked some tentative questions about what was on her mind, but, receiving very noncommittal answers and perhaps seeing the manic glint in her eye, decided not to push it. They ate a wordless breakfast, and she packed him off to work with an absent-minded kiss. Once Nick was gone Hattie ran through the plan one last time, then made preparations for her own departure.

She was nearly out of the door when her phone buzzed with a text message from Angharad the lighting tutor. It began:

Apocalypse!!!! 99% certain the course is being axed...

Hattie dismissed the message without reading further. She had neither the time nor the appetite for Angharad's ghoulish predictions at the moment. It did occur to her that she must be very near the deadline for the statement Mark had asked her to prepare, but at the moment there were more important things to worry about.

She took the tube to the heart of theatreland, alighting at Leicester Square and making her way north into Seven Dials. She arrived in Tower Court a little after 9 o'clock and soon found the doorway, with the little brass plaque saying 'GDP Ltd'. Was she too early? Would anyone be in yet? Would he even be back in London yet? There was only one way to find out.

She pressed the doorbell, and moments later was rewarded by the click and buzz of the door being unlocked electronically. She pushed it open and made her way up the stairs inside.

'Good morning!' a young woman at a small desk at the top of the stairs greeted her warmly. 'Who are you here to— Oh! Hattie!'

Hattie frowned. Who was this? She recognised the face but couldn't place it. The missed night's sleep wasn't helping. She blinked, then tried again: oh yes!

'Hello, Lorna,' she said, forcing a smile. 'I hope the work experience is going well. I need to speak to Geoffrey. Is he here?'

'Uh… yes, but I think he's in a meeting,' replied Lorna, her smile faltering. 'Unless… do you have an appointment?' she asked hopefully.

'No, but it's important,' Hattie assured her.

The space at the top of the stairs was slightly too small to make a comfortable reception area. It held a sofa for visitors, a desk and chair for the receptionist, and beyond that was largely featureless apart from a frosted glass door leading deeper into the building. This door now opened to reveal Geoffrey's assistant, Louise, who emerged bearing an armload of photocopies.

'Babe, can you work your hole-punching magic? Oh. Hi.'

Louise smiled, but Hattie's attention wasn't on her. It was on the closing door, behind which she'd caught a fleeting glimpse of a large and familiar figure.

'I need to talk to you!' she called out, loud enough for him to hear through the glass.

'Do you want to sit down and have a cup of tea?' asked Louise, nervously.

'No. I need to talk to him.'

'I do understand, but Geoffrey is rather busy t—'

'It's about Lel. I know who killed him.'

'I know, I know, but he's been arrested, you don't need to worry—'

'It was Calvin!' Hattie found herself yelling. 'Calvin murdered Lel!'

He took her into the office meeting room and sat her down on one side of the large conference table, while he instructed Louise to make some tea before sitting down on the other side. The walls were adorned with posters from his production company's greatest hits: shows like *The White Hotel*, *Airportland!*, *A Collection of Roses* and, an obvious recent addition, *The Guilty*. There was a large stretch of the wall to the right of these posters left bare, which seemed like a deliberate statement of intent.

Geoffrey looked weary and somewhat exasperated, but his tone was kinder than Hattie had been expecting. 'Well. When you left on Monday that put me in a difficult position, and I think there's rather a lot that we need to talk about. But before we talk about what *I* want to talk about, you obviously have something you need to say. So I think I'd better just let you say it, and then we'll see where we stand.'

Hattie nodded, and drew a breath while she considered where to begin. She had rehearsed this entire speech in her head the previous night and on the journey over, but now that she was here she couldn't for the life of her remember how she had planned to start.

'I think,' she said eventually, 'we'd better begin with Delphine. You know about that business on *The Guilty*: she got on Lel's bad side, and he had her axed, didn't he? He was like that: if he took against someone, and he did frequently take against people, he wasn't interested in hiding it. He'd just take whatever steps he thought necessary to get them out of his way as quickly as possible. That happened with Calvin, didn't it? After years of working together, for some reason he got on Lel's bad side, and quick as you know it, Lel dropped him as the fake face of his music for *Fall*, and decided he wanted him replaced by Teri. With me so far?'

Geoffrey frowned and opened his mouth as if to disagree, then stopped himself and simply shrugged, so Hattie continued. 'And Calvin's been following Lel round like a puppy for years, hasn't he? Paying his dues, hoping for a moment to shine. He thought it was going to be *Fall*, got all excited by it. And then abruptly he finds himself dropped, and very soon after Lel finds himself dead.'

'Now look, Calvin is many things, but—'

'Oh I know, I know, he's so sweet and harmless, wouldn't hurt a fly, that's what everyone sees who doesn't know him well. And most people don't know him very well. But sometimes people get to know him, just a little bit. Tom did. And Tom didn't like what he saw.'

'Are you talking about their little tryst? Tom gave me all that gossip, he can't help himself. Yes, that all sounded a little bit dark, but I don't think a predilection for some rough stuff in the bedroom necessarily correlates to a propensity for murder.'

'It's not just that,' Hattie insisted. 'Think about the peacock.'

'The what?'

'Peacock. Well, peahen. You didn't see it, but it was ripped to pieces at the bottom of your garden. Just after Calvin had been complaining about it disrupting his singing rehearsals.'

'Hattie, I… I don't know what to say. Peacocks? Do you hear yourself?'

Hattie felt her frustration boiling into anger. 'Look, I know. I *know*, all right? It's just lots of little things. But it adds up. Look, I've been through something like this before. Last year, at the Tavistock. I'm not just some mad old lady. I've thought this through. Calvin had a reason to be angry with Lel, there's a reason to believe he gets out of control when he's angry, he spent the whole workshop admitting he was *haunted* by Lel, and he was there, in the theatre, right when it happened. He said he was with Louise, but he only met up with her afterwards, he's got no story for where he was at the moment Lel was killed, and most importantly… most importantly, there's no one else it could have been. If it wasn't Eoin, and it wasn't you… then it must have been him. So you have to go to the police. You have to tell them about who really wrote the music for *Fall*, and how it involved Calvin. You have to tell them he killed Lel. They'll believe you. They won't believe me.'

She stopped. She'd run out of words.

Geoffrey gave her a sympathetic look. 'Hattie, you look terrible. None of this is any the better for you not having enough sleep. You are, when you're yourself, the most calm, level-headed person I know, and I want you to understand that I give a lot of weight to anything you say because of it. But at the moment you are talking nonsense. To give just one small example, if you were to take the briefest moment to apply some critical thinking, I am absolutely sure you would be a little less hasty to lay the not entirely regrettable demise of my neighbour's peacock down the bottom of my garden at the feet of a harmless repetiteur, *when there are so many other more credible explanations*. Even the smallest amount of investigation – such as, for example, asking me – would have revealed that my neighbour on the other side recently acquired a Maine Coon, and it's a bloody monster that keeps traumatising the gardeners. But you didn't ask me. You didn't investigate. You didn't apply critical thinking. You are not yourself. Frankly, I think you've not been yourself since Lel died, and I've been too slow to notice it. Go home. Rest. Restore yourself. Then we'll talk. Yes?'

He stood, and motioned for Hattie to do the same, so she started to lever herself to her feet.

'I know I'm a mess,' she said. 'I didn't get any sleep last night, and I'm probably not making total sense. If I go and sort myself out and come back, and I can explain this all more clearly later, will you agree to go to the police?'

Geoffrey met her pleading look with a pensive one.

'No,' he eventually replied. 'There's nothing you can say that would convince me to take an accusation against Calvin to the police. I'm sorry, but it's true. I don't want to string you along.'

Hattie felt herself slumping in defeat. 'Why?' she asked. The word came out as barely more than a whisper.

'For three reasons. The first is that Lel didn't want to drop Calvin as the stand-in composer. Calvin asked to be dropped, because he felt uncomfortable directly lying. He's a sweet man, outside the bedroom at least, and hopelessly naïve in many ways, but we all wanted to preserve his innocence, so we agreed to use Teri instead.

'The second is that Calvin only arrived at the theatre just *after* Lel's body was discovered. Prior to that he had been in a meeting with me and my assistant Louise, the very meeting in which we decided that he would no longer be the face of the music. Calvin stayed behind with the lawyers to get up to date with the paperwork – and I promise you my lawyers are thorough, and work as fast as you'd expect from a profession used to charging by the hour. He then followed me and Louise to the theatre, arriving at least half an hour after us, by which point Lel's body had already been discovered. He simply could not have been on the fly floor at any point prior to then. Maybe he did lie to you about being with Louise, but what he was trying to conceal from you will have been the fact that at the time he was signing some very secretive paperwork, not that he was off committing a murder.

'The third reason is one you would do well to listen to and try to *hear*. You may have seen in the news that on Monday your pal Eoin was arrested. What has not yet made the papers is that it came about because he handed himself in at a police station, and my contacts have since informed me that he has made a statement in which he unambiguously confessed to Lel's murder. Whatever you think you know that has you convinced of his innocence, you must listen to this: you are *wrong*.'

With that, he took her by the arm, and silently led her out of the meeting room, through the reception and down the stairs to the street, Hattie too stunned to say a word in response. She hesitated in the doorway, but with a meaty hand he propelled her slowly onto the pavement.

'Goodbye, Hattie.'

23

The room could almost have been a school cafeteria. The chairs were more substantial and bolted to the floor, and the tables were smaller and lower and not designed for eating off, but the easy-clean, hard-wearing plastic flooring, the panelled ceiling with strip-lights and the pervasive smell of disinfectant were all distinctly familiar.

A few other people were clustered in different corners of the room, muttering. Some looked anxious and stressed, others as though they could have been down the local on a Friday night, stretched out on their seats, laughing and chatting. Hattie, who had never been in this sort of place before, was firmly in the former category. She picked a table on one side of the room, as far from any of the other inhabitants as possible, and sat stiffly, her hands in her lap, waiting. She hadn't been allowed to bring her handbag or phone in with her, and she missed having something to fiddle with.

After about a quarter of an hour he appeared through the door in the far wall, accompanied by a uniformed guard who then stood at ease in the corner while he ventured further into the hall. His eyes scanned the room, eventually lighting on Hattie when he was a few yards away, and as they did so he faltered, and a look of horror suddenly shot across his face. But then he set his jaw, strode across to her and took a seat on the chair opposite.

'I suppose you feel that I've wronged you, and that I owe you an explanation,' he said, matter-of-factly.

'I don't know that you owe me anything,' said Hattie quietly. 'I've made quite a fool of myself over you, I will confess. But I only have myself to blame for that. I would *like* an explanation, though.'

Eoin shrugged. 'Very well. I killed Lel. He was my only friend, and he betrayed me. You know about that now, don't you? About how he and Geoffrey conspired to replace me and my script, to cut me out and leave me in the dirt. You got there in the end, although I had to practically spoon-feed it to you. I found out that night, at the Revue, and I got so angry I killed him.'

'Why?'

'What do you mean? I just told you.'

'No, I mean… why did you spoon-feed it to me?'

'Because if I'd told you that I'd just found out about Lel and Geoffrey screwing me over, you'd have been quicker to realise that I'd killed Lel. I had to play dumb so you'd believe I was innocent. Ask you to do me a small favour by going to Lel's studio, use that as a stepping stone to a bigger favour, let you find out in your own time what was going on, so that you came to see Geoffrey as the villain. I… I wouldn't have chosen you, Hattie, if there was someone else. But it had to be you.'

'It did, didn't it?' Hattie nodded. 'Because when you broke into Geoffrey's London office – it was you who broke in, wasn't it? The new intern told me about it. Anyway, when you broke in you didn't find the score, but you did find out details of the workshop. And you saw my name somewhere, on some piece of paper. You knew you couldn't get to Trevelyan House directly. But you could get to me.'

She frowned. 'I still don't understand what you were trying to achieve, though. Were you hoping I'd tell the world about what Geoffrey did? Get your revenge, that sort of thing?'

'Pretty much,' said Eoin, but there was something off in his delivery. Hattie wasn't sure it *was* that sort of thing.

'Then why give up just as I was putting it all together?'

HATTIE STEALS THE SHOW

'You took too long. I suppose I had too much faith in you. Again. The police were closing in, and at that point it was just about cutting my losses. I knew that I'd get a better sentence if I handed myself in and cooperated and so… well, here we are.'

Again, there was something not quite right here. Eoin seemed uncomfortable with the words coming out of his mouth.

'Here we are,' echoed Hattie. Then she laughed.

'What's so funny?'

'You know, everyone, *everyone* told me you'd been the one to do it. And I didn't believe them. I said to myself, *I know him better*. And now you're telling me you did it yourself, and in my heart of hearts I can't bring myself to believe you.'

'But that's just it, Harriet. You don't know me. You remember me as some innocent young boy, and leaving aside the fact that a few decades of the world constantly kicking you in the ribs would knock the sweetness out of anyone, you forget the fact that even back then *you were the only one who liked me*. I was lazy, I was rude, I lied *constantly*… You remember I pretended to have vertigo to get out of going up ladders? Utter, shameless fabrication, and only you were clueless enough to believe me. And even though you'd seen the physical proof that I wasn't scared of heights, you still believed that lie when I repeated it to you *a month ago*. You're naïve, Harriet. You just immediately believed the picture I painted of myself. And maybe one day you'll come to terms with the fact that you were wrong about me, but if I'm honest I doubt it. In which case, well, more fool you.'

Eoin sat back, his arms crossed, his face defiant.

Hattie looked back at him. 'You seem like you're having a go at trying to make me angry with you,' she said, eventually.

'I don't care how you feel about me,' he shot back.

'Maybe you don't,' she said. 'But I notice that you still pick at your thumbs when you're agitated. How did you get in, by the way?'

'What?' said Eoin, who, in the middle of glancing involuntarily down at his hands, was caught off guard by the question.

'The Revue? I don't think you broke in there, did you? The police didn't say anything about signs of forced entry.'

'I walked in through the stage door, just like you.'

'Followed someone in, did you?'

'That's right,' said Eoin. 'Now why—'

'Who? There weren't many people around, were there?'

'It was the… guy. Colin. The one you suspected at first'

'I don't think so. He wasn't there that night.'

'Then it was someone else. I didn't ask his name. It was some guy.'

'Some guy,' echoed Hattie.

Eoin twitched irritably. 'For God's sake, give it up. I killed Lel. Do you hear me? I killed him.'

'All right,' said Hattie gently. 'If you say so. I suppose all I want to know is: was Louise actually in the room at the time, or…?'

She let the question hang, watching Eoin to gauge his reaction. She didn't need to watch too closely. He stiffened, his eyes widened, and Hattie was pretty sure he stopped breathing. He even stopped picking at his thumbs.

Hattie waited. She knew she couldn't control what happened next. She had played the one card in her hand. Now it was up to him.

A few seconds of complete stillness were punctuated by a sudden ragged breath from Eoin. He looked momentarily as though he was about to cry, then he screwed up his face and said, in a very small voice, 'Don't. Please.'

As gently as she could, Hattie replied, 'Look. I've spent a lot of time in the past few weeks coming up with theories, and more times than I'd care to mention, when I've laid them out in front of someone I've made a fool of myself. I don't know what happened. All I know is that Louise was in the theatre at the time Lel died.

She denied it to me, but then Geoffrey said she arrived with him. I didn't spot her while I was walking round with Donna, so she wasn't anywhere obvious backstage. And it sounds to me like she's the one who let you in, so it seems at least *possible* that for the next little while she was with you.

'Now, you seem pretty keen to sell me the notion that you killed Lel out of, what? Spite? Jealousy? And you've been working quite hard these last few minutes to convince me that I'm wrong about you, that you're actually nasty and manipulative, and that you've been lying to me all along. It's been quite a convincing performance. And… well, it rings quite true because you *have* been lying to me all along, at least about some things. But something doesn't add up. I think up until today you've been lying to me to make me believe you're innocent, but now… now I think you're lying to me to make me believe you're guilty. And in the last few minutes I've changed my mind, to be honest: after all I've been through on your behalf, I think you *do* owe me an explanation. For once, I want you to tell me the truth. I can't make you, of course, but if you don't tell me I can't promise that I won't carry on digging and trying to piece it together for myself. I'm not the fastest, but I normally get there in the end. So. What's it going to be?'

Eoin looked truly pained, and he twitched once or twice, as though on the very edge of jumping up and bolting. But eventually, with a snort of frustration, he leaned forward and muttered to Hattie in a voice barely above a whisper, 'I can tell you if you *promise* not to tell anyone. You take this to your grave.'

'Do you really set all that much store by promises?'

'No. But you do.'

Hattie shrugged. 'Fair enough. I promise.'

Eoin looked around to check no one else was listening in, then started speaking, low and fast.

'Louise let me in. She didn't want to, but I twisted her arm. I was pretty shitty about it to be honest. I already knew about what

Geoffrey and Lel were planning. Because Louise told me. We were… friends. Of a sort. Maybe. I don't know what we might have been. I liked her, and she's very vulnerable. Maybe she brings out my protective side.

'But, because I'm a bastard – and I am a bastard, Hattie – I used her. After Louise told me what was going on I tried to have it out with him, but he was avoiding me, I suppose out of guilt. When Louise mentioned she'd be at the Revue for a meeting between him and Geoffrey, I turned up and twisted her arm into letting me in. Then I went and found Lel. I just wanted to talk it out. I honestly would have walked away from the show if it was what he really wanted, but I needed him to say it to my face. And Lel got defensive. You know what happens: you get caught in a lie and you get angry because it's easier to be angry than ashamed. Louise stuck around, I think she sensed it might turn ugly. And when the question came up of how I'd *known* about his deal with Geoffrey… she admitted that she'd been the one to tell me.

'Lel went ballistic. He started yelling and swearing, calling Louise a stupid bitch, and saying he'd have her out of a job within an hour. Then he lunged for her, like he was going to smack her – I'm afraid that wasn't out of character for Lel – and to her eternal credit, Louise smacked him first. It was pure instinct, I'm sure of it, and it's not like she knows how to throw a punch. But she reached for the closest thing to hand and swung it at him, and the closest thing turned out to be a cast iron counterweight with sharp edges. It took everyone a minute to understand what was going on, then suddenly we realise Lel's bleeding from the temple… and then he *went* for her. I'd only seen him like that once or twice, normally when he was blind drunk and couldn't do anything about it. But this time he was sober, and he was angrier than I'd ever seen him. He picked up a weight of his own. He'd have killed her.

'And so I… stopped him. Or at least, I tried to. He was bigger than me, and stronger, and he kept lunging at her. He just kept clawing and kicking, and I was losing my grip on him. So I hit him. Hard. On the temple. With the weight. And then he was on the floor, not breathing.'

Eoin sat back.

'You hit him,' said Hattie.

'Yes.'

'Not Louise.'

'No.'

'Even though she was the one holding a weight, and she was the one he was going for, and your hands were full trying to hold back Lel.'

Eoin said nothing. Hattie decided not to push it. 'So then what?'

Eoin shrugged.

'Lel was dead on the floor. It looked really, really bad. Louise panicked. I knew I had to get her out of there. No one had seen her since she let me in, so I knew if she could get out of the theatre unseen she could claim she'd been outside the whole time and no one would contradict it. So I told her to get out of there, then I moved Lel's body to try to make it less conspicuous and then made a break for it myself. Only to walk straight into you.

'I spoke to Louise later that night, after we'd had some time to think. She said we should make a clean breast of it. She thought if we explained what had happened there's no way we'd get in trouble. I knew better. You can't just show up next to a corpse and claim it was self-defence. Lel was liked; I was hated. He managed to hide the darkness inside him; I never did. And Louise was a nobody. Even if she backed me up, at the end of the day she struck the first blow. And besides, she'd have to tell everyone *why* Lel went for her, which would mean admitting that she was the one who told me about what Lel and Geoffrey were cooking up. Which would be her career over immediately. And what you have to realise about Louise is that, for all that she's just the lowest grunt in the GDP operation, doing all the boring bits for almost no money... she really loves that job. She lives for it.

'So I convinced her to keep her mouth shut. If I was going down either way, better not to take her with me. I knew they'd get to me eventually, and I was... I was honestly okay with it. If prison is where I belong, well... I don't have much worth holding on to on the outside. But I wasn't ready to hand myself in without doing something to protect Lel's legacy. He was a monster, but he was my monster. I owed him that m— No. I'm lying to myself. I wanted to protect *my* legacy. I wanted *Fall* to exist. My version. *Our* version. It was stupid, really. But it mattered to me.

'I tried to get the score from Lel's studio, and when I realised it wasn't there, I broke into Geoffrey's office.'

'Did Louise help?'

Eoin shook his head. 'No, there was no way I was going to get her into *more* trouble. I had to work out how to get in there on my own. And as you say, I saw your name on a memo and... it felt like fate. I really should have given up then, but I really... as much as anything else, I wanted to see you. It's so selfish of me, but you were one of the few people who ever saw any good in me. And I so wanted to have *someone* not hate me. Ironic really, because I showed up at your door and all I did was lie to you. I'm sorry, I'm so sorry...'

His voice suddenly cracked, he covered his face with his hand, and was silent for a while. Then he took a deep breath, sniffed, and, tears in his eyes, looked up at her, and continued. 'You know the rest. Well, most of it. I wasn't in Norfolk to see you, I was there to try to catch Louise. She'd said that the police had started asking Geoffrey more questions, and that he'd started asking *her* more questions, and she was having a hard time lying about it. I tried to convince her to stay the course, but she said she couldn't take it. Which was when I knew it was over. I handed myself in and made a full confession, so that she'd be left alone.'

Eoin was calm now. He sat back, blew out a long breath, and smiled a small, sad smile.

'I have to ask,' said Hattie, gently. 'Louise. Are you in love with her?'

He shook his head.

'But you're throwing your life away just to protect her.'

'My life ended as soon as Lel's did. That bit is inevitable. But she's blameless, and she was only in the room because I put her there. I was given the chance to *not* ruin her life, and I'm taking it.'

He stood up. 'Now you know. And you've promised not to tell. Haven't you?'

Hattie hesitated.

'Haven't you?'

'Yes,' she said ruefully. 'I have.'

'Well then.'

'I can visit,' she said, suddenly. 'If you want someone to—'

'No Hattie,' he said. 'You're nice. Too nice. I don't want to drag anyone down with me. I want to be left alone. Forget about me.'

He turned away, and suddenly, vividly, reminded Hattie of that last parting, so many years ago. The setting was a hospital ward, not a prison visiting room, but there was a similar smell of disinfectant and desperation.

A few years had passed since she'd last seen him. In the meantime, she'd got used to her new criminal record. It was, the puffed-up lawyer her parents had hired to represent her insisted, farcical that the CPS had ever *dreamt* of charging her. The passing of the Child Abduction Act was recent enough that it had yet to be fully tested by the courts, and in their enthusiasm to explore its potential they were over-reaching, drastically over-reaching. He was *almost* certain that he could get her off if the case made it to trial.

'*But*,' he added with a wince, 'I do appreciate that you have no appetite to go before a court, and that risk of failure is not something any of us want hanging over our heads. *Whereas*, I believe if we show a willingness to work with the CPS we can guarantee you a simple suspended sentence. No fines, no community service, certainly no prison time. There will be some paperwork, but other than that you can go on with your life as if nothing had happened. Although certain career paths will be closed off by your criminal record.'

So that was what happened, and Harriet the assistant stage manager became Harriet the assistant stage manager and child abductress.

For the most part she could ignore this new title entirely: in the world of theatre it was relatively easy to reinvent oneself. Thanks to her old contact Oli she eventually got her first touring gig and used that as an excuse to move out permanently from her flat. She started referring to herself as Hattie rather than Harriet (and was only too happy when she later got married to become a Cocker rather than a Fowler). And from then on she gently steered away from any gigs that involved a background check.

A few years later she saw a positive review of a play in London by an up-and-coming writer called Eoin Norell and rejoiced to see that her friend had also escaped Knapesfield. She got in touch with him a few times to try to arrange a catch-up, but they were both always so busy, and so frequently off working on productions in far-flung parts of the world, that somehow it never quite happened.

And then came the call, the once-familiar voice on the other end of the phone line asking her, quietly, if she would come to the hospital, and that he wouldn't have bothered her, except that there was no one else who he could ask. Not for this. She dropped everything and got on a train.

He met her at the main entrance. She was worried she wouldn't recognise him, but as soon as their eyes met she knew it was him, and he raised a hand in greeting, and even in these bleak circumstances neither of them could resist a smile. He wasn't a boy any more, but there was still something boyish about his expression. Hattie was reminded of just how much she had missed him in the intervening years.

'Are you sure?' she asked. 'You don't owe him anything.'

'It's not about what I owe,' he said. 'But come on. I don't think we have long.'

They set off down the maze of corridors that linked a thousand ominously but vaguely named areas: the Acute Medical Ward, the Urgent Treatment Unit, the Interventional Care Suite. Hattie was entirely lost almost immediately, but Eoin led her confidently through it, until they reached a couple of sofas and a vending machine outside a double door with a placard that said 'Lamb Ward (Palliative Care)'.

'This is as far as I got when I tried to come by myself. I think he's through there.'

He reached for her hand, and she gave it to him with what she hoped was a reassuring squeeze. Perhaps it was what he needed: after a second he reached forward and opened the door.

The Lamb Ward was a sorry place. A circular corridor connected a series of small rooms, each containing between one and four beds, all inhabited by frail figures whose unifying feature appeared to be that they were not long for this world. Most were very old. From some of the rooms came groans and sobs, but most people here were quiet and still. A few nurses and orderlies hovered around, with none of the bustle and hurry that could be observed in the rest of the hospital. Maybe it was to preserve an atmosphere of calm and reverence appropriate to the proximity of the great beyond. Maybe it was because there was very little that could productively be done for these patients.

Eoin walked round to Bay 2, Room 6 where, crumpled and pale, moored by a dozen cables and tubes and serenaded by beeping equipment, his father lay. Unlike Eoin, he really was unrecognisable. He looked thirty years older than Hattie remembered, even though in reality only half a decade had passed. He was sallow and waxy-looking, and the left side of his face was entirely slack. He lay with his head turned to the side, his eyes open. Hattie and Eoin were in his eyeline as they entered, but he didn't react to their arrival. Hattie briefly wondered if they were already too late, but a moment later she saw his chest move fractionally as he took a weedy, wheezy breath in.

'It was a massive stroke, apparently,' said Eoin quietly. 'And no one found him for a long time. I don't know if they could have done anything if they did, but either way, there's no coming back.'

'I don't... I don't know what to say. Or what to think,' Hattie confessed. 'Given, you know, who he was. And what he did. How are you feeling?'

'It doesn't matter how I feel,' said Eoin. 'Not right now.'

'Oh. Okay. Is there... is there something you want to say to him?'

'No.'

'Did you just want to see him, then?'

'Not really.'

'Then... sorry, this is terrible, but... why are you here?' Hattie whispered, feeling acutely self-conscious under the dead-eyed gaze of the man in the bed, unsure if he could even hear them.

'Because no one else would come,' Eoin replied, simply.

'Oh,' said Hattie, and lapsed into silence.

Eoin picked up the spindly-legged chair from the corner of the room, brought it over to the bedside and sat down. Then he reached out and took his father's hand and held it gently.

'You can go now,' he said, after a while. 'I needed help getting into the room, but I'm here now. Thank you. I really appreciate it. I know you've travelled a long way. I'd love to catch up properly, but maybe in different circumstances.'

'I'd like that too, when this is... when... well, some other time,' said Hattie, feeling more awkward than she had done in a long time. 'And it's no problem. I'm happy to help. Maybe I'll go, then.'

She made it a couple of steps back towards the door, then dithered, and said, 'I think it's very noble of you that you're still able to love him, even when—'

'I don't love him,' Eoin cut in quietly. 'I hate him. He bullied me, he tried to crush me, he beat me, oh, he beat me so many times, and he hurt my mum in so many ways. He broke her, and he tried to break me. I hate him, and I can never forgive him. But the one thing more awful, more crushingly terrifying than being alive in this unsympathetic universe is dying in it. And no one should die alone. So I'll sit with him until it's over, and then I'll leave, and I'll go back to my life, and I'll never allow him to trouble my thoughts again.'

All this was delivered without emotion, and Hattie saw that Eoin's eyes were locked onto his father's all the while. His father, in response, gave two small, strangled groans, but was otherwise entirely still.

Hattie watched them for a few seconds more, feeling at last that she understood at least part of what had brought Eoin to the bedside. She felt a moment of almost unbearable sadness, but her sympathy was not directed at the dying man in the bed.

'You're a good man, Eoin. Better than I think you realise,' she said.

He didn't reply, so after a moment or two more she turned and left, with a strong and as it turned out correct premonition that it would be a very long time before she saw him again.

And now once again, many years later, Hattie and Eoin parted, and her heart ached in a way she would have struggled to put into words. Then she manoeuvred herself up out of her chair, and walked unsteadily back towards the exit.

Epilogue

Hi Mark,

Sorry it's taken me so long to write this. I've had a little bit of trouble working out what to say. Also I've been quite busy recently. But I know this is important to you, so here's my statement about the value of the ACDA technical course.

Theatre isn't a normal industry. People don't get into it because it's the rational thing to do. They join because they can't help themselves, and because they don't fit anywhere else. The theatre is the only place they can be, but that doesn't mean they're ready for it. Because it's also an incredibly brutal place.

That's why ACDA is valuable. It gives them a safe place to learn. Yes, they're here to learn the craft, but actually the most important thing they need is to learn about themselves. A drama school like ACDA gives them a chance to do that, and in particular to learn what they need. What they need to get from the industry, and what they need in order to be able to contribute to it. They come to us, and we create an environment where they can learn about the unique way that they're

broken that led to them towards the theatre in
the first place.
  Some of them will eventually learn that the
theatre isn't right for them, or they aren't right
for the theatre, and they can go in a different
direction. That's absolutely fine, and maybe as
valuable a lesson as any other. On the other hand,
some of them will waste the chance they're given
and not learn anything. Maybe they're blinded by
their own preconceptions, or stuck in the past, or

Hattie was interrupted by the sound of the doorbell, and she was somewhat grateful for it. She was beginning to feel that she was getting rather out of her depth with the statement. She'd never been one to express herself well in writing. Taking a break seemed like a decent idea. She got up from her chair and hobbled – the last couple of days her hip had been particularly bad, keeping her practically housebound – through the hall and down the stairs to the front door. Opening it, she was surprised to see the now-familiar face of Lorna looking awkwardly back at her.

'Hullo, my love. Am I in trouble with Geoffrey, then?'

'No,' replied the girl. 'Well, I mean… yes. I think he's pretty angry with you. Um. I think he's possibly going to tell some other people not to hire you. At least, he said he would. I don't know if he's joking, or…'

'I see,' said Hattie. 'Well, thanks for letting me know.'

'Oh. Well. Yes, you're welcome, but… that's not why I'm here.'

'No?'

'Actually… actually my work experience ended yesterday. They offered me an extension, but I didn't take it. It was horrible!' she suddenly burst out, before lowering her voice guiltily. 'I mean… he's horrible. I didn't realise it at first, he's so jolly, and friendly. But he's not nice. And the way he does business, it's not… nice.'

'No, I rather think you're right,' said Hattie, still mystified as to why Lorna was pouring this out on her doorstep. 'Sorry, is there something I can help you with?'

'No. Yes. Sort of. Um… they decided that they don't want to credit Lel with the music after all. Not even when the rights expire. Geoffrey said that it's just "too messy". They talked the other composer, Teri, into saying explicitly that she'd written the whole thing. She didn't look happy about it, but she signed a document about it anyway. Um. And I don't think that's fair. I mean, I don't know if Lel had any next of kin, or who would be entitled to the money that he, you know, deserved for writing the music. But either way, it just didn't seem right to me.'

'No, it's not right,' said Hattie. 'That's not right at all. That's… I dunno, fraud or something.'

But almost as soon as the impulse towards indignation and outrage entered her body, it left again, chased out by a fatalistic pragmatism. 'But there's nothing you or I can do about it. Even if we had cast-iron proof it'd do no good. He's a knight, a millionaire and a ruthless bastard. We're nobodies. It's grim, but there it is.'

'I know,' said Lorna. 'I know. But the thing is, pretty much the last thing they asked me to do was shred this.'

She reached into her bag and withdrew a thickly stuffed A3 envelope.

'Calvin had it while he was transcribing it into the music software he uses, and he brought it back a couple of days ago. He asked what they should do with it, and that was the point where Geoffrey said it would be simpler to forget about it. So Louise gave it to me to dispose of. But I couldn't do it. So I just sneaked it into my bag and took it home. But then I started to worry about how much trouble I'd get in if anyone ever found it on me. I don't want it, but I don't want to throw it away. And I thought, maybe… you…?'

She tailed off, and held out the envelope shyly. Hattie looked at it suspiciously.

'Are you saying that inside there is Lel's original score for *Fall*?'

'Yup. The whole thing. In his handwriting. With Eoin's lyrics. It's even got his name and a date on it. If Geoffrey ends up producing it, and saying Teri wrote it, well, it's a—'

'Hot potato,' Hattie said with a nod. 'You probably wouldn't get very far if you tried to make it public, and it'd almost certainly be career suicide whether you succeeded or not. No wonder you want to be shot of it.'

'So will you take it?'

'Didn't you hear what I said? It's a hand grenade! I don't want it any more than you do!' exclaimed Hattie.

Lorna crumpled and looked crushed, and Hattie realised that, for all her words, her fingers were itching. It only took her a moment before she relented and reached out to take the packet. 'Oh for goodness's sake. Well then. You'd better scarper before anyone sees you.'

Lorna nodded.

'Wait,' said Hattie. 'I need to know about Louise. Is she… I mean, when you saw her, was she… Oh, never mind. Off you go. If anyone asks, you were never here. Right?'

'Thank you,' Lorna said as she left.

Hattie took the envelope upstairs and put it down on the kitchen table. Then, after a moment's hesitation, she picked it up again, opened it and pulled out the top sheet of paper just enough to see, on the top corner, the neatly handwritten letters 'T.F.O.A.T.H.S.'. Hattie quickly tucked the sheet back in, then went into the sitting room and, stretching up on tiptoes, plopped the envelope onto the top of the bookshelf next to the shoeboxes, where it was invisible from almost every viewing angle.

She could go public. Send it to a journalist or post it on some sort of whistleblowing website – there were whistleblowing websites, weren't there? Like the one that Swedish fellow ran – and kick up a stink. Maybe, just maybe, if she resigned herself to never working again, and being sued into oblivion, she could get the word out. Perhaps she could get others to corroborate her story. Jala, Calvin, Teri, they all knew about it. But Jala and Calvin didn't seem to mind, and Teri was almost certainly too spineless. Perhaps Louise could… No. Not Louise.

Hattie started to reach up for the envelope, stopped, started again, stopped again, sighed and dropped her hand down by her side. She didn't have the fight in her for this. If it would have helped Eoin that would have been different.

I'm not forgetting about it, she thought to herself. *I'm just not going to think about it quite yet.*

She made herself a fortifying cup of tea and was just steeling herself to sorting out her tangle of a statement for Mark, when her phone rang.

Speak of the devil…

'Hullo, Mark, I was just writing that statement for—'

'Don't bother,' he cut her off. 'There's no need any more.'

'Why? I thought the meeting was later this week. Did Jolyon have a change of heart?'

'No, he didn't. Quite the opposite.'

'What do you mean?'

'He's… he outplayed me. He got wind I was trying something, so he went round all the Governors one by one and talked them round, then persuaded them to nominate him as their proxy.'

'I'm sorry, I don't understand what that means.'

'It means there's no point submitting any statements because no one will be at the meeting to hear them besides Jolyon. The votes have already been cast, the meeting is now just a formality to count them. Which means that it's over. As of next week the technical theatre course will no longer exist.'

'I… oh. Well. That's a bit of a shock.'

'I thought I'd made it pretty clear this was on the cards. And

Angharad's been keeping you abreast of all the updates, hasn't she?'

'I've not been paying much heed to Angharad recently. I've been rather distracted by... Well anyway, what about the current students?'

'They'll walk away with an HNC for their first-year work, but nothing more. I think some of the other drama schools can be persuaded to take them, hopefully along with some of the incoming first-years who thought they'd be starting in September. But it's a mess. And you understand that the staff are all being made redundant, don't you? I'm afraid that you've not been with us long enough to qualify for any severance pay.'

'I understand,' said Hattie, although in truth, having spent her entire career freelancing, it wouldn't have occurred to her even to think about severance pay had Mark not mentioned it.

'I hope that project with Geoffrey has gone well,' Mark continued. 'If there's any chance of getting more work out of that I'd jump on it if I were you.'

'Well... I'm not counting on it,' said Hattie, miserably. 'But what about you?'

'Me? I'll be fine. They'll have to keep me on for a few months to tie up loose ends, and after that I've got a back-up plan.'

'Still, this can't be fun for you. I'm guessing you've had to make quite a lot of difficult calls today.'

'You're not wrong. But honestly, don't worry about me. This is the job I signed up for.'

'Well, it's been a pleasure working for you. I'm sorry it didn't work out.'

'Me too, Hattie. Well, I still have some calls to make. You take care of yourself.'

'Goodbye, Mark.'

Hattie put down the phone.

'Oh... *bugger*,' she muttered to herself. A spurt of pain flared up in her hip, and she winced and gingerly sat herself down on the sofa. A print copy of the most recent edition of *The Stage* lay folded up next to her. After a minute spent in silent thought, she picked it up, unfolded it and matter-of-factly thumbed her way to the jobs section.

Acknowledgements

I'm deeply grateful to Carolyn Mays and the excellent team at Bedford Square Publishers for their staunch support of Hattie. I'm so glad they gave me the opportunity to give her a second outing.

Thanks also to my agent James Wills for providing feedback and suggestions on the first couple of drafts, and always gently pushing me to make improvements.

Finally I'd like to thank my mother in law Christine and my wife Ellie, both of whom offered sage advice on the tricky issue of deciding who, when you get right down to it, dunnit.

About the Author

Photo courtesy of Patrick Gleeson

Patrick Gleeson has a degree in philosophy and classics, another one in technical theatre and stage management, and one more in business administration. He has worked as a theatre sound designer, an 'interpretive naturalist' at an aquarium, a software developer, a business mentor to fledgling entrepreneurs, and a voice actor.

He composed the music for a musical about taxidermy that *The Stage* said 'put to shame the hackneyed standards of the contemporary musical scene', and has been performed in London, Edinburgh, Suffolk and, weirdly, Alaska.

He now lives in Norfolk with his wife, two children, and a pair of malevolent demons who have yet to make their peace with having manifested on Earth in the form of ragdoll kittens.

patrickgleeson.com

NO EXIT PRESS
More than just the usual suspects

CWA DAGGER AWARDED BEST CRIME & MYSTERY PUBLISHER

'A very smart, independent publisher delivering the finest literary crime fiction' **Big Issue**

MEET NO EXIT PRESS, an award-winning crime imprint bringing you the best in crime and suspense fiction. From classic detective novels, to page-turning spy thrillers and literary writing that grabs the attention. Our books are carefully crafted by some of the world's finest writers and delivered to you by a small, but passionate, team.

In over 30 years of business, we have published award-winning fiction and non-fiction including the work of a Pulitzer Prize winner, the British Crime Book of the Year, numerous CWA Dagger Awards, a British million-copy bestselling author, the winner of the Canadian Governor General's Award for Fiction and the Scotiabank Giller Prize, to name but a few. We are the home of many crime and noir legends from the USA whose work includes iconic film adaptations and TV sensations. We pride ourselves in uncovering the most exciting new or undiscovered talents. New and not so new – you know who you are!

We are a proactive team committed to delivering the very best, both for our authors and our readers.

Want to join the conversation and find out more about what we do?

Catch us on social media or sign up to our newsletter for all the latest news from No Exit Press.

f fb.me/noexitpress **X** @noexitpress

noexit.co.uk